A Killer's Christmas in Wales

ALSO BY ELIZABETH J. DUNCAN

A Brush with Death
The Cold Light of Mourning

A Killer's Christmas in Wales

A PENNY BRANNIGAN MYSTERY

Elizabeth J. Duncan

Thomas Dunne Books

St. Martin's Minotaur

New York

THOMAS DUNNE BOOKS.
An imprint of St. Martin's Press.

A KILLER'S CHRISTMAS IN WALES. Copyright © 2011 by Elizabeth J. Duncan. All rights reserved. Printed in the United States of America. For information, address St. Martin's Press, 175 Fifth Avenue, New York, N.Y. 10010.

Library of Congress Cataloging-in-Publication Data

Duncan, Elizabeth J.
  A Killer's Christmas in Wales: a Penny Brannigan mystery / Elizabeth J. Duncan.—1st ed.
      p. cm.
  "A Thomas Dunne book."
  ISBN 978-0-312-62283-1
  1. Murder—Investigation—Fiction. 2. Wales—Fiction. I. Title.
  PR9199.4.D863K55 2011
  813'.6—dc23

                                                2011026223

First Edition: November 2011

10 9 8 7 6 5 4 3 2 1

For the Bothwell family
Bob, Marjorie, Duncan, Alexa, and Jeremy

Thank you for sharing your beautiful home with us at Christmas—
and in happy anticipation of all the Christmas puddings to come!

Acknowledgments

*L*ike all good things, novel writing saves the best for last—when the author gets to reflect on the work just completed and to acknowledge those who made it possible. So I begin with a few words about the late Ruth Cavin, for it was she who called me on a blustery March day in 2008 to tell me I had won the Malice Domestic/St. Martin's Press award and that St. Martin's would be publishing my first novel. Ruth died earlier this year and the mystery community mourns her loss. She was ninety-two when she died, still working as an editor. Ruth taught us many things, including that one is never too old to enable the dreams of others.

As I pay tribute to Ruth, I thank my new editor, Toni Plummer, who enhanced many aspects of this novel. She caught errors, suggested clever bits of dialogue, and suggested many other improvements, as did my agent, Dominick Abel, and friends Carol Putt and Madeleine Matte.

If you love the wonderful Dorothy Martin mystery series by Jeanne M. Dams as much as I do, watch for a special guest appearance in this novel. And be sure to see if you spot a familiar character in Jeanne's next Dorothy Martin, *The Evil that Men Do*. Warm thanks to Jeanne for her contribution.

On the home front, I am always grateful to my son, Lucas, for his encouragement, support, and the occasional, unexpected cup of coffee, and to Dolly, who brings boundless joy into my life.

In Wales, it was great fun getting to know Peter and Sylvia Jones. Sylvia is an ex-pat American who has settled into her life in Wales rather like Penny. It was in their Conwy kitchen that I discovered the Rayburn cooker and airing rack.

With apologies to the Arriva train system that connects North Wales, I look a liberty with one of the routes and had the Llandudno-bound train make a regular stop at Conwy. However, everything else described in the town is as it should be.

And finally, to my friend Eirlys Owen in Llanrwst, I am grateful for her Welsh translation skills, helpful suggestions (the window-dressing competition and Welsh love spoon were her ideas), her hospitality, and above all, her friendship.

New York City,
May 2011

A Killer's Christmas in Wales

One

On a dark gloomy morning in early November, Penny Branigan placed her spoon in her empty cereal bowl, finished her cup of coffee, looked up from the newspaper spread out on the table before her and, taking off her reading glasses, gazed about the small kitchen with both pleasure and anxiety. Work on the charming period cottage that was now her home was almost finished, and while she was pleased with the results, the spa was turning out to be a different story.

Not for the first time, she wondered what she had let herself in for. Just a few short months ago her life had been relatively uncomplicated and uneventful. She'd owned a small manicure shop in a picturesque North Wales market town where people went quietly about their business, she belonged to an artists sketching group, and she enjoyed rambling about the beautiful country-side painting watercolours and selling them in local galleries. She was reasonably content with the way her life was turning out and the universe had been unfolding as it should.

But recently, following the death of retired schoolteacher Emma Teasdale, Penny had inherited a cozy cottage that was now undergoing a complete makeover while she and her friend and business partner, Victoria Hopkirk, were converting a derelict stone building beside the River Conwy into an up-market spa. And bearing silent witness to the enduring accuracy of Murphy's Law, that if something can go wrong it will, the spa renovations had gone wildly wrong when workmen discovered skeletal remains in the ductwork. Remains both human and animal that so far, despite the best forensic efforts of the North Wales Police Service, remained unidentified, although it had been determined that the bones were those of a female with an estimated age of twenty-five to forty and that the animal skeleton was that of a cat.

There had been the kinds of setbacks and complications that come with any major building project and some, like human remains in the ductwork, that no one could have anticipated. But beyond the inconvenience of the decades-old bones, their discovery raised troubling questions that had awakened her in the middle of the night more than once.

Who had this woman been in life? What had she looked like? How had she died? What had gone so terribly, tragically wrong that someone, for some reason, had removed grille work, stuffed the remains of a woman and a cat bundled in a tatty old duvet into the ductwork, and replaced the grille, leaving the remains to decompose in their dark, secret place for decades?

While the police had been dusting off old missing persons records and reviewing computer databases, Penny had gone through back issues of the local newspaper to see if she could turn up anything. She scanned microfiche copies going back years, searching for a story of a local woman gone missing. Although she had found nothing, she knew that the answer was out there somewhere. It always is. Someone knows, she thought. Someone always knows. The police had told her that the DNA results were expected soon and she hoped that encoded within them would be the information to reveal the identity of this poor woman. If not, she wondered if the police would go to the trouble and expense of having a forensic sculptor create a facial reconstruction based on the woman's skull to attempt to reveal what she might have looked like at the time of her death.

Enough of this, she told herself firmly, bringing her thoughts back to the morning about to unfold. Victoria will be wondering where I've got to. Best get on. She pushed her chair back, gathered up the newspaper for the recycling, and set her cup and bowl in the sink. As she opened the back door to get a sense of the weather, as she did every morning, a draught of damp, frosty air rushed past her. Her eyes swept over the walled garden, taking in the pile of brittle, withered leaves that had been blown into the corners, and then turned upward, toward a sky the colour of a bruised plum. It'll be tipping down rain, and a cold rain at that, before the morning's over, she thought. Swirls of mist wreathed the trees and shrouded the ancient hills that overlooked the town, cloaking them in mysterious foreboding. She closed and locked the door and, crossing her arms over her chest, headed upstairs in search of a warm sweater to wear under her raincoat. She'd need both.

A trim, smart-looking woman in her early fifties, Penny had arrived in the town of Llanelen many years earlier as a recent university arts graduate looking for a place to stay for a night or two. Days turned into weeks and still she stayed, reluctant to leave but not knowing quite what was binding her to the town.

Temporary accommodation became permanent as she began to acquire the necessary things of daily living, small and few at first, then larger and more of them, those items that add comfort, familiarity, and civility to one's life, like books and art supplies and clothes for a new season. And one day, she realized that while she had been making friends, starting and growing her manicure business, drawing and painting, twenty years had slipped away. She rarely thought of her native Canada and the few family members she had left behind. Her life was here now.

As she was looping a scarf around her neck, her mobile rang. She checked the number, then smiled.

"Hello, you."

Detective Chief Inspector Gareth Davies of the North Wales Police. Another recent addition to her life and, without question, the most welcome complication of all.

She listened for a moment.

"So there's no match. That's disappointing." The DNA results were in on the skeletal remains found in the spa ductwork, he'd told her, but unfortunately they did not match anything on file.

"We have to find out who she was and how she came to be there," Penny told him. "You will keep looking, won't you?"

Davies reassured her, and after they said their goodbyes, Penny hung up and looked at her watch.

There's so much still to be done, she told herself as she opened the front door, reaching in her pocket for her gloves. And what with Christmas still to sort out and the spa to get up and running, there's no time to dwell on anything else, even an unidentified body.

And today, being Thursday, she'd have to make sure everything in the shop was ready for her most demanding client.

She checked to make sure she had her house key, pulled the door behind her, and set off for her salon.

Two

Evelyn Lloyd picked her way slowly down the path that led from her bright red front door to the street, lifting her feet up and placing them down carefully with each cautious step. Although the cold rain of the past two days had eased into a light, misty drizzle, the overnight temperature had dropped below freezing and yesterday's shallow puddles had become today's invisible patches of smooth, slippery black ice. Like most people her age, she was desperately afraid of falling. One moment you're perched atop a kitchen chair reaching for a can of peaches and the next minute you're laid out on the linoleum with a broken hip. She'd mourned the loss of several dear friends over the past few years and for one or two of them, a nasty fall had meant the beginning of the end. Just yesterday she'd sadly crossed two names off her Christmas card list. No, in this weather, she was taking no chances.

Still, she was glad to be able to get out to the shops after a day or two of being cooped up indoors. She paused for a moment to glance up at the pale, watery sun that hung low in the mid-afternoon sky and then, just as she was about to take her next step, she heard her front door opening behind her. She turned around.

"Don't forget to pick up one or two navel oranges," Florence Semble called out to her. "I need the zest for that new short-bread recipe I want to try." Florence had recently moved in with Mrs. Lloyd as something of a cross between a companion and a lodger and had happily taken on the responsibility for cooking their meals. Mrs. Lloyd considered the fact that Florence loved baking a delicious bonus.

Mrs. Lloyd raised a gloved hand to acknowledge she had heard and then, reaching the safety of the stone wall that separated her house on Rosemary Lane from the street, she clung to the wall to steady herself while she unlatched the wrought-iron gate. Stepping onto the pavement, she closed the gate carefully behind her, and after hearing the satisfying click of the latch settling into place, she turned toward the High Street and set off eagerly, not knowing she was headed for a date with destiny.

An active, robust woman in her mid-sixties, Mrs. Lloyd favoured the old-fashioned look of a crisp white blouse paired with a pleated skirt, and on chilly days like this one, a buttoned-up cardigan underneath her winter coat. Now retired from her life's work as postmistress of the North Wales town of Llanelen, Mrs. Lloyd liked to think she took good care of herself mentally and physically: her permed grey hair was washed and set every Monday at 9 A.M. and she treated herself to a weekly manicure at the Happy Hands manicure salon every Thursday afternoon so her hands would look their best on her bridge night. Today was that day.

She soon arrived at the salon and, pushing open the door, stepped gratefully into its warmth.

"Hello, Eirlys," she called out as the young manicurist working at the treatment table looked up and gave her a warm smile. "Hard at it, I see. Makes me wonder how Penny got along without you." Penny emerged from the small preparation room, wiping her hands on a fluffy white towel, and smiled at her customer. "Hello, Mrs. Lloyd. On time as always."

Mrs. Lloyd took off her coat and draped it on the coatrack. "So glad you took my advice, Penny, and took Eirlys on as a junior staff person."

Eirlys smiled to herself and exchanged a quick glance with Penny. She doubted very much her recent employment had anything to do with a suggestion or recommendation from Mrs. Lloyd. It probably had to do with the fact that her employers, Penny and Victoria, were about to open a new spa, and while their attention was focused on the new venture, they needed to entrust their existing business to someone pleasant and reliable.

But Eirlys, and Penny, too, for that matter, like most of the Llanelen townsfolk, wouldn't dream of contradicting Mrs. Lloyd.

"If you'd like to have a seat, Mrs. Lloyd, Eirlys will be with you in about ten minutes." Eirlys glanced at the hands of the client she was working on and then at Penny. "Actually, better make it fifteen. We don't want to rush Mrs. Owen, do we?"

Mrs. Lloyd sighed, then reached for her coat.

"No, of course we don't. I am a little early, and as I've a few errands to run, I think I'll just nip out to the shops."

"Well, mind how you go, Mrs. Lloyd," said Penny. "It's slippery out there."

"I am well aware of that, thank you, Penny, having just walked over from Rosemary Lane." Mrs. Lloyd gathered up her handbag and hooked it over her arm. "I'll be back in about ten minutes." She glanced at Eirlys, who gave Mrs. Lloyd a brief smile and then returned to the task of applying the first coat of varnish to her client's nails. Little wisps of black hair escaped from behind her ears as she bent forward in concentration. Penny closed the door behind Mrs. Lloyd and returned to the preparation room.

Mrs. Lloyd walked down Station Road and then ventured onto the rough, uneven cobbles of the town square. Although the weather forecasters were predicting the coldest, snowiest winter in Britain in more than twenty years, she, like most townsfolk, was not well prepared. In her mind, practical, rubber-soled galoshes folks used to wear belonged in the past; like everyone else she had gotten through the recent mild winters in ordinary walking shoes.

After paying for a few groceries, she emerged from the small supermarket, toting her shopping in the reusable carrier bag from a major department store chain she had brought with her. Having lived through the days when British housewives carried all their shopping home in string bags, she was delighted to see the end of the era of disposable plastic bags and the return to sensible shopping bags.

As she shifted her handbag higher up on her arm, her foot caught on a shard of ice that had formed between the cobbles and went out from under her. She instinctively dropped the shopping bag and stretched out her arm to try to balance herself. As her other arm came up as a counterbalance, she felt a strong pair of hands under it, steadying her. A moment later, her centre of gravity restored, she felt in control again and looked to see who had come to her rescue.

A handsome man whom she judged to be in his late fifties smiled at her, his hand still resting lightly under her forearm.

"Steady on, my dear," he said. "Are you all right now?"

Mrs. Lloyd nodded and clutched at her collar with her other hand.

"I don't know what happened; I think I must have slipped," she said. "It all happened so fast, but I think I would have gone right down if you hadn't been there. Thank you."

His eyes crinkled at her.

"Not at all. I'm so glad I was here to help."

He looked at her carrier bag lying on the cobbles, its contents spilling out. Two oranges had managed to escape and roll a little distance away.

"If you're okay to stand there for a minute, I'll get your bag," he said, releasing her arm. Mrs. Lloyd stood motionless as he bent over and picked up the bag, then scooped the wayward oranges into it.

"There we go," he said. "No harm done, I hope?"

"No, I'm just fine, thank you," she said, gesturing vaguely at her shopping bag. "I must go or I'll be late for my appointment."

"Perhaps you would allow me to escort you." The man smiled, offering her his arm.

"Oh, really, that won't be necessary," Mrs. Lloyd protested. "I'm just going a little way up Station Road to the manicure salon. I'll be fine."

"It's no trouble. Let's get you there safely," he replied and, tucking her arm in his, led her the few metres across the square and then along Station Road to the door of the salon. Just as they arrived, Eirlys opened the door.

"Oh, Mrs. Lloyd there you are," she said. "We were beginning to wonder."

"Well, you had nothing to worry about," Mrs. Lloyd replied. "Penny was right, it is a bit slippery out and I very nearly took a tumble. But this gentleman has very kindly seen to me and I'm perfectly all right." She smiled at her companion as she took her shopping bag from him. "Well, thank you again," she said as she handed the bag to Eirlys and started to enter the salon.

"Good-bye," he said, with a broad smile that revealed well-cared for teeth. "I do hope we'll meet again. Mrs. Lloyd, is it? Harry Saunders. It's been a pleasure." He offered his hand, which she shook. She stood in the doorway of the shop and watched as he turned away and strode off confidently.

Mrs. Lloyd gave a wistful sigh and a few minutes later, after Eirlys had shaped her nails, was dipping her fingers into a bowl of lavender-fragranced soaking solution.

"You know, Eirlys," she said happily, "you always get the temperature of my soaking solution just right. With Penny, it's so hot she must think my fingers are made of asbestos."

"Hmm," murmured Eirlys. "I'm glad it's okay for you." She glanced at the shelf of bright nail varnishes. "Have a little soak and while you're doing that, I'll just fetch two or three bottles for you to choose from."

She walked over to the selection of nail polishes, and after a few moments pulled one, then two more. She returned to the treatment table and set them down. Mrs. Lloyd looked from one to the other, and then nodded at the one in the middle.

"That one looks nice; I'll have it. Turn it over and let me see what it's called."

She squinted at the label and then smiled.

"Chicago Champagne Toast!" She shook her head. "Well, it'll look nice for the bridge game tonight." Her smile faded. "If there is one, that is. I'll have to ring to find out. With these cold temperatures, all that rain we've had is freezing. When you get to my age, Eirlys, you can't be too careful." She peered over to admire the young manicurist's work.

"Such a nice job you do choosing the colours for me, Eirlys love," she said. "You know exactly what I like. What did you say the name of this polish is?"

Eirlys repeated it.

"I wonder. That gentleman I just met out there in the square. Harry Saunders, did he say his name is? From his accent, do you think he's an American?"

"He might be. He sounded a bit like Penny, but she's a Canadian." Eirlys lowered her voice. "I find it really hard to spot the differences in those North American accents. They all sound the same to me." She shrugged. "We don't get too many Americans or Canadians, either, round here this time of year."

"That's true," Mrs. Lloyd agreed. "Not like in the summer." A comfortable silence fell between them as Eirlys applied two coats of polish and then a top coat. Mrs. Lloyd watched her intently, the way she always did, and then allowed her gaze to wander to the window.

"Do you want to sit for a few moments to give your nails a chance to dry?" Eirlys asked when she had finished. "We have some new magazines you can look at, if you're careful."

Mrs. Lloyd shook her head and stood up.

"I think I'd just like to be on my way, if you'll bring me my shopping bag. But before I go, I need a word with Penny. I've just remembered something I need to tell her. Be a love, will you, Eirlys, and ask her to come here."

A few minutes later Penny appeared.

"Ah, Penny, there you are. Good. Now I was speaking to the deputy lady mayoress herself a day or two ago, and this year they

11

want to do something a little more formal about the Christmas window dressings in the shops and businesses. There's going to be a proper competition and I suggested that they couldn't do better than having you and Victoria as the official judges."

Heading Penny off before she could protest, Mrs. Lloyd held up her hand.

"Now, none of that. I know what you're going to say. That you're opening the spa and you're too busy. But, Penny, my dear, you've lived in this community longer than some of us who were born in these parts, like Eirlys here, and you're one of us now and have been for some time. So with that comes responsibilities and you should be happy that I've found this way for you to contribute to the life of our little town."

"You won't be taking no for an answer, I guess," said a deflated Penny.

Mrs. Lloyd smiled at her.

"No, I certainly will not." She looked at Eirlys, then back to Penny.

"Anyway, you might enjoy it. You have artistic taste and Victoria has a wonderful business sense, so between the two of you, you'll be perfect for the job.

"All right, Eirlys, let's be having my coat now, please."

"You won't be able to wear your gloves," Eirlys warned as she held up Mrs. Lloyd's coat. Eirlys and Penny watched as Mrs. Lloyd threaded her arms carefully down the sleeves, not allowing her tacky nails to touch the lining. Eirlys then handed Mrs. Lloyd her handbag and shopping. "I hope your hands won't get too cold on the way home."

"It's not far," Mrs. Lloyd assured her. "I'll be fine."

"Right, well, we'll see you next week."

Penny nodded.

"Mind how you go."

Mrs. Lloyd set the shopping bag down on the kitchen table and stood by as Florence began rummaging through it.

"Oh, good, I'm glad you remembered the oranges," she said.

Mrs. Lloyd gave her a sharp look. "Of course I remembered them. There's nothing wrong with my memory, thank you very much!"

"I didn't mean that, Evelyn," Florence replied evenly. "It's just that, me, I need to make a list or things slip my mind, so you're doing better than most of us."

Mrs. Lloyd threw her a dismissive glance, pulled out a chair, sat down heavily, and sighed.

"I do hate these short November days," she grumbled. "Look at it!" she said, pointing at the pewter grey sky. "Barely gone four and already it's starting to get dark. So dreary." She removed her scarf, folded it, set it down on the table, placed her hands on top of it, and admired her fingernails.

"Well, I guess I'd better call Huw to see if the bridge game's still on for tonight. With these freezing temperatures and the streets so slippery, it may be that some of the players won't be too keen to venture out."

"Oh, you've just reminded me," said Florence, reaching into the pocket of her blue-and-white striped apron and pulling out a slip of paper. She glanced at it, then handed it to Mrs. Lloyd.

"Here you go. As I said, me, I have to write everything down or I forget. Sometimes I don't think I'm as sharp as I used to be. Forget my head if it wasn't screwed on! I've even got a little notebook now for my to-do lists and all the other bits and pieces I don't want to forget. Anyway, Huw called and said to tell you that one of the members had decided not to go, but the game's still on because they found a replacement at the last minute. An American. Apparently he used to give bridge lessons on one of those fancy cruise ships, so if you play your cards right, maybe you'll get him for your partner."

Mrs. Lloyd cocked her head.

"An American? I think I met an American man this afternoon in the square. I almost took a tumble and he came to my rescue."

"Then it was lucky he was there."

"Yes, it was, now that you mention it," agreed Mrs. Lloyd. "Seemed very friendly." She glanced at her fingernails. "But Americans do have that reputation for being friendly, don't they?"

She studied the message and then gingerly reached into her handbag, pulled out a compact and examined her face critically, turning this way and that, holding the little mirror at different angles. She stroked the skin on her neck and sighed. After a few moments she snapped the compact shut.

"Well, Florence, while you're figuring out what we're going to have for our tea, I think I'll go upstairs and lie down for an hour or so. Do you know, I'm that tired. Do my eyes look puffy to you?" Without waiting for an answer, she added, "I think a little nap will help. I want to look refreshed this evening." She headed down the hall toward the stairs, then stopped and turned back to Florence.

"I don't suppose we have any cucumbers in, do we? They're meant to help with puffy eyes."

Florence shook her head as she watched Mrs. Lloyd disappear up the stairs. She turned back to the counter and picked up an orange. Thoughtfully, she began grating the rind into a bowl and soon a zesty citrus aroma rose toward her. She glanced out the window, but the garden was now bathed a dusky darkness.

Salmon, she thought. We'll have some nice salmon fillets with a parsley sauce and rice. Up until a few weeks ago she had been barely scraping by on a meager pension in Liverpool, and she still had difficulty believing that, thanks to Mrs. Lloyd's kindhearted generosity, she could have almost anything she wanted for dinner.

Penny Brannigan stood in the centre of the reception area of the about-to-open Llanelen Spa and turned slowly around. Although the space was still littered with leftover construction debris, the walls had been painted a soft, sophisticated shade of green, the recessed lighting was subdued and restful, and the space gave off a feeling of calm serenity. She smiled at her business partner and friend, Victoria Hopkirk, who was pointing at a closed tool box set squarely in the corner.

"They'll make sure their tools are neat and tidy, right enough," Victoria grumbled, and then, gesturing at a paper coffee cup lying on its side beside an empty paint can and a few scrap ends of hardwood flooring, "but they leave all this rubbish lying around."

"We'll soon have it all cleared away," Penny said soothingly. "The furniture will be delivered in a few days and we're in really good shape for our grand opening."

She held her arms out to the room.

"You've done a brilliant job, Victoria. Just a couple of months ago this place was a filthy, run-down, abandoned old building that nobody wanted, and everyone was thinking we were mad to take it on. It's just amazing what you've done."

Beautifully situated on the bank of the River Conwy, a stone's throw from the town's historic three-arched bridge, the charcoal grey, three-storey stone building that had been converted into the new Llanelen Spa had seen many incarnations over the past hundred and fifty or so years. It had begun life as a rather fine coaching inn and then, as horses gave way to the automobile, had gradually lost its way until the Second World War when it had seen service as a billet for the Allied soldiers who trained in the nearby hills. When the war ended and once again it no longer had a defined purpose, the building descended into a long period of decline, decaying by the decade. Penny had always admired its façade and loved its location and so, a few months ago, she and Victoria had bought it and poured hundreds of thousands of pounds into its renovation and refurbishment. The structure had been stripped down to its stone walls and rebuilt. Now, modernized and restored beyond its former elegance, the building had never looked better, and municipal officials were excited about the positive economic impact the new business was sure to have on the town.

"And the lighting seems perfect any time of day," Penny continued. She turned to her friend. "Have you ever noticed that a room might seem cold and grey first thing in the morning but in the late afternoon, when the sun pours in, it seems to come alive, all warm and cozy? I noticed that in Emma's cottage when I first moved in. The mood shift in the sitting room was very noticeable. Dramatic, even."

Victoria smiled. "I think that's the artist in you talking, Penny. I doubt most people notice things like that. Rooms seem pretty much the same to us—the lights are either on or off." She paused. "But I'm glad you approve, and the great thing, O business partner of mine, is that we've all those bookings lined up well into March."

"And soon you'll be moving in here, yourself."

"Oh, I'm so looking forward to that! Not that there's anything wrong with your old flat, I hasten to add, but my rooms here have a wonderful view of the river. It changes all the time. It never looks the same, depending on the weather or time of day." Her voice trailed off. "I think I see what you mean." She laughed. "You should see it by moonlight! It's magical."

She sighed and looked at her watch.

"Well, I guess you should be heading back to the salon to close up for the day. I'm going upstairs to the new flat to measure up for curtains. Or should I say window treatments. I'm not sure exactly what I'm going to do yet, but I did see some beautiful fabric with Latin words on it." She smiled and shrugged. "On second thought, perhaps more suited for a posh library."

Penny nodded and, after one last look around the room, gathered up her handbag.

"By the way, as if we weren't busy enough already, Mrs. Lloyd has volunteered us to judge the commercial window displays this year. But the good news is that Eirlys is doing really well at the salon. I think she really enjoys taking on the extra responsibility when I leave her in charge." She turned to go, and then stopped.

"The smell of this place," she said. "The new paint and all the new materials . . . When I was in grade seven, I was moved to a new school and I seem to remember that we started our classes before the construction was even finished. I think the paint and plaster on the ceilings were still damp. Anyway, this project just reminded me of that time. Funny how the smell of something can instantly take you back."

Three

Mrs. Lloyd studied the cards fanned out in her newly mani-
cured hands and then smiled across the bridge table.

"Three no trump."

The bidding continued and a few minutes later her partner
laid down his cards on the table, in descending order and by
suit, so she could play the dummy's hand in the last round of the
evening.

A few minutes later, with the scores tallied, Harry Saunders
leaned across the table to take her hand.

"Well played, partner! And your hands look lovely, by the
way."

Mrs. Lloyd smiled broadly.

"Oh, I can't tell you how much I enjoy having you as a partner," she exclaimed. "You're such a clever player. On every hand
you just seemed to know what my next move was going to be!"

Saunders smiled at her, then glanced toward the back of the multipurpose room where the other players were starting to gather.

He shot Mrs. Lloyd a quizzical look.

"Oh! Yes, one of the ladies always organizes a little snack for us afterward," she explained as she pushed her chair back. "Sandwiches with pickles and a cup of tea. Come along now, or the best ones will be snapped up. Oh, I do hope Glynnis made those egg and cress ones I like!"

"Glynnis?"

"Yes, Glynnis Bowen. She's married to Huw Bowen, who organizes our card evenings here in the community centre." She lowered her voice. "He's quite controlling. Insists on everything being just so, but I guess you have to be that way, sometimes, if you want things to run smoothly." She gave Harry a conspiratorial smile. "Bit of a stuffed shirt, really, but I suppose you'd expect that from a bank manager."

Mrs. Lloyd prattled on as the two made their way to the white-clothed table where she eagerly helped herself to several sandwiches. With a nice little selection carefully arranged on her plate, she stood by Harry's side as the other card players approached him, welcoming him to the group, hoping he'd be able to come again and asking polite questions about what had brought him to Llanelen. Did he have family here? Distant ancestors and tracing his roots, perhaps? After a few words with each of them, he disentangled himself and turned to Mrs. Lloyd.

"Would you mind if we sat down over there for a moment? There's something I'd like to ask you," he said, pointing to one of the empty card tables.

"Oh!" breathed Mrs. Lloyd. When they were seated, he leaned forward.

"I thought you played the hands you were dealt very well tonight, Mrs. Lloyd," he said. "I enjoy playing cards with a partner who knows what she's doing. Those preemptive bids of yours really had our opponents on the run."

"Oh, do call me Evelyn, please," Mrs. Lloyd said, and then added, as if to try out the taste of his name on her lips, "Harry." Harry gave her a broad, encouraging smile. "And that's very high praise coming from you," she continued, "as I understand you give bridge lessons on those big fancy cruise ships. I've never been on a cruise, but I'd like to hear all about it. Is the food really as good as they say it is?"

"Indeed, it is." Harry laughed. "But there's much too much of it, I'm afraid." He patted his stomach which showed no signs of excess. "You have to be careful not to overdo it. Most passengers gain at least five pounds a week."

Mrs. Lloyd leaned toward him.

"What was it you wanted to ask me?"

"Do you know, sitting here with you, it's gone right out of my mind."

"Well, I'm sure you'll think of it. It'll probably come to you later."

By now the card players were beginning to set their empty teacups down on the table and head off to the cloak room to collect their coats. The volunteers who looked after the refreshments, led by Glynnis Bowen, talked quietly as they stacked and rinsed used cups and saucers and packed leftover sandwiches and biscuits into plastic containers. At the other end of the room, the community centre caretaker emerged from a small office under the stairs and began folding up card tables, snapping their folding legs into place with a metallic click, and carrying them off to a storage cupboard.

"Well," said Mrs. Lloyd with a sigh, "that's it for another evening. We'd best hand in our cups and be on our way."

"May I see you home?" Harry asked. "Or perhaps Mr. Lloyd will be coming to pick you up?"

"Oh dear me, no," Mrs. Lloyd said. "Sadly, I lost my Arthur several years ago. He wasn't much of a bridge player, but he was wonderful on the dance floor. I do miss those days." They set their cups down on the table, thanked the volunteers for a lovely evening, and jostled along with the others reaching for their coats in the cloakroom.

"It's funny you should say that because I've just remembered what I wanted to ask you," Harry said as he held Mrs. Lloyd's coat for her. "Besides giving bridge lessons, I'm also a certified dance instructor and I wondered what you would think of the idea of my offering dancing lessons here in the community centre. Do you think there'd be any interest in that?"

Mrs. Lloyd's eyes lit up.

"Oh, Harry, I think that would be a brilliant idea! Get us out on the long winter nights, and it would be such fun! Perhaps Huw or Glynnis would even help you organize it. You'd need to book the hall, arrange for the music and all that, but I think it would be very popular."

"Well, then!" said Harry. "I'll look into it."

They left the building together and stepped out into the bracing cold of the November night. Under a canopy of a thousand bright stars glittering above them, Harry offered her a friendly, protective arm, and together they set off on the short walk to Mrs. Lloyd's charming two-storey stone home.

While the caretaker stood by to switch off the lights in the community centre, Huw Bowen helped his wife into her coat.

"What did you think of the American chap, then?" he asked her.

"I thought he was very nice."

"Hmm. Wasn't giving much away, though, was he? 'Where do you come from?' 'Here and there.' 'What do you do?' 'This and that.' I don't trust the fellow. What's he got to hide?"

Glynnis turned around and faced her husband. "Huw, I'm tired. Let's just go home, shall we?" She picked up her bags and started toward the stairs, with her husband following.

The caretaker switched off the lights behind them and locked the door.

Four

"ancing lessons?"

Mrs. Lloyd laughed as she cracked the top of her soft-boiled egg.

"Florence, you sounded just like that old Dame Edith what's-her-name playing Lady Bracknell!" Mrs. Lloyd did her best imitation of the famous "A handbag?" from *The Importance of Being Earnest* and then did it again, this time changing the words to "dancing lessons?"

Even Florence had to smile at that.

"I thought it was very enterprising of him to suggest it," Mrs. Lloyd said. "Getting out once a week for some dancing will liven us all up and we'll get some exercise into the bargain. I'm certainly going to sign up." She thought for a moment. "You know, I haven't been dancing since Arthur and I used to go to the Grand Hotel in Llandudno on Saturday nights."

She sat back in her chair and gave a small, airy gesture.

Oh, here we go, thought Florence.

"It was such great fun, Florence. You'd get all dressed up in a lovely frock that moved and swished when you danced, silk taffeta maybe, and wear your best fragrance. How special I felt giving myself a little spritz of Shalimar, knowing that my Arthur was waiting downstairs for me! And the men all looked so handsome in their suits with a flower in their lapels. And there would be a real orchestra, too, with the musicians in crisp white jackets. So romantic. . . . Arthur could hardly wait to get me home!"

She giggled and then gave herself a little shake, as if to help herself return to the present.

"Anyway, I'm looking forward to it. Will you go, do you think?"

"I doubt it," said Florence. "Dancing was never something I particularly felt drawn to. Now," she said, changing the subject, "have you given any thought as to what you'd like for tea?"

"Well, something light," Mrs. Lloyd replied as she picked up her knife and reached for the butter. "I'd like to lose a few pounds. I'm planning to go into Llandudno today to see if there's anything new and smart in the shops and I'm not really sure what time I'll be back." She withdrew her knife before it could reach the butter and glanced at Florence. Sensing disapproval, she added defensively, "I've been wanting a new outfit, anyway. There's also the grand opening of the new spa coming up and we're sure to be invited to that, so you see I really could do with a new outfit for the holiday season."

Florence buttered her toast and said nothing.

"Do you think you'll go to the spa opening?" Mrs. Lloyd continued. "I expect everyone will be there and it will be a good opportunity for you to meet folk."

"I don't know," Florence replied. "Depends on whether or not I'm invited."

"Oh, you're a right old stick in the mud, you are," Mrs. Lloyd said. "Even if you were invited, you probably wouldn't go. It'd do you good to get out and about more. So do think about coming dancing with us. There's sure to be a good turnout. We're desperate around here for fun and excitement." She thought for a moment and then brightened. "Do you think there'll be disco dancing? I always wanted to give that a go."

Before Florence could reply, the sound of the letter slot being pushed open, followed by the soft thud of the morning's post landing on the hall carpet had Mrs. Lloyd setting down the spoon she had been using to stir her coffee and springing from the table.

She returned to the dining room a few minutes later, holding a small stack of colourful envelopes in one hand and waving a letter opener in the other.

"I think our invitations to the grand opening have arrived," she said, as she slid back into her chair. She handed two pieces of mail to Florence, then slit open a stiff, cream-coloured envelope.

"Yes! Here's the invitation to the opening. Mrs. Evelyn Lloyd and guest." She leaned over and eyed Florence's envelopes. "Did you not get one?" Florence shook her head. "Well, perhaps they assumed you'd be coming as my guest." She thought for a moment and then brightened. "Or maybe yours will arrive on Monday."

She glanced again at the invitation, then set it down and took a sip of coffee.

"You know, Florence, that Penny Brannigan and Victoria Hopkirk . . . they fancy themselves brilliant amateur lady detectives. Ha! The next time a good mystery comes to town, we should show them we're just as smart as they are. You and I, we could give them a good run for their money!"

27

Florence frowned. "But I heard that Penny woman's courting a rather high-up police detective. Surely he gives them clues and tips. They'll have inside information we wouldn't have access to."

Mrs. Lloyd's eyes narrowed slightly. "Courting is it? Gosh, I don't think I've heard that term used since, well, I can't remember when." She shook her head. "I don't think it's got that far yet. I'd have heard. No, they're just good friends, but he is definitely keen on her. I've been in the salon and seen the way he looks at her."

Florence raised her eyebrows.

"Well, whatever their relationship is, we could still beat them at their own game, no problem." She leaned forward. "You see, we have local knowledge on our side and you can't beat that!"

"You might," said Florence, "but I don't have any local knowledge. I've only been here five minutes."

She reached over and picked up Mrs. Lloyd's gold-coloured letter opener. After admiring the pineapple on the end of the handle and holding the opener in both hands, she turned it over to reveal an inscription:

ARTHUR LLOYD, N. WALES GOLDEN PINEAPPLE AWARD, 1988

"What's the golden pineapple award?" Florence asked.

"Oh, that was from the fruit and veg vendors association," Mrs. Lloyd said. "Arthur belonged to that group for years, although what good it did him I could never tell. Still, it got him out of the house once a month or so, and I guess that's something."

"He had a fruit and vegetable shop, then, did he?"

"Indeed he did," replied Mrs. Lloyd. "You'll remember those

days before the supermarkets took over, when there was the butcher, the dairy, the fruit and veg shop, the dry goods place. All separate, like. You'd go from one to the other with your basket." After a moment she continued. "It was a lot more time-consuming, of course, but you bought just what you needed for the day and cooked everything fresh. There was no processed food and ready meals back then. And you got to socialize with the shopkeepers. That's how I met Arthur, in fact. His shop was where the supermarket is now, just down the road from the manicure salon, and the post office was across the square, where it is now." She sighed. "Oh, just thinking about it brings it all back. All the changes we've seen in the town over the years and not all of them for the better, let me tell you."

Florence handed the letter opener back to Mrs. Lloyd who began to slit her way through the rest of her post, which seemed to consist mainly of bills, with one or two Christmas cards. She chewed thoughtfully on her toast and looked around the well-appointed dining room with its heavy drapery and dark, old-fashioned furniture. Soft morning light slanted through the tall windows and a carriage clock on the mantelpiece ticked away the seconds.

"I was wondering how long you and Arthur lived here," Florence said, breaking the silence. "The house is so big—it must have seemed very empty after he died."

Mrs. Lloyd looked up from the last piece of her mail.

"He went much too soon, Arthur did," Mrs. Lloyd said. "And he was practically a vegetarian, so it couldn't have been his diet." She set down her letter opener and wiped her hands on her napkin.

"We lived here from the day we were married. Of course, it wasn't our house then, it belonged to Arthur's aunt. A spinster, as unmarried women were called back then. We planned to stay with her just until we saved up the down payment for a little place of our own, but she grew rather dependent on us and, well, we just never left. And when she died, she left it to Arthur, and when he died, he left it to me."

"You don't have any children, do you? You've never mentioned them."

"No," Mrs. Lloyd said. "Sadly, Arthur and I were never blessed with children of our own, so there's just my niece, Morwyn. Of course, she's like a daughter to me, but it's not really the same, is it?"

A small, soft sound coming from the front of the house attracted their attention, and two heads turned toward it, and then back to each other.

"Sounded like mail landing on the carpet, but the postman's been," Mrs. Lloyd said.

"Perhaps he forgot something and came back," Florence replied. "I'll go and see what it is."

A few moments later she returned with an envelope which she handed to Mrs. Lloyd.

"Delivered by hand, it looks like," she said.

"Oh," Mrs. Lloyd replied, surveying the paper that littered the table. "What did I do with my letter opener? Oh, there it is," she said, turning over an envelope.

She slit open the envelope, pulled out a piece of paper, and then smiled.

"Oh! It's from Harry. He's inviting me out to dinner tomorrow evening."

"Well, I hope you're going to tell him you're busy," Florence said.

Mrs. Lloyd gave her a puzzled look. "But I'm not busy, so why on earth would I tell him I am?"

"Because Wednesday is the cut-off day for accepting an invitation from a gentleman for the weekend," Florence said. "After that, you're supposed to say you're busy. Otherwise, it makes you look desperate."

Mrs. Lloyd laughed lightly. "Desperate, is it? Oh, my dear Florence, no, I am not desperate, but I do enjoy a man's company and how often these days does one invite me out for dinner?"

She looked at her watch.

"If I get my skates on, I can just make the ten thirty bus into Llandudno."

Clutching the note from Saunders, she got up from the table and hurried off down the hall. Florence watched her go, and then began sorting the morning post into three little piles: one to keep, one to shred, and one to recycle. When she was finished, she set the pineapple letter opener squarely on top of the keep pile, and then settled back in her chair to finish her coffee.

Five

She's taking a long time to get ready, Florence thought as she puttered about in the kitchen. With Mrs. Lloyd out for dinner, Florence thought she'd just have something light on a tray in front of the television. She'd read somewhere that the queen and Prince Philip often take their evening meal that way on a rare night off from their busy round of social engagements.

The sound of the doorbell startled her and she set down the bowl she had been drying and went to answer it.

"Well," she said to the middle-aged man standing on the front step, "if you're Harry Saunders, you'd better come in."

"Thank you," he replied as he stepped into the entry hall. "I didn't realize Evelyn would have someone with her."

"Oh, didn't she say? I'm Florence Semble and I live here with her."

Saunders's eyes narrowed slightly and then he smiled at her.

"Well, I'm sure that's very nice for both of you. Are you related?"

"No, we're not. And if you'd just like to come through, she said to tell you that she'd be down in a minute. I'd offer to take your coat, but I don't think she'll be that long." Florence led the way to the sitting room with Saunders following her, unbuttoning his coat as he went. He eased himself into the squishy depths of a floral easy chair, crossed his legs, and took in the details of the room under Florence's watchful eye. A few moments later he stood up and crossed over to the fireplace and, after making a show of warming his hands on the gas fire, turned his attention to the items displayed on the mantelpiece.

He casually picked up the invitation to the spa opening, glanced at it, set it down again, and moved on to a figurine of a Siamese cat with a pink bow around its neck. He picked it up, tipped it over, and turned toward Florence, apparently about to say something.

She cleared her throat and fixed him with a steady brown eye. He returned her gaze with a blank, cold stare.

"Sorry." Saunders grinned sheepishly as he returned the cat with its pointed ears to its mantelpiece home. "So many interesting, lovely things, couldn't help myself."

The sound of Mrs. Lloyd descending the stairs broke the awkwardness of the moment, and the two turned toward the doorway as Mrs. Lloyd, hand outstretched to Saunders, sailed through. She was wearing a long-sleeved turquoise dress with fancy pleating across the bodice, which put Florence in mind of some kind of mother-of-the-bride outfit. And something about her posture seemed different. She carried herself very erect, shoulders back in a way that looked stiff and somehow unnatural.

"Evelyn, my dear, how lovely you look," Saunders said. "Shall I just help you on with your coat and we'll be off?"

"Did Florence not offer you a drink?" Mrs. Lloyd asked. "Oh, Florence, whatever will Harry think of us? Harry," she said, turning to him, "do let's have a drink before we go. Let me see. I'll bet you're a whisky man." She beamed at him. "Florence, why don't you pour us all a whisky and, Harry, do take your coat off. There's no rush, is there?"

"Well, our reservation is for seven thirty," Harry said, pushing up a monogrammed shirtsleeve so he could consult his watch. "Still, I guess we have plenty of time. We'll call for a taxi after we've finished our drinks. Oh, just a ginger ale for me, please, if you've got one."

Florence walked over to the drinks table and poured two glasses of whisky and a ginger ale. With a glance at Harry, she abruptly left the room and returned a few moments later with a few ice cubes in a small cut-glass bowl.

"As you're an American, I expect you take yours with ice," she said curtly. He nodded and she added a few cubes to one of the glasses.

"Well, cheers, everyone," said Mrs. Lloyd, raising her glass.

"Here's to a very special evening," added Saunders. Mrs. Lloyd smiled at him, then gestured to the other two that they should sit down.

"Now, then, Mr. Saunders," said Florence, leaning forward with her arms resting on her knees, holding her glass in two hands. "Why don't you tell us a bit about the part of America you call home."

Saunders took a sip of his drink. "I come from sunny Palm Beach."

"Palm Beach," repeated Mrs. Lloyd. "I forget now. Is that in California? Sounds as if it should be." She smiled at Florence. "Sounds so wonderfully exotic, doesn't it, Florence?"

"Florida, actually," Harry said. "You may be thinking of Palm Springs. That's in California."

"And what did you do in Palm Beach?" Florence continued.

"Well," said Harry, meeting Florence's eyes, "not too much of anything, really. You see, thanks to a trust fund from my mother's side of the family, I've never really had to earn my living, although managing my investments portfolio takes up a lot of my time. So I get to do what I like and what I like to do is keep busy." He smiled at Mrs. Lloyd. "Like playing bridge, and giving dancing lessons. All just for fun, really."

He drained the last of his ginger ale and was about to place his empty glass on the table beside him when Florence jumped up and took the tumbler from him.

Saunders cleared his throat. "Now, Evelyn, I really do think we should be off," he said.

"Yes, all right," Mrs. Lloyd agreed. "Florence, while I'm getting my coat on, would you mind ringing the taxi? The number's right there beside the telephone."

A few minutes later Saunders was holding the front door open for Mrs. Lloyd, and the two disappeared into the night, Mrs. Lloyd leaving a whiff of Shalimar in her fragrant wake. This is bound to end in tears, thought Florence. Good thing I'm here to pick up the pieces.

She returned to the living room with a small tray and collected the glasses. She glanced at the table where Saunders had been about to set his glass and reached into her pocket for the little notebook she used to jot down to-do lists, the names of books she wanted to read, programs coming on the television she didn't want to miss, and the countless other small details that made up her life.

Coaster, she wrote.

Snug in her best winter coat with its black mink collar, Mrs. Lloyd settled herself comfortably in the backseat of the taxi, holding her handbag with both hands on her lap. She turned slightly toward Saunders and felt a small frisson of excitement as their knees touched. Saunders smiled at her and gave her hand a friendly pat. They rode the short distance to the restaurant in silence, and as the taxi pulled up in front of the Red Dragon Hotel, Saunders withdrew a slim billfold from his pocket.

He took out a bill, folded it in half, and leaning forward, passed it to the driver.

"Here's a twenty, driver," he said, with a subtle emphasis on the twenty. "Keep the change." Turning to Mrs. Lloyd, he told her to stay where she was and that he'd get the door for her. As she shifted toward the passenger door, Saunders leaned forward to adjust his coat and, as he did so, wedged the cheap, now-empty wallet between the seat and the side of the vehicle. He opened his door, walked around behind the car, opened Mrs. Lloyd's door and, offering her his arm, helped her alight.

The driver smiled to himself as he watched this display of old-fashioned gallantry, then drove off. At the next streetlight he slowed and unfolded the ten-pound note Saunders had given him. It barely covered the fare.

"Tosser," he muttered under his breath.

————

After hanging up their coats, Saunders and Mrs. Lloyd entered the welcoming, cozy warmth of the hotel dining room. Mrs. Lloyd had had lunch there many times and the restaurant staff nodded to her as the couple crossed the heavily patterned, carpeted floor to a table under one of the tall windows. In daylight, the window tables offered a clear view past the car park to the new Llanelen Spa beside the River Conwy.

Harry pulled out a chair for Mrs. Lloyd and, when she was seated, gently pushed it back into the table. As he took his place across from her, she looked eagerly around the room, hoping that someone she knew would be there to see her being taken out for dinner on a Saturday evening by a gentleman with such good manners. When she didn't see anyone she knew, she turned her attention to the large menu that the waiter had placed in front of her.

"Hmm. Not sure what I feel like this evening, but I think I'll have the melon as a starter and then I might have . . ." She raised her eyes to Harry and was taken aback by the way he was gazing at her.

"Whatever is it?" she asked.

"I was just thinking how lovely you look tonight," he said. "Is that a new dress? The colour is very becoming on you."

Mrs. Lloyd laughed and shook her head.

"New? No, I've had this old thing for ages!"

Florence Semble had spent many Saturday nights alone in a cramped, cold Liverpool bedsit, so she was not the least bit unhappy at having been left home alone in Mrs. Lloyd's spacious, warm home. After eating a poached egg on toast for her supper, she tidied up the kitchen she was starting to think of as hers.

Then, after browsing the television listings in the *Radio Times,* she sank into a comfortable chair, put her feet up, and with a cup of tea on the small table beside her, settled in to watch a variety show. She enjoyed the dancing well enough, although the costumes were a little on the skimpy side. But after listening to the wailings of two young singers she'd never heard of and thought remarkably talentless, she began to get restless, and when a comedian came on, telling off-colour jokes, not in a saucy, humorous way, but in a manner Florence thought vulgar and obvious, she gave up.

She thought about watching a DVD, *My Fair Lady,* perhaps, but the television system was complicated and she wasn't sure how to switch over to the DVD setting. She felt a sharp pang of longing for a simpler time when a television set was either on or off and there were four channels to choose from. And if there was nothing on that you wanted to watch, you simply went to bed with a good book. With a small, disappointed sigh, she switched off the television. But perhaps it was just as well there was nothing on the television she wanted to watch, she told herself.

Mrs. Lloyd had told her not to wait up and Florence knew what that meant: if Mrs. Lloyd returned with that man, they would want the downstairs to themselves. Florence shuddered at the very thought of it.

She switched off all the lamps in the sitting room except one, which cast a small pool of light over one end of the sofa. Normally, she wouldn't dream of leaving a light on in an empty room, but she didn't want Mrs. Lloyd tripping over anything in the dark.

After a backward glance at the living room, she rinsed out her cup in the kitchen, and then climbed the stairs and headed down the hall to her bedroom. Passing Mrs. Lloyd's room, she saw a light seeping under the partially opened door. Such an unthinkable waste that was, a light burning in an unoccupied room.

She pushed the bedroom door open so she could go in and turn the light off. As she reached the bedside table to switch off the lamp, a pile of tissue paper, bags, and packaging on the bed caught her eye, and unable to resist, she began to sift through it. She noted the posh carrier bag from the most exclusive ladies' dress shop in Llandudno and beside it a tag that Mrs. Lloyd had apparently cut off her new dress.

She picked up the tag and looked at the price. Almost one hundred and fifty pounds! For Florence, who had not bought anything in decades that she didn't absolutely need, and even that had to be on sale or from a charity shop, one hundred and fifty pounds seemed like a small fortune. She dropped the price tag, pinched her lips together, and picked up a plastic bag with a cardboard insert. As she started reading the package insert, a knowing smile spread slowly across her face.

A shapelier, slimmer, lovelier you!
. . . The revolutionary new BodySlimline is a firm, natural-looking way to help control, shape, and smooth. Three-ply tummy panel helps eliminate bulging . . . guaranteed to improve your posture while it makes you look younger and slimmer. Lose a dress size instantly! Guaranteed!

So that's why Evelyn Lloyd had walked so stiffly into the sitting room, with her back ramrod straight and shoulders back, Florence thought. She'd been compressed into this torturous device, whatever it was. Florence turned the package over and looked at the photograph of the full-length body shaper. Anyone over a certain age who had ever had any experience with a girdle would have recognized the power of this foundation garment, which reached from just above the knee practically to the neck, compressing and squeezing everything in between. It was a 1950's girdle on steroids.

Florence was tempted to gather up all the packaging, tissue paper, and tags and cram it all in the large, heavy paper shopping bag from the dress shop, and maybe even turn down Mrs. Lloyd's bed, but decided she should leave everything as it was. She switched off the light that had beckoned her into the room and, closing the door behind her, walked along the patterned carpet runner to her own bedroom.

"That was absolutely delicious," said Mrs. Lloyd, licking the sweet stickiness of cherry brandy off her lips. She set down the small glass and smiled at her dinner companion.

"Very nice indeed, but the best part, of course, was the company," Saunders replied as the waiter approached their table with a coffeepot. Catching Mrs. Lloyd's eye, he raised the pot and she shook her head.

"That'll be all, I guess," Saunders told the man. "Just the bill, please."

A few minutes later their server returned, bearing the bill on a small plate, which he set down at Saunders's place. Saunders reached for the bill with his left hand and patted the inside breast pocket of his jacket with the other. A small look of alarm flashed across his face as he reached inside the jacket. A moment later he replaced the bill on the plate and, with an apologetic look at Mrs. Lloyd, shoved his hands in his jacket pockets.

"That's funny," he said. "I must have left my wallet in my coat pocket. But I always keep it right here," he said, tapping his breast pocket, "so I know where it is." He stood up. "Just give me a moment, Evelyn, I'll be right back."

Mrs. Lloyd's shining eyes followed him as he headed off to the coatrack and then gazed contentedly around the room, taking in the few remaining diners. She was disappointed that no one from her immediate circle of friends had seen her dining with Harry. It would have been nice, she thought, if Reverend Thomas Evans and his wife, Bronwyn, for example, had come into the hotel tonight.

Saunders returned and from the worried look on his face, she knew that the news would not be good.

He shook his head as he sat down. "I'm terribly sorry, Evelyn," he began, "but I seem to have lost my wallet. So embarrassing."

"Nonsense," Mrs. Lloyd replied cheerfully. "You'll have left it in the taxi, that's all. After all, you paid the fare, so you had it then, didn't you?"

She smiled at the look of relief that crossed Saunders's face.

"Of course," he said, "that'll be it. I'm sure someone will hand it in. Perhaps if you tell me what firm you used we could call them and see if anyone found it."

"Well, I'm not just sure which taxi firm Florence rang," Mrs. Lloyd said in a slightly evasive manner. "But why don't you come back to mine for a nightcap and we'll soon find the number and sort this out."

Saunders nodded and Mrs. Lloyd reached for the bill.

"Now, why don't I take care of this and you can . . ." "reimburse me later" hung unspoken in the air between them.

Mrs. Lloyd opened her purse and set a credit card down on the small plate beside the bill. As the waiter took the plate away, she reached into another section of her purse and withdrew two twenty-pound notes.

"Now you're not to argue with me, Harry, but I want you to take these," she said, holding the banknotes out to him. "Go on, take them. I insist." She thrust the notes closer to him. "You'll need a bit of walking-around money until you get your wallet back. Go on now."

"Well, I feel terrible," said Harry, taking the money. "Of course, I'll . . ."

"Reimburse you later" again hung unspoken in the air between them.

"Yes, of course, you will," Mrs. Lloyd said.

The waiter returned to present the credit card receipt for signature and Mrs. Lloyd did a double take when she saw it. That much? she thought. Of course, Harry had ordered the best wine on the menu, and his menu choices were at the top of the price list, too.

Well, she reassured herself, you don't mind paying when you've really enjoyed yourself, and anyway, he'll be reimbursing me. She added a generous tip, smiled at Saunders as she gathered up her handbag, and the two of them prepared to leave the dining room.

"Don't forget your credit card, Evelyn," Saunders said as he handed it to her.

He helped Mrs. Lloyd on with her coat. A moment later, as they approached the front desk to ask the hotel clerk to ring for a taxi, the young woman smiled and nodded toward the door.

"Already here," she said. "Just dropped someone off. I asked him to wait as I thought one of our customers would likely need him."

"Oh, well done, you," said Mrs. Lloyd. "Come along, Harry, we mustn't keep him waiting." A sudden thought made her smile. "Now wouldn't it be wonderful if it was the same fellow who drove us here? We could get that wallet business sorted out right away."

"That would be great," Saunders agreed. But he didn't look as if he really meant it.

Six

Come Dancing!

Group Dance Instruction

Tango, Fox Trot, Waltz, Quick Step, Rhumba, and Swing!

Great fun! Great exercise!

Classes begin Friday, 12 November in the community centre, 7:30 P.M.

Register now to avoid disappointment!

Penny and Victoria joined the small group peering at the hand-lettered sign in the newsagent's window.

"Do you think we should go?" Victoria asked. "Would Gareth come, do you think?"

Penny smiled. "I know he likes gardening, but I'm not sure about dancing." She shrugged. "It might be fun. Why don't we take down the number and think about it." As she reached into her bag for the notepad and pencil she now carried everywhere with her, Mrs. Lloyd joined the little group.

"Good morning," she said. "What's all this, then?" Penny pointed to the sign and a broad, knowing smile lit up Mrs. Lloyd's face. "Oh, so the sign's up, then, is it?" She beamed at Penny. "That's my friend Harry who's teaching the class. And if he's half as good at dancing as he is at bridge, we're in for a treat, I can tell you."

"Oh, you'll be going, then, will you?" Victoria asked.

"Of course I will," Mrs. Lloyd replied. "It was my idea, after all. Wouldn't miss it for the world." She thought for a moment, then added, "And Morwyn will be doing a write-up about it for the newspaper, I shouldn't wonder. After all, how often does someone come from Palm Beach to give us dancing lessons?" As she shifted her shopping bags from one hand to the other, she missed the quick exchange of glances between Penny and Victoria as Victoria mouthed *Palm Beach?*

"Well, I must get these bags home," Mrs. Lloyd said. "Florence is doing a nice chicken casserole for our tea tonight. Now, girls, I do hope you'll sign up for the dancing lessons as we want a very good turnout for Harry. If we don't get enough people, the classes won't be able to go ahead and that will certainly be a disappointment to some of us. And don't forget they begin in just a few days."

"We're definitely leaning toward going, Mrs. Lloyd," Penny told her.

"Yes, we are," Victoria echoed. A couple of people standing nearby murmured their assent, and as the group began to disperse to get on with the busy morning that lay ahead, Penny raised a hand to brush her hair back from her eyes and gave Victoria an almost apologetic smile.

"We must be starved for excitement because I'm starting to think I wouldn't miss this for anything," she said. "And who's this Harry when he's at home?"

"No idea," replied Victoria as they turned to go, "but we won't have to wait very long to find out." They walked on for a few metres behind Mrs. Lloyd. Just as she was about to turn down the road that led to her house, she stopped and, noticing Penny and Victoria, raised a hand and headed back toward them.

"Something I meant to ask you. If you wouldn't think it terribly rude, I wondered if I might bring two guests to the grand opening of your new spa. Florence, of course, having only just moved to Llanelen doesn't know anyone so it would do her good to get out and meet some new people. If she'll agree to come, that is. And well, Harry and I have started seeing each other, I think you might say, so naturally he would want to be my escort. I'm sure your opening will only benefit from having an extra person or two, to help fill the room. People always say they're coming and then don't turn up." She looked from one to the other.

Victoria's eyes widened slightly and Penny nodded.

"Of course, Mrs. Lloyd, we'd be delighted if you brought your guests," Victoria said. "In fact, we're meeting with Gwennie later this afternoon to sort out the catering, so we appreciate your letting us know so we can figure out the numbers."

"Oh, Gwennie's doing the catering, is she? Well, that'll be lovely, then. Do you think she'll make those little petit fours I like so much?"

"We'll ask her to make them just for you, Mrs. Lloyd," Penny replied.

Mrs. Lloyd let out a little squeak of disappointment.

"On second thought, better not. I've just started a bit of a slimming regimen and her petit fours would be so tempting."

"Right," Penny said. "No petit fours, then. We'll have a nice veggie tray for you."

Mrs. Lloyd groaned. "Do you know, I've never been particularly fond of vegetables, even though I was married to a greengrocer all those years." She gave a little shudder. "And especially not raw! Still, I appreciate the thought." She shifted her bags. "Well, must get these things home. Florence will be waiting for them. See you at the dance lessons, if not before."

Penny and Victoria headed off to the salon where their morning's work awaited them. On the way, they discussed how they should go about judging the Christmas displays in the merchants' shop windows and the kinds of categories they should create. "Most creative?" suggested Victoria.

"Like it," agreed Penny, adding, "Most beautiful?" And then they both agreed there would have to be a best in show.

In Llandudno, about fifteen miles away, Harry Saunders inserted a key into the front door of a bed-and-breakfast inn near the railway station. He opened the door quietly, hoping he would not attract the attention of the owner, a robust, bossy woman in her early sixties.

As he entered the small hallway, with its faded brown floral-patterned carpet, he was greeted by a hovering smell that put him in mind of decades of boiled vegetables and wet dog. To his dismay, he heard his landlady clumping up the stairs from the breakfast room in the basement.

"Is that you, Mr. Sanderson?" she called. "I need a word if you don't mind."

Harry sighed.

"Ah, there you are," she wheezed as she closed the basement

door behind her. "I've been meaning to speak to you. Are you planning to stay on?"

"If that would be all right with you," Harry replied with a weak smile.

"Perfectly all right," she replied, "only we'll need to square up the money. You've paid until today, so if you're going to stay for another week, I'll need to have your money by this afternoon. Same rate as last week, and you know what I charge."

Harry nodded.

"Yes, I'll just slip out this afternoon and cash a few travellers' cheques. No problem."

"Right, then."

Harry climbed the stairs to a small room on the second floor, overlooking the street. He closed the curtains, lay down on the single bed and, tucking his hands under his head, stared up the ceiling.

Where could he get sixty pounds by this afternoon, he wondered. He had a few pounds left over from the money Mrs. Lloyd had given him. He thought about a woman he'd met recently in Chester and decided to give her a call. He didn't have any time to lose and this affair with Mrs. Lloyd was taking longer than he liked to get going. But he had high hopes there. She just needed a little more cultivation, but if his experience was anything to go by, she'd be well worth it in the end. Oh yes, he had high hopes with that one. And then the dancing classes would bring in a bit of money, but it would have to be cash. He'd have to make sure Huw Bowen didn't try to take advantage of him.

The bedsprings creaked under his shifting weight as he got up.

He kept his one suitcase in the small closet and made sure it was locked each time he went out. He'd had problems before with prying landladies, but so far, this one seemed to be minding her own business.

He reached into his coat pocket and withdrew a small key, unlocked the case, and pulled out a brown envelope. He sat back down on the bed and opened it. In it were two black-and-white photographs. He took out one and examined it.

It showed a young woman holding the hand of a small boy dressed in shorts and a Fair Isle vest and wearing sturdy boots. He smiled awkwardly at the camera, as if the photographer had told him to. The woman gazed down benignly at the boy, her face lit up from within as if by love.

Behind them was a closed wooden door, set into a sturdy stone frame with rosebushes growing up each side. On the door was a knocker, in the shape of a dolphin.

Saunders's fingers brushed lightly over the image. Oh Mum, he thought for the millionth time. Why did you leave me? What happened to you? Where are you? He ran his fingers lightly over the photo and then, with a small sigh, replaced it in the envelope, tucked the envelope into a corner of the suitcase under a larger envelope, locked the case, and then pocketed the key. He wanted to find out what happened to her, but if he started asking too many questions, that could spell trouble.

He reached into an inside pocket of his coat and pulled out a small black book held closed with an elastic band. What was that Chester woman's name again? He pulled off the elastic band and riffled the pages. Oh, yes, here she is. Widow, married daughter. Have to be careful when grown-up daughters are in the frame. They don't approve of mum taking up with a man at her age. Worried about their inheritance, more like. Women without interfering children, like Mrs. Lloyd, were much better bets.

Still, Chester it would have to be. He thought about the

woman and wondered which he despised more about her: her foolish gullibility or her little moustache.

He reached for his mobile.

"Supper? I'd love to, sweetie," he was saying a few moments later. "I'll catch the next train to Chester and be with you by late afternoon. I'm counting the minutes, too. Good-bye, my dear."

He ran his hand over his face and decided there was just enough time for a quick shave. In his line of work, you had to look your best.

A few nights later, Penny and Victoria joined the queue of eager, aspiring dancers at the community centre who were lining up at a table where bank manager Huw Bowen, who ran the bridge club evenings, was taking in money, checking names off a typed list, and handing out name tags.

"This is proving much more popular than I thought it would," said Penny, looking around the room as she peeled off her HELLO! MY NAME IS PENNY badge and slapped it on her sweater.

"Too bad Gareth couldn't make it, though," Victoria replied. "There seems to be more women than men. But I guess there usually are at something like this." After a moment she added, "And don't forget, it's just the first night, so people will be here out of curiosity and to see if they like it. Some of them won't be back next week."

"Gareth said pretty much the same thing. But he also said that he'd try to come to the second class, if there is a second class," said Penny, glancing over Victoria's shoulder and raising her hand. "Oh, look, there's Thomas and Bronwyn. Let's go over and join them."

"Well, what do make of all this, then, Penny?" asked Bronwyn Evans with a vague hint of a mischievous smile.

"Not sure, yet," Penny replied, "but Victoria and I were just saying there seems to be a pretty good turnout for a cold November night when it's much easier to stay home."

"I think some people feel the same way about going to church of a Sunday morning." The Reverend Thomas Evans smiled. "Of course, I can hardly get Bronwyn to leave the house these days because she doesn't like leaving wee Robbie home alone."

"Well, he misses me," Brownwyn said, referring to the cairn terrier the couple had found cowering in the churchyard a few months earlier. In their kind and loving home, the abused, frightened dog had become a loving, trusting pet.

She seemed about to say something else when a trim man who appeared to be in his fifties took the centre of the floor and clapped his hands. He was smartly dressed in a casual way, in an open-necked white shirt under a navy blue blazer, with a blue-and-white polka-dot handkerchief peeking cheerfully from the breast pocket. Improbably, he was lightly tanned and looked as if he had just spent a long weekend yachting in the south of France.

"Is that him?" Victoria whispered. "He looks a little young for Mrs. Lloyd." Penny flashed her a knowing look and the two turned their attention back to the speaker.

"Now, ladies and gentlemen, if you'll just gather round for a moment," Harry began, "I'd like to explain a few things and then we'll get started. We're going to begin our dancing this evening by learning the fundamentals of that most graceful of dances, the waltz. This is the most classic and traditional of all the ballroom dances."

A tiny murmur of anticipation rippled through the small group as they exchanged nervous glances.

"Here's a bit of history for you. The waltz originated as a seventeenth-century Bavarian country folk dance before finding its way into European ballrooms in the early 1800s, and since then it's been one of the most popular of our formal dances and, if I may say so, when done properly, the most beautiful."

He gave Mrs. Lloyd a warm look, as if seeking reassurance, and then continued.

"Now watch closely. The basic movement is a three-step sequence that consists of a step forward or backward, a step to the side, and then a step to close the feet together." Saunders demonstrated as he talked, holding an imaginary partner in his arms. "So let's everybody try doing that, just on your own. You'll partner up in a moment. So, all together, start off by stepping back on the right leg, then to the side, then together, then forward, side, together."

He continued his demonstation as he spoke. "Don't lift your feet too high. You are not prancing ponies. Glide! Glide! And again and again."

He watched with apparent satisfaction as the group shuffled self-consciously about.

"Now," he said, "take your partners, gentlemen placing your hands on the small of your partner's back." He turned to Mrs. Lloyd, held out his hand, and pulled her toward him.

"Don't look at each other. Heads to the side, hands just so, and now let's try doing your little box step."

Giggling, Penny and Victoria were about to take each other as partners when Philip Wightman, the town undertaker, stepped forward. "May I have this dance?" he inquired in an old-fashioned way, holding out his hand to Victoria. She gave Penny a quick glance and then placed her hand in his. "I'll be back for you next time, Penny," said Philip.

Penny smiled at him and walked off to watch from the sidelines as the pairs took their first tentative steps.

"Good, good, very good. That's it." Harry and Mrs. Lloyd paused for a moment so he could observe the other couples. "Are we ready to try it with music?" He nodded at a teenager seated in the corner in front of a couple of large speakers and a hefty CD player. "And once we've mastered the basic steps, we'll add in some turns and work on our movements. I want to see you sway, rise, and fall away smoothly in time to the music. Remember, this is an elegant, sophisticated dance. Your steps should be smooth and confident.

"Right then. Here we go."

The opening strains of a Viennese waltz filled the room and the dancers took their first tentative steps. They moved awkwardly at first, many of them seeking reassurance by looking at their feet.

"Don't look at your feet," Harry called out. "They're right where you left them!"

The dancers laughed and mumbled apologies as they stepped on their partners' shoes or lurched backward when they should have glided smoothly and confidently to the side. Most of the people who had turned out had taken to the dance floor, Penny noted, although with the shortage of men, a couple of women were partnering each other.

As the music ended, the dancers applauded and inquiring eyes turned to Harry.

Holding a beaming Mrs. Lloyd by the hand, he asked if they were enjoying themselves, and in response, the little group applauded. Their enthusiasm seemed to encourage him, so he demonstrated a few more steps, and as the music started up again, the dancers set to work incorporating the additional steps into their routines.

Keeping an eye on the dancers, Penny wandered along the length of the hall to the end nearest the kitchen where a few chairs had been placed. She sat down and a few minutes later was joined by Glynnis Bowen, whose husband Huw organized most of the events in the community centre. At least a decade younger than her husband, the local bank manager, Glynnis was still attractive in a faded, what-might-have-been kind of way, and while she hadn't exactly let herself go, she didn't take the same care with herself as she had before she was married. At one time, Penny recalled, she had been a regular in the salon; now she booked a manicure only at Christmas, if that.

The two women greeted each other.

"I hear the new salon is coming along well," Glynnis said, sliding onto the chair beside Penny. "I'll be sure to make an appointment when you open. When will that be, do you think?"

"We're aiming to have everything up and running in time for Christmas," Penny replied. "Things have gone pretty well, all things considered. We've had some setbacks, that's for sure."

Glynnis nodded. "Penny, I've been thinking about asking you this for some time now. When I was younger, I used to really enjoy drawing and I wondered if I might come along with your sketching group sometime."

"Yes, do." Penny smiled at her. "We'd love to have you. We're just an informal group, but we enjoy our day out together and you'd be most welcome to join us. Why don't you give me your number and I'll ring you. Not sure where we're headed for next, but there's no shortage of beauty spots in these parts. And our Christmas lunch is coming up soon. We're going to a smart new restaurant in Conwy for that."

A few years ago Penny and Alwynne Gwilt, who looked after the local museum, had started what they called the Stretch and

Sketch Club. Members, mostly middle-aged women, got together once a month or so to ramble over the rolling green hills and through the leafy, wooded areas that surrounded the town. Some brought sketchbooks, others brought easels and paints. They usually had a destination in mind and would set up when they got there, drawing and sketching the natural beauty that lay before them. In spring, it might be wildflowers peeking through the hedgerows, in summer a flock of sheep grazing contentedly in the high pastures, or in winter the rugged handsomeness of Mount Snowdon, its snow-covered summit basking in celestial light.

A warm, friendly man transplanted from Yorkshire had recently joined them, taking stunning photographs, which he incorporated into an award-winning blog.

Penny sold her watercolours in local gift shops and during the high tourist season found it difficult to keep up with demand. She wondered, though, if that would change with the greater demands on her time of running the spa.

Realizing that she had missed something Glynnis had said, she turned her attention back to her.

". . . don't you think?"

"I'm so sorry, Glynnis. I was miles away. What were you saying?"

"Oh, nothing, really. I was just saying that Mrs. Lloyd seems very animated tonight. I think she's really enjoying dancing with that man."

Penny followed her gaze to the centre of the room where the dancers were just finishing the waltz.

Something about the wistfulness in Glynnis's voice caught her attention.

"Did you not want to dance, Glynnis? Surely Huw would give you a turn or two around the floor?"

Glynnis shook her head.

"No, not one for dancing, is our Huw. He likes playing bridge, but that's about it. He's really more interested in organizing the events because he likes to make sure the community centre is well taken care of. For some reason, he feels very proprietary about it." She shrugged. "He just likes things to be done right, I suppose, and the right way is always his way." She glanced at the group of dancers. "But I might ask the same thing of you. Would you like to join the dancers?"

"I'm not bothered. Really, I think I'd rather just watch."

The music stopped and the dancers broke away from their partners. Penny and Glynnis looked up as Mrs. Lloyd led Harry Saunders over to them.

Talk about proprietary, thought Penny.

"Oh, Penny," she exclaimed, holding her right hand over her heart. "I told Harry I'd sit this one out with you and give someone else a chance to dance with him. What about one of you?" She looked brightly at Glynnis. "How about you, dear, since Huw doesn't seem up to it? Harry will show you the steps and you'll catch on in no time."

Harry held out a hand, and with a small shrug, Glynnis took it. As the two joined the dancers, Harry gave the signal and the music started up. Mrs. Lloyd and Penny watched as he put his arm around Glynnis and they started to waltz. They moved smoothly in time to the music, turning gracefully and rhythmically.

"Well, what do you think, Penny?" Mrs. Lloyd asked. "You can't have enjoyed yourself very much sitting here on the sidelines. You'll have to get the policeman of yours here next week."

"You're right, Mrs. Lloyd, I will."

"Why isn't he here tonight?"

"He's with the major crimes unit, Mrs. Lloyd. You know how it is. It's always something."

"Well, I'm sure it is, but he shouldn't let his police work get in the way of his personal life. Policemen tend to put the job first. They should pay more attention to all that talk about balance in their lives that everybody's going on about these days. In my day, you went to work and you came home. You arrived on time and you left on time, and that was it and nobody thought any more about it. I think the problem is all these mobile devices everywhere. No one can survive five minutes without checking their e-mail. Is everybody so important the world's going to come to an end if they don't check their e-mail? Or send one of those awful text messages."

Penny knew from long experience with Mrs. Lloyd in the salon that once she was off and running it was best just to wait it out, with the odd "mmm hmm" and "you may be right" sprinkled in every now and then to let her know that she had your full attention.

"And Harry and I have come up with the most wonderful idea for New Year's Eve. He's going to announce it at the end of the class tonight. You'll want to get your policeman in on this, that's for sure."

At the end of the dance Harry returned with Glynnis, and Mrs. Lloyd stood up, smoothing down her skirt.

"Last dance," Harry announced. "Evelyn, may I have the honour?" He turned to Glynnis. "Thank you, my dear, it was a pleasure."

As the dancers resumed their positions, Glynnis turned to Penny.

"I'd better go," she said. "Huw will be wanting me to help him close up. But please call me. I'd love to go sketching with your group."

Penny assured her she would and then turned her attention to the dance floor. The difference in the dancers' confidence and ability in just two hours was amazing. They smiled at their partners, held their heads high, and seemed to be really enjoying themselves.

"Now then," Harry was saying, "Evelyn and I have a little surprise for you. Over the next few weeks we're going to work on our dancing skills and then on New Year's Eve, we'll have a wonderful, old-fashioned evening of dancing. Best bib and tucker!"

Mrs. Lloyd beamed as the dancers broke into applause.

"Now next week, we're off to sunny Argentina to learn how to tango. I hope you all enjoyed yourselves tonight and that you'll be back next week. And tell your friends!"

Penny smiled as Victoria made her way over to her.

"Well, that went well," Penny said. "You danced all evening with Philip."

"It was fun. He's a surprisingly good dancer." Victoria smiled. "You don't expect that from an undertaker."

"No, I guess you don't," Penny agreed, "although I've always thought he's a lovely man."

"Yes, he is and I think he rather fancied you, at one point." She lowered her voice. "But honestly, what do you think of Mrs. Lloyd and that dancing instructor? She seems really taken with him. Do you think he's all right?"

"I don't know, but what I can't figure out is what he's doing here. What would bring someone like him to this small town?"

Victoria gave her an ironic smile.

"The same thing that brought you?" And as an afterthought she added, "And me, too, I guess."

Penny nodded.

"So I wonder what he's running away from."

"Or who."

As usual, Glynnis and Huw Bowen were the last to leave the community centre.

"Well, I think that went well, all things considered," Huw said as he checked to make sure the door was locked behind them. "But he might have consulted me about that New Year's dance before making his big announcement. Now I suppose we'll have to go and I was looking forward to watching it on telly."

"You don't have to go if you don't want to, Huw," his wife replied. "I'm sure we could manage without you for one night."

"'We'? You don't mean you'd come without me, do you?"

"Yes, I think that's exactly what I meant." She let out a bored, tired sigh. "Oh, I don't know what I meant. Never mind."

Mrs. Lloyd said good night to Harry on her doorstep. She had decided not to invite him in as she was tired and anxious to clean her face, slather on the expensive apple-serum rejuvenating moisturizer she had just bought, and slip into her nice, warm bed. The dancing had definitely tired her out.

She held her face up and he kissed her cheek.

Then, putting her key in the lock, she let herself into the still, dark house and stood there for a moment before tugging one by one at the fingers of her gloves.

"Had a good time, did you then?" came a voice out of the dark silence.

"Oh! Really, Florence, you scared the life out of me. What on earth do you mean by creeping up on me like that?"

Mrs. Lloyd switched on the hall light to discover Florence in her tattered dark green dressing gown with large red dragons winding around the sleeves.

"Sorry, I'm sure," Florence said. "Only when I heard you come in and realized you were alone, I thought I'd just see if you wanted anything. Cup of tea before you head up?"

"Well, now that you mention it, that might just hit the spot, if you're making one anyway," Mrs. Lloyd agreed. "I'll get my coat off while you get the kettle on."

A few minutes later, settled on the sofa lifting a cup of tea to her lips, Mrs. Lloyd beamed at her companion.

"Oh, Florence, I do wish you'd come," she said. "We all had such a wonderful time and everyone had such high praise for Harry. It wasn't any time at all until everyone was waltzing away and having the time of their lives."

She sat back against the plump cushions, waving away the biscuits Florence held out to her.

"No, Florence, and you must not tempt me again. I am determined to lose at least half a stone before the grand opening of the new spa. And that reminds me"—she leaned forward and set her teacup down—"I've decided that we're going to give a little party of our own. We'll talk about the date tomorrow, but I'd like to have a few friends and neighbours in for a Christmas drink one afternoon. Just a few mince pies and a glass of sherry. Nothing too complicated, but it is, after all, the season of good-will, and we're going to show some."

She stood up.

"And now I must be off to my bed. Thank you for the tea.

Don't worry about the cups tonight. You can tidy up in the morning."

Florence dropped a little curtsey to Mrs. Lloyd's disappearing back.

"Yes ma'am," she muttered. "Whatever you say."

Seven

"You know, Penny, when he took me in his arms, I could have danced all night!"

"You certainly seemed to be enjoying yourself, Mrs. Lloyd," Penny said as she leaned forward to apply a base coat to her client's nails.

"Well, it wasn't just me enjoying myself, Penny, in case you didn't notice. Everyone was."

"Yes, they certainly seemed to."

Penny had barely been able to contain her astonishment when Mrs. Lloyd entered the salon for her standing Thursday afternoon manicure. Penny had quickly caught Eirlys's eye and given a quick shake of her head. Following her lead, Eirlys returned to her client after giving Mrs. Lloyd a quick smile and, beyond the expected polite, cheery hello, said nothing.

Gone was Mrs. Lloyd's rigidly permed, iron-grey hair, replaced by loose chestnut curls. At first, Penny had thought she was wearing a wig, but when she caught a glimpse of pink scalp, she realized Mrs. Lloyd must have spent hours that morning at the hair salon. With the dieting, hair colour, and softer hairstyle, Mrs. Lloyd was in full makeover mode. Soon would come wardrobe changes. She's got it bad, Penny thought. If she had been married, her husband would have huge cause for concern. She was displaying all the classic symptoms.

"I'm going into Llandudno tomorrow to get some new clothes," Mrs. Lloyd was saying, as if she had just read Penny's mind. "Normally, Angharad Roberts makes my dresses, and a very good job she does, too, but I think I'll go for something off the rack. I'm so tired of just about everything in my wardrobe. It all seems so frumpy and dated, and we need something new every now and then to perk ourselves up, don't you think?"

"Yes, Mrs. Lloyd, we certainly do," Penny agreed. "What are you thinking you might get?'

"Something a bit more youthful. A flirty skirt! A stylish top! Both!"

Penny grinned. "Go for it, Mrs. Lloyd! Why not?"

"Why not indeed. And that reminds me. I've decided that Florence and I are going to hold a little holiday open house, so you might want to mark your calendar. It'll be from two to four in the afternoon and you and Victoria should both come. Oh, and of course bring that policeman of yours, too, if he's a mind to come. That's if he's not too busy with, what did you call it, major crime." Mrs. Lloyd gave Penny the date. "We chose the day so it wouldn't conflict with your grand opening. But between the two of us, we're all going to have a very busy holiday season this year. I always say Christmas will be here before we know it, and every year it just creeps up on us and proves me right."

Mrs. Lloyd selected a rich, deep burgundy polish that she said would go nicely with a smart jacket she had recently bought.

"It's in the Chanel style, you might say. And with my pearls, it should be just right for the bridge game tonight."

After a moment's thought, she leaned closer and gave Penny an intent look.

"Would you mind terribly if I asked you a question? What are your thoughts on tights?"

"Tights?"

Victoria looked up from her computer where she had been entering numbers into a spreadsheet.

"Yes, tights. She read in a magazine that they're considered outdated and aging. She wondered if that was just true for young women or for everyone. She wonders if she should stop wearing them but wonders if it would look strange for a woman her age to go about with bare legs."

"Oh, Lord." Victoria laughed. "It doesn't bear thinking about. Not in this weather, anyway." After a moment she added, "I still wear them. Do you?"

"I do. I can't stand the way my feet feel in shoes without socks or stockings. But I know that young women don't wear them. I really don't know what the rule is for older women or where the cutoff point is."

"Well, anyway," said Victoria, pressing a button on the computer and then sitting back with her arms folded, "the good news is that we're still within budget on the renovation— just—and they tell me the work will be done on time. How did you get on with Gwennie?"

"Oh really well," Penny replied. "She's happy to do the food for the opening and she'll take care of the other things, too, like tablecloths and plates and cutlery. I've given her the guest list so she knows how many are coming and I ordered the flowers."

"And the wine?"

"Right, that's done, too. Oh, and Mrs. Lloyd is having a little get-together a couple of days before our event, so it's shaping up to be a busy holiday season."

"It'll be fun, though. I love Christmas. Such a happy time of year. Peace on earth and all that."

"And this year, it might be a white one. They're predicting snow and lots of it this winter."

In Llandudno, at the North Wales Police station, Sergeant Bethan Morgan looked up as her supervisor, Detective Chief Inspector Gareth Davies, carrying a small, sickly looking plant, passed by her desk on the way to his office.

"Afternoon, sir."

"Afternoon, Sergeant. Thanks for holding the fort. The meeting with the district commissioner went on longer than I thought it would." He gestured at the plant. "Rescued this poor thing from his office. So what's been happening today?"

"It all seems pretty quiet. There's just one thing. Been some thefts reported in Llanelen."

Davies set the plant on her desk and waited.

"I've had a call from one of the charity shops. Apparently a few small items have gone missing and the woman who runs it thinks there's a shoplifter on the loose."

She glanced down at the notebook beside the telephone and pointed her pencil at it.

"Funny stuff. Odds and ends. Let's see." She picked up the

notebook and, after a quick look at Davies to make sure he was listening, read from a short list. "A biography of John Lennon. A serving plate with a daffodil pattern in the centre. A couple of packets of blank note cards. A wooly sheep with horns. A figurine of a shepherdess, complete with crook and lamb."

She set down the notebook.

"The woman said there may be more items, but they don't have a bar code kind of inventory system, naturally, so it's difficult for her to know."

"Did you ask her if another shop assistant could have sold any of these items?"

Morgan gave him a withering look.

He held up a hand. "Yes, of course you did," he said good-naturedly. "How did she come to notice the things were missing?"

"She said that someone wanted the John Lennon book for her grandson but didn't have much cash on her. The shop doesn't do debit or take credit cards, so the woman said she'd go to the bank and do a bit more shopping and then stop back later. The charity shop woman said when the customer returned in the afternoon the book was gone, but she hadn't sold it to anyone. They looked all through the books in case someone had moved it, but it wasn't there." Bethan took a sip of her coffee. "She felt bad that she hadn't put the book aside for the customer."

"Anybody unusual or suspicious in the store that day?"

"No, just the usual townsfolk. Some dropping off donations, others browsing. A few sales. But nothing out of the ordinary."

"Well, I don't know there's much we can do at this point, but we'll keep an eye on the situation and see if any more reports come in." He picked up the plant and seemed about to move on.

"I can't tell you how glad I am it wasn't ladies' knickers disappearing from clotheslines." He gave a little shudder. "For a moment there when you said things have been disappearing . . . Haven't had one of those cases in years and don't want one, either."

"Well, not too likely, sir. People don't dry clothes outside much anymore and anyway, it's winter."

"People used to hang their laundry out to dry all year round," Davies said. "When I was a lad, my mother used to hang out the wash in the winter and it would freeze on the line. Then she'd bring it all back in the house, frozen stiff, and hang it all up again inside. I could never understand the point of hanging it out."

He smiled at her. "The good old days. You won't remember them. You weren't born yet."

The dancing class was proving more popular than Harry Saunders had hoped. Instead of the numbers dropping off, they increased and the next week, as word got round, a few more couples showed up. Mrs. Lloyd, who was starting to fantasize about being Harry's partner in bridge, in dancing, and hopefully, in the not too distant future, in life, was over the moon.

"I told you the dancing lessons would be a great success," she remarked to Florence on the morning of their open house.

"Yes, Evelyn, you did and you were right, as usual," Florence replied as she polished a glass.

"Now, have we got everything we need for this afternoon?"

"Yes, it's all set. I've just a few more things to put out. Leave it to me and you get along to church. You don't want to be late."

Mrs. Lloyd, now looking a few pounds slimmer, gave an airy wave and disappeared into the hall. Florence heard her rustling about in the cupboard, and a few minutes later, the front door was pulled shut behind her.

Florence plumped a few pillows and then, noticing a few envelopes on Mrs. Lloyd's desk, opened the top drawer and slid them inside. She then turned her attention to the dining room and, after straightening a row of forks, gave the table one last approving nod. Mrs. Lloyd's benefactor, the aunt of her late husband, would have thought the table magnificent. Her fine old china, a pattern featuring fruit on a cobalt blue background, had been washed and neatly arranged on a crisply ironed linen cloth. Gleaming silverware flanked a centrepiece of silver candelabra with space in the middle for a floral arrangement of festive red carnations. A plaid table runner gave everything a seasonal look.

Florence had set out small glasses for sherry and larger ones for wine. She was determined that her spread would be at least as good as the one at the spa opening and knew that because many of their guests would be going to both events, comparisons would be inevitable. In the kitchen, she opened the fridge door and peered inside. The large cheese tray she had prepared last night, tightly covered in cling film, a fruit tray, small quiches, packets of smoked salmon waiting to be opened, sliced lemons for garnish, and more awaited their guests.

At precisely five minutes to two, Florence would place all the trays on the table and the party would begin. She was happy to look after the food and drink, leaving Mrs. Lloyd to circulate and socialize. Florence not only knew her place but liked it very much. It was definitely starting to feel like home.

And now, there was nothing to do but wait for the guests to arrive and the party to start.

———

As Florence set the last platter on the dining room table the sound of ambient chatter began to fill the adjacent living room.

"Oh, Penny, of course you already know my friend Harry, but, Harry, I don't think you've met Penny's friend Inspector Gareth Davies." Saunders seemed momentarily taken aback but recovered his composure quickly and held out his hand. Davies shook it and casually asked Saunders where he was staying.

"Oh, an old friend of mine has a place not too far from here, farther up the valley," Saunders replied. "He's in the States for a few months and said I could use it while he's away."

"And how long will you be staying with us, do you think?" Davies asked.

Saunders let out something that might have been a wheezy chuckle and turned to Mrs. Lloyd.

"Does he give all your guests the third degree or is it just me?"

Davies' eyes narrowed slightly and he smiled at Penny who gave an eloquent, apologetic shrug.

"Now, Inspector," said Mrs. Lloyd, "I was telling Penny just the other day that you should get out and about and have more fun. Come to the dancing classes with us, why don't you! But for today, you're off duty and among friends so we'll have no more of your questions. Just enjoy yourself. And now," she said, turning to him and touching Saunders gently on the arm, "you and I need to circulate amongst our guests. There are others who would like to meet you. Oh, look, there's Huw and Glynnis Bowen. And Bronwyn and Thomas Evans. Such a good turnout."

The room had filled up as they'd been speaking. Penny waved to the rector and his wife who had just arrived. Davies' eyes followed Saunders and Mrs. Lloyd into the living room. Keeping his eyes on them, he inclined his head toward Penny.

"Later, I want you to tell me everything you know about him."

"Do you know this inspector well, Evelyn?" Saunders was saying.

"No, not really," Evelyn replied as she led him to the food table, where they admired Florence's spread. "I hear he's very taken with Penny Brannigan. Now, I'd like you to come over here, Harry, and meet Bunny, an old friend of mine. We go way back." Catching herself, she added, "Well, not that far back, of course."

Saunders examined the table and seemed to focus on a tray of hot nibbles that Florence had just brought out of the kitchen.

"And this Penny, now, is she . . . ?"

"Penny?" Mrs. Lloyd gave him a quizzical look. "Oh, Penny, she's just the person who does my nails."

Saunders helped himself to a stuffed mushroom, which he balanced on a red paper napkin, and then gave Mrs. Lloyd his best smile.

"Introduce me to Bunny, why don't you. I'm dying to meet her."

As the last of the guests departed, Mrs. Lloyd sank gratefully into a comfortable chair and, with a sigh, slipped off her shoes and rubbed the toes of one foot against the toes of the other.

"Oh, that was wonderful," she said. "I enjoyed myself enormously and I think all our guests did, too." Saunders lowered his eyes and watched Florence as she picked up several used paper napkins and stuffed them into an empty glass. She loaded several glasses onto a large tray, added the plates of leftover food, and then disappeared into the kitchen. They soon heard the sound of running water followed by the closing of the kitchen door. A few seconds later, the doorknob turned silently and the door opened an imperceptible crack.

Saunders sat on the couch and patted the seat beside him. "Come on over here, Evelyn," he said. "I've got something to ask you."

With a surprisingly shy smile, Mrs. Lloyd did as he asked. "Yes, Harry? What is it?" After a quick glance at the kitchen door, he leaned toward Mrs. Lloyd and put his arm around her.

"I thought you looked especially lovely this afternoon, Evelyn," he said softly. "In fact, ever since I met you, you've been getting more beautiful in my eyes."

"Perhaps that's because you bring out the best in me, Harry." Mrs. Lloyd smiled at him. "You make me feel alive again. I feel younger when I'm with you."

"Oh, I don't think it's anything to do with me at all. You're a very special woman, Evelyn." He gave her hand a friendly, reassuring squeeze and cleared his throat. Although she was bursting to hear whatever it was he wanted to ask her, Mrs. Lloyd waited.

"As you know, my dear, over the past few weeks we've become rather close and I was wondering what you would think about us becoming partners."

"Partners?" exclaimed Mrs. Lloyd. "What do you mean exactly, by partners?"

"Well, we're bridge partners and dancing partners and I've got something else in mind."

"Oh, Harry, really?"

"Yes," he said. "I'm offering you the chance to make a lot of money. I thought you might like to consider becoming one of my investment partners."

As a look of profound disappointment crossed her face, Mrs. Lloyd gazed down at her hands and twirled her wedding ring. Harry raised an eyebrow and nodded at her.

"Well, I say business partners, but I do hope that it might one day be more than that," he went on. "You mean a lot to me, Evelyn, even though we haven't known each other very long, and I think, well, at least I hope, that you feel something for me, too."

"Oh, I do, Harry, I do!"

"Well, perhaps we could, um"—he glanced again at the kitchen door and spoke softly—"I guess it might be a little awkward if I were to stay over, what with Florence and all, much as I would want to." His voice trailed off.

"She'll be off to spend the weekend with her sister in Liverpool," Evelyn said eagerly. "Oh, what are we like? Planning to spend a weekend together as if we were a couple of kids and having to wait until the grown-ups leave so we can have the house all to ourselves." A thought seemed to cross her mind and she became serious. "If I'd known I was going to meet you, Harry, and how we would come to feel about each other, I never would have asked Florence to stay. You're right. It does make things awkward for us, having her here."

Harry gave her a quizzical look and lowered his voice.

"Does it have to? After all, this is your house and surely you decide who you want to have here with you."

Mrs. Lloyd was about to reply when the kitchen door opened and Florence emerged carrying a tray full of clean glasses. She gave the couple a little nod.

"Don't mind me. I've just got to put these best glasses back in the sideboard before they get broken."

Mrs. Lloyd and Saunders remained silent as Florence lined up the glasses on the sideboard shelf. They made a soft scraping sound as she slid them into place.

"Well, give some thought to what I said, Evelyn," Saunders said as Florence disappeared back into the kitchen.

"I will, Harry," Mrs. Lloyd replied. "What exactly do you mean by business partner? What would I have to do?"

Harry waited for the sound of the kitchen door closing before he spoke.

"Well, I run an exclusive syndicate of carefully chosen investors. We pool our money equally so we have more to invest. We buy hedge funds on margin and derivatives when they're down and then we sell them when the market rebounds. All in U.S. dollars, of course. Sound as a bell. So far I've made quite a bit of money for the investors, I can tell you. As for you and me, we'd just need to set up a joint account at the bank, we contribute equally to it, and then I take care of everything," he said. "And then a few weeks later, I give you a nice cheque. Your original investment back, plus a tidy profit."

Mrs. Lloyd cleared her throat.

"Well, I don't know. Huw Bowen at the bank manages my investments for me. I don't know very much about that kind of thing."

She hesitated.

"And while we're speaking of money, Harry, I hate to bring this up, but there is one thing," she began tentatively. "That night we had dinner at the Red Dragon Hotel, you remember, the night you lost your wallet, you did say you would reimburse me and I am so sorry to mention it but . . ."

"Oh, my goodness!" exclaimed Harry. "Did I not . . . well, here, let's sort that out right now." He shifted forward on the sofa and withdrew a sleek, black leather wallet from his back pocket. He held it in front of him for a moment revealing a glimpse of the two intertwined Gs for Gucci, then opened the billfold section allowing Mrs. Lloyd to see at least an inch of folded bills. He withdrew several and gave them to her.

"There you are, my dear, that should cover it. And please accept my apologies for being so tardy in repaying you. Forgot all about it! Won't happen again, I promise!"

Mrs. Lloyd settled deeper in the sofa and leaned her head on Saunders's shoulder. He moved his arm to accommodate her, and then turned it ever so slightly so he could check his watch.

"How did you sleep?" Mrs. Lloyd asked Florence the next morning. "What time did you go to bed? I didn't hear you come up."

"I wanted to leave the kitchen shipshape," Florence replied. "I can't abide coming downstairs in the morning to a sink full of dirty dishes. No matter how late, I like to have everything tidied away before I head off to my bed."

She held a steaming pot of freshly brewed coffee in her right hand and reached for Mrs. Lloyd's cup with her left. At that moment, the post dropped through the letterbox and Florence set down the coffeepot. She trotted down the hall, picked up the cards and letters, and returned a few minutes later.

"Your letter opener wasn't on your desk," she said to Mrs. Lloyd as she handed her a few colourful envelopes. "I looked in the most likely places but didn't see it."

A small frown creased Mrs. Lloyd's forehead as she picked up an envelope and tugged it open with her fingers.

"Well, it must be somewhere," she said. "You probably put it in a drawer or something when you were dusting or tidying up.

We'll have a good look for it after breakfast." She shrugged and turned her attention to the Christmas card in her hand. "Oh, look, it's from Huw and Glynnis. How nice of them to send the card through the post when I saw them only yesterday." She stood the card on end and admired the image of a plump robin sitting on a little branch lightly dusted with glitter.

She picked up the next envelope in the little stack and, after a quick glance, offered it to Florence.

"I think this is your invitation to the opening of the Llanelen Spa."

Florence smiled as she tucked the envelope in the pocket of her blue-and-white-striped apron.

"Well, good," said Mrs. Lloyd. "I take it you're pleased and I expect that means you'll be going."

"Oh, yes," said Florence, giving her pocket a pat. "I can't wait."

Mrs. Lloyd's eyes narrowed slightly as she shifted in her chair.

"Harry will be joining us for dinner this evening. He likes chicken and has a good appetite, I've noticed. Do you think you could make that casserole with the dumplings? It was very good last time and I'm sure he'll enjoy it. Oh, and as we'll be discussing pressing business matters, it would really be best if it were just the two of us. You wouldn't mind having your dinner in the kitchen, would you?"

"Of course not, Evelyn," Florence replied. "I understand completely. I could even have a tray in my room, if that would suit you better." She slid into her chair and placed her napkin on her lap.

"Evelyn?"

"Hmm." Mrs. Lloyd looked up from her plate. "Yes, Florence, what is it?"

Florence hesitated. "Well, it's about that Harry Saunders. You will be careful, won't you?"

"Careful? Whatever do you mean?"

"Well, it's just that I wouldn't want to see you get hurt, that's all, and—"

Mrs. Lloyd interrupted her. "Oh, and I'm a big girl, Florence, and I can take care of myself. Careful! Whatever do you mean?"

"Well, there's something about him that I don't think is completely trustworthy. In fact, I—"

Mrs. Lloyd held up her hand. "That's enough now, Florence. I won't hear anything said against him."

Florence nodded. "What time would you like me to serve dinner?"

Eight

*P*enny finished applying her lipstick and stepped back to examine her reflection in the mirror. When she thought about it, she found it difficult to believe that she was in her fifties, and she was always mildly astonished that the woman in the mirror who looked back at her was not in her mid-twenties. Where did those years go, she asked herself with a resigned sigh as she replaced the cap on her lipstick and set it down in a little pewter dish on the vanity table.

With a small, satisfied smile, she took in the tranquility of her new bathroom with its gleaming shower, soft lighting, fluffy white towels, and pale grey walls. After taking possession of the cottage, Penny had lived in it for a few weeks to get a feel for the place before tackling the renovation, and now that the work was complete, she was very pleased with the results.

The downstairs had been opened up, so the formerly small

sitting room, dining room, and kitchen were now one generous living space with what real estate agents liked to call open flow. A thoroughly modern kitchen with custom cabinetry clad in wenge paneling and stylish lighting fixtures had been installed, but Penny had insisted on keeping the original slate flooring and the now highly prized Rayburn cooker. Above the cooker, attached to the ceiling, was a laundry drying system, with a complicated set of ropes and pulleys to lower the rack for loading and then hoist it back to the ceiling where towels and sheets could dry in the warmth from the range. Emma had told her once that the airer, as the British called it, was also sometimes known as a Sheila Maid.

In the living area, the outdated, brown soft furnishings were gone, replaced by a cream-colored sofa highlighted with plump floral pillows and a pair of elegant wing chairs. Small side tables had been repositioned, and with Emma's clutter and collectibles gone, the space was airy and inviting.

Gareth Davies sat now in one of the wing chairs and looked around him. In the early fall he had sat in the same place, knowing that once Penny had completed her renovation the cottage would resemble something right out of the pages of an interior design magazine. And he had been right.

He stood up when he heard her footsteps on the stairs and his eyes lit up when he saw her.

"You look lovely tonight," he said, as she stepped off the bottom stair and into his arms. A moment later he held her at arm's length. "Let me look at you."

Penny was wearing a long-sleeved woolen dress in a soft red. A narrow red ribbon encircling her waist and tied in a neat bow at the front provided detail and interest.

Gareth reached into his pocket and pulled out a small red leather box.

"I got you a little something to mark the opening of your new business," he said as he handed the gift to her. "I hope you like it."

Penny smiled at him as she opened the box and then gave a little gasp.

Nestled on a bed of midnight blue silk was a brooch in the form of a delicate, sparkling snowflake.

"It's beautiful," she said as she pinned it to the shoulder of her dress. "I love it. Thank you." She gave it a little pat and then smiled up at him.

"Would you mind if we skip the drink and just go? I'd rather be off now so we can get there a little early."

"Of course." He helped her on with her winter coat, and together they walked to his car. The night was cold, with the promise of snow before morning.

Davies, who had been banned from the spa for weeks in the run-up to the big reveal, was astonished by the transformation. While the conversion had maintained the character and charm of the old stone building, inside it was now unrecognizable. Gone were years of decay and decrepitude, peeling paint and worm-eaten floorboards, replaced by light, style, and the promise of a wonderful experience.

"Hello, Victoria," he said as she greeted them at the door. "You look lovely tonight, too." With her shoulder-length blond hair tied back in a small black velvet bow that complemented her little black dress, makeup expertly applied, and wearing rather high heels, Victoria looked expensive and well cared for. The spa's clients would identify perfectly with that look.

"Thank you, Gareth. Coats over there," she said, gesturing

to a small room off the main hall where a large coatrack brought over from the hotel had been set up.

"Now then, the bar's over there and Eirlys will be along in a few minutes with food. But Penny will look after you. I've just got a few last-minute things to see to." She smiled at both of them and disappeared.

"Let me show you around," Penny said. "We'll start over here, at the manicure salon. It's like the old place, only better."

Besides the manicure salon, their ground-floor tour included a hairdressing salon with two stations, three massage/treatment rooms, walk-in supply cupboards, and a restaurant-quality kitchen filled with gleaming stainless-steel appliances. As they entered, a small woman in a white uniform artfully arranging canapés on a silver tray stopped what she was doing and stood back from the table holding her tiny hands in front of her bosom.

"Don't let us interrupt you, Gwennie," said Penny. "Just giving Inspector Davies here a quick look round before the guests arrive." She took a closer look at the prepared trays waiting to be sent out and then gave Gwennie a broad smile.

"They look wonderful, Gwennie. You do such wonderful work. But those trays you're using, they aren't ours. Did you . . . ?"

"Yes, I did, Miss Penny. They're from the Hall and the finest silver they are, too. I asked Mr. Emyr if we could use them tonight and he said certainly we could. Said I could borrow anything I needed." She sighed. "It's not as if he ever does entertaining, rattling around like he does all by himself in that big house. When he's home, that is." Her meerkat-like eyes moved from Penny to Davies. "I don't know what's to become of him, or the Hall, to be honest. Since his fiancée died last summer, he's just had no interest in anything. He travels a lot, but his heart doesn't really seem to be at home or anywhere else, far as I can tell."

"Well, you know that we want you to come and work for us," Penny said. "Victoria's explained everything to you, and we need you. If there's not enough work at the Hall to keep you busy, there's plenty for you to do here." She shot a quick glance at Davies who was reaching toward the tray Gwennie was working on.

"Yes, sir, do take one," Gwennie said to him. "Two, if you like. There are lots more. And these ones with the smoked salmon spread are quite nice."

She checked her watch.

"And Eirlys is coming in to pass them round, is she? I'd expect to see her any minute now. It's almost time."

A light bustle in the doorway signaled that Eirlys had arrived, and with a broad, excited smile, she bounded into the room.

"Hi, Penny, Gwennie," she greeted the two women, adding, "I wore the white blouse and black skirt just like you told me to, Gwennie."

"Hi, Eirlys," said Penny. "This is my friend Detective Chief Inspector Davies. I don't think you've met him."

"Oh, hello," said Eirlys, extending her hand. "I'm happy to meet you."

"Right, well, we'll leave you to it," said Penny as Gwennie held up the tray so Davies could sample a couple more canapés before they moved on.

"Where would you like me to start?" Eirlys asked Gwennie.

"First things first, young lady," said Gwennie as she set the tray down. "What's the first thing we do in the kitchen before we touch food?"

"Oh, right," said Eirlys as she immediately turned and walked toward the sink.

Penny and Gareth left the room to the sound of running water as Eirlys washed her hands.

The reception area had begun to fill up and several guests were sipping wine and gazing around in awe.

"Well, it certainly has that wow factor," Mrs. Lloyd was saying to Harry Saunders. "You would never have believed what this place used to look like. Disgusting it was. It's amazing what money can do, isn't it?"

"Oh, yes, Evelyn," he replied, pursing his lips. "Absolutely amazing."

Florence Semble trailed after them, left out of the conversation. But she didn't mind. She'd been to lots of parties on her own, and she wasn't so much interested in the socializing as she was in the food.

She helped herself to a small sandwich from the tray that Eirlys was passing around and, after examining it critically, took a delicate nibble and then ate the rest of it. Across the room a flash of red caught her eye, and recognizing Penny, she headed over to her.

"Oh, hello, Florence," said Penny, "so glad you could make it. How are you? Getting something to eat? Can we offer you a drink?"

Florence took a step closer and shook her head. "No, thanks, nothing to drink for me right now. But I was hoping to have a word with you. When it's convenient, like."

Penny and Victoria exchanged glances and Penny stepped away.

"Is there something the matter, Florence?"

"You know me well enough by now, Penny," she said in a low voice, glancing slightly behind her. "Some folks might think I'm a little blunt, but I speak as I find and you always know where you are with me, so I'm going to come right to the point." She looked across the room where Mrs. Lloyd, holding Harry's arm, was talking animatedly with the rector and his wife, Bronwyn.

"Is there someplace we can go for a quiet word?"

"Yes, there is," said Penny. "Just through here. Follow me."

She led the way down a well-lit hall and into a small room that faced the river. She switched on a lamp and then turned to face Florence.

"We had this bit of extra space so I decided to make it into a little reading room. Please, have a seat."

The room was a serene little haven with two comfortable chairs, bookshelves displaying a few best sellers, and a low coffee table with new fashion and style magazines. It would be the perfect spot for a quiet chat over a cappuccino with a new friend, or if a guest wanted a private place to check e-mail, think, or read.

"Oh, this is very attractive," Florence said, impressed despite herself. "But it's Evelyn I wanted to talk to you about. Evelyn and that man."

"Harry Saunders."

"Yes, Harry Saunders." His name curdled on her lips. "That's the one. He's a charmer. What used to be called a cad. He's wormed his way into her affections and she can't see it. It's so obvious he only wants her for her money."

"Well, maybe he does," said Penny, "but I don't think there's anything you or I can do about it." She thought for a moment. "You know, maybe you should speak to Mrs. Lloyd's niece, Morwyn. Have you met Morwyn? They're very close and perhaps she could have a word with Mrs. Lloyd."

"I thought of that," said Florence, "but she's just gone to Spain for six weeks. On holiday, like."

"Well, listen, Florence, if you're that concerned, maybe you should suggest that she come home."

Florence pinched her lips together. "I don't know how I would contact her. I have no idea where she's staying and I don't have her mobile number. And if I tried to get it, Evelyn would want to know why."

Penny acknowledged the truth of that.

"What makes you think he's after her money?" Penny asked.

Florence groaned. "You've met him! What's he like? Comes across with all that charm, but I see him for what he is, even if no one else can. There's so much about him that's not right." She leaned forward. "He says he's from some posh family in Florida. Old money. Ha! He's got about as much class as a re-claimed brick. He makes you feel like you want to count your fingers after you've shaken hands with him."

She gave her fingers a little twiddle and then raised a hand to her cheek.

"You know, I came from a very poor family and we didn't have much, but my mother always used to tell us that good manners cost nothing. She made sure we grew up knowing what a butter knife is for and little things like that. Now the first time that Saunders character came to the house he didn't seem to know enough to use a coaster. What kind of civilized person puts a wet glass down on a nice wooden table? And last night, when he came for dinner, he cut his bread roll in half and buttered the whole thing. Just slathered it on!"

She sat back with a triumphant look.

Penny inclined her head. "And the bread roll is important because . . ."

"Because anyone his age who came from a fancy Palm Beach background would have been taught that you break a little piece off your bread roll and butter that. You don't slice the thing in half."

"Of course. Anything else?"

"Well, yes, there is. I think he's after Mrs. Lloyd to let him move in with her, and once he gets his feet under the table . . ."

"You'll have to move out? Florence, is that what this is really about?"

Florence looked at her hands and then raised her lined, care-worn face. Penny and Victoria had met her a few months earlier in Liverpool when she had been living in a suburban bedsit and struggling to make ends meet on a tiny pension. Her face had filled out since then, Penny realized, taking years off her appearance. Being with Mrs. Lloyd in her safe, comfortable home must seem as if she'd landed in the lap of luxury.

"You and Mrs. Lloyd hadn't known each other very long or very well before you moved in, had you?" Penny asked gently.

"No. But we were getting along just fine until he came along. We had our routine and I was happy to take on the cook-ing and do what I could around the place. Making sure every-thing runs smoothly, like. I've settled in now and I want to go on living there," Florence said. "I gave up my place, such as it was, in Liverpool to move here. I'll never find another place now at the rent I was paying at my old place."

Penny sighed and touched Florence on the arm.

"I'm sorry, but Victoria will be wondering what's happened to me. I had better get back to our guests."

"Yes, you better had," agreed Florence.

"Right. Well, Florence, you know where to find me if you want to talk some more. In the meantime, I don't know what to tell you. It is Mrs. Lloyd's money, after all, and she can do with it what she likes." She brightened. "But if it's any help to you, the flat over the manicure shop will be vacant in a day or two when Victoria moves out." Florence gave her a dark look. "No, well, I suppose not."

Penny stood up and opened the door.

"But you've certainly given me something to think about, Florence," Penny said as the two women prepared to rejoin the party. Penny found the conversation unsettling, but she wasn't sure why. Perhaps something Florence had said didn't ring true or maybe it was something she didn't say. But whatever it was, like a wisp of chimney smoke carried away on a wintry wind, it eluded her. And she had to get back to her guests.

Nine

"Are you quite sure you want to do this, Mrs. Lloyd?" asked Huw Bowen. "It's a lot of money."

"I'm perfectly well aware of how much it is, thank you, Huw," replied Mrs. Lloyd stiffly. "And yes, I wish to transfer twenty thousand pounds from my savings account into the joint account Harry and I are opening today. And he's depositing a cheque for the same amount." She looked at Harry, who held up a small piece of blue paper, and then back at Bowen. "Now, then, where do we sign?"

Bowen took the cheque from Harry and examined it carefully. "This is drawn on an American bank and it is not certified," he said, clipping it to the inside of a beige file folder that contained two or three documents. Looking at Mrs. Lloyd, he said carefully, "You will need to allow thirty days for this cheque to clear. You do understand that you will not have access to this money for that time. It will be as if the money isn't there."

"Oh, we're not going to be spending it," Mrs. Lloyd replied. "Not as such. Harry will be investing it when the right opportunity comes along."

Bowen took off his glasses and rubbed his eyes. He wished there was something he could do to stop Mrs. Lloyd from going ahead with this scheme, and although he hoped he was wrong, he feared that she would pay a very high price for her involvement with this man, who had struck him the minute he clapped eyes on him at the bridge game on that frosty November night as being completely untrustworthy.

"Well, with this account, then, Mrs. Lloyd"—he tapped the documents on his desk—"let's set it up so that a withdrawal will require both of your signatures. I strongly recommend that you do that."

As Mrs. Lloyd hesitated, Saunders smiled at her and gave his head the tiniest shake.

"No, we'll have it so that either of us can access the funds," Mrs. Lloyd said. "It'll be easier and faster that way. Harry's business ventures are very demanding and sometimes he has to travel."

Bowen put his glasses back on. "I wonder if I might just have a quick word with you in private, Mrs. Lloyd." He gave Saunders a pointed look and then, pursing his lips slightly and folding his hands on his desk, turned his gaze back to Mrs. Lloyd. She met his eyes with a look of resolved indignation.

"You know, Huw, I'm starting to think you're afraid that Harry's going to do so much better as my financial advisor that you'll find yourself out of the job." She sat back in her chair and folded her arms.

Suppressing a sigh, Bowen pushed a piece of paper across the desk to Mrs. Lloyd and offered her a pen.

"Very well. If you'll just sign here, please."

Saunders gave him a muted look that Bowen would come to think of later as triumph mixed with a generous swirl of contempt.

"Right, well, that's that, then," said Mrs. Lloyd as she stood up and pulled on her gloves. She jammed the fingers of one hand down between the fingers of the other and then turned around for her heavy wool coat that Saunders had hung on the rack in the corner of Bowen's office. He removed Mrs. Lloyd's coat, helped her on with it, and then returned to the rack for his own. He hesitated for a moment seeing two green anoraks but realizing quickly that the top one must be his, lifted it off the rack and put it on. He put his hands in the pockets and pulled out a pair of black gloves.

"Well, then," said Bowen, as he opened the door for them. "Good luck," he said neutrally and then, with a little more emphasis directed to Mrs. Lloyd, "Do call me if you have any questions or if, ah, any problems arise."

"Oh, we're not anticipating any problems, are we, Harry?" Mrs. Lloyd replied.

A minute later they were standing in the town square outside the bank. The sky had turned a pewter colour and dark clouds rested sullenly on the hilltops.

"I'm so excited, Harry," Mrs. Lloyd said. "I just know our investments are going to do really well."

"Of course they will, Evelyn."

"There's just one thing that's bothering me, though. I'm having second thoughts about that joint signing business. It might have been a good idea, just to keep everything . . ."

"Now, Evelyn," Saunders said with a smooth smile, inclining his head toward her, "either you trust me or you don't. You do trust me, don't you?"

"Yes, of course I do, Harry."

He gave her a broad, boyish grin, and then as it faded, he consulted his watch. "Now then, will you let me take you to lunch to celebrate our new partnership? I thought perhaps the hotel. Some nice cream of leek soup to warm us up. I know you like that. What do you say?"

Mrs. Lloyd touched his sleeve, then tucked her arm through his, as they began walking in the direction of the Red Dragon Hotel.

"I have a better idea, Harry. Florence is going to Liverpool this afternoon, so why don't you come round for dinner this evening. She'll have left something nice." Mrs. Lloyd gave his arm a friendly little squeeze. "And she'll be stopping in Liverpool for the weekend, so you won't have to rush off."

"That sounds delightful, Evelyn," Harry replied. "What time would you like me?"

"Well, let's say about seven. We'll have a lovely evening. Oh, I have so been looking forward to this!"

"Oh, me too, Evelyn, me too." He gave her a little peck on the cheek and then stood back. "Well, only another hour or so and the markets will be open in New York, so I'd best be off. Let's hope there are some good mutual funds available at fire sale prices!"

Mrs. Lloyd laughed and set off for the short walk home. Saunders watched her until she turned the corner, and then he started walking slowly in the other direction.

"Only me!" Mrs. Lloyd called out as she pushed open her front door. Noticing Florence's battered, old-fashioned suitcase in the hall, she smiled to herself as she pulled off her gloves, stuffed them in the pocket of her coat, and draped the coat over a chair. After a moment she picked up the coat and hung it in the hall closet her late husband Arthur had had put in a few years before he died.

Mrs. Lloyd walked through to the kitchen where Florence was finishing her lunch. "I wasn't sure what time you'd be back," she said, "and I thought you might even have your lunch out, so I didn't make anything for you. But I can make you a sandwich, if you like. Tea's just brewed," she added, pointing at the pot. "Would you like me to pour you a cup?"

"Well, actually, Florence, that would be perfect," Mrs. Lloyd replied. "No, I didn't have lunch. Came straight home after the appointment at the . . . well, never mind that. I am hungry, though, so a cheese sandwich would really hit the spot. I'll just go and change my shoes. I really shouldn't be walking all over the place in these. I wonder what I did with my slippers."

Florence buttered two pieces of bread, scraped the cheese slicer across a hefty slab of mature cheddar, added some thin slices of red onion, and cut the sandwich in two. She set it down on the table and sat down to wait for Mrs. Lloyd.

"Cheese and onion," said Florence, "just the way you like it."

"Oh, I don't think I'll have the onion today, thank you." Mrs. Lloyd smiled as she opened the sandwich, picked out a few onion slices, and set them down on the edge of her plate. "Harry's coming for dinner."

"I thought he might be, so I've left a nice fisherman's pie in the fridge for you," Florence said. "All you've got to do is heat it up. And there's a treacle tart for pudding. I was going to make some custard to go with it, but there's some pouring cream, so you can have that with it, instead." She paused for a moment and then added as an afterthought, "Custard doesn't really keep all that well, does it? Gets that nasty skin on it if you don't put the cling film right down on top of it."

Mrs. Lloyd nodded and took another bite. The onion slices were piling up on her plate.

"Have you ever been to his place, Evelyn?" Florence asked, breaking the silence. "Have you seen where he lives?"

Mrs. Lloyd stopped chewing and looked at her.

"It's just that I was wondering if maybe he might be, well, you know, married. Or otherwise spoken for."

"Hah!" said Mrs. Lloyd. "And here's me thinking that you've been thinking it's my money he's after."

"Well, I did wonder."

"Now, let's just consider that for a moment, Florence, shall we? What is it about me that makes you think that he couldn't like me just for myself? Am I so unlikable, so unattractive that a man wouldn't want me just for me? To enjoy my company? To go dancing? To have as a bridge partner?"

"I'm sorry, Evelyn, I didn't mean to imply any of that. It's just that I've been worried about you, that's all."

"Well, I don't need you to worry about me, Florence. You and I have only known each other five minutes and, forgive me if I speak frankly, but it's really not your place to meddle in my affairs. I've given you a lovely home here, at practically no rent in exchange for doing a few simple things about the place and now you're worried about me having a friendship with a nice man?

"I think it's you that you're really worried about, Florence. I think you're worried that Harry's going to be moving in here and where will that leave you? Back in a shabby—" Mrs. Lloyd, looking somewhat aghast at where her thoughts were taking her, stopped abruptly. "I'm sorry," she apologized. "That came across as much harsher than I meant it to. I'll say no more. Least said, soonest mended."

Florence gathered herself up with as much dignity as she could muster.

"Good-bye, Evelyn. I hope you have a lovely weekend. If it's all right with you, I'll be back on Sunday afternoon, by teatime, I should think."

"Of course, Florence. You get off now and enjoy yourself. You don't want to miss the bus. Oh, and it's suddenly got quite cold when I was out. There could be some bad weather coming in."

Mrs. Lloyd remained at the kitchen table, and a few minutes later she heard the front door closing quietly. She got up from the table and peered down the hallway. As she expected, the little suitcase was gone.

Now then, Mrs. Lloyd thought, as she ran a bath later that afternoon, I wonder if I should wait until Harry gets here to put the fish pie in the oven, or would it be more welcoming if he were to be greeted by the aroma when he walks in the door? But maybe he won't want to eat right away and we'll have a drink first. The timing is always tricky on something like this.

Oh dear me.

Never mind the fish pie. What should I wear? I don't want to seem too eager. But not too casual and not overdressed, either. Still, I don't want something for every day, like a skirt and blouse. Or do I?

She added some fragrant lavender bath salts to the warm water and then settled in for a nice, long soak. She lay back, resting her head on a towel, and thought about those scenes she had seen on television in which a young beautiful woman, eyes closed, relaxed in a soothing bath with candles all around the tub. Mrs. Lloyd closed her eyes and thought about scented candles. When she opened her eyes, the water had turned a tepid grey and her fingertips looked like prunes.

Wrapped in a warm bathrobe, she slid her garments along the clothes rail assessing each one as it passed by. Too tight. Too severe. Too old looking. He's seen that. I hate that old thing— must give it to the charity shop. I look like hell in trousers. There's a button missing on this blouse and anyway it pulls across the bust. One by one she assessed the items in her wardrobe and found nothing to her liking.

She sat down on her bed and sighed. She was regretting those hurtful things she had said to Florence. I'll ring her later, she thought, and put things right with her. And then she remembered that Florence couldn't afford a mobile phone and had not left a telephone number where she could be reached.

Mrs. Lloyd stood up and returned to the task of rummaging through her closet, finally taking out a black skirt and a tailored white blouse. I'll dress that up a bit with my pearls and put on some black stockings. She rummaged around in her drawer, found a new pair of tights, and started getting changed. She slipped on a pair of low-heeled black shoes, checked the time on her bedside alarm clock, and after taking one last look around her bedroom to make sure it was invitingly tidy, closed the door behind her. She took a few steps down the hall and then returned to her bedroom. There was something she had forgotten to do.

She sat down on her bed and picked up the photo of her late husband, Arthur, that she kept on her bedside table. She looked fondly at his kind, handsome face, gazing cheerfully back at her from its silver frame, never growing any older, always watching over her as she slept.

She gave the image a little kiss and then gently placed the photo in the top drawer of her nightstand. After a moment's thought she twisted off her wedding ring, placed it on top of the photo, and then closed the drawer.

The heaviness of the afternoon sky, filled with fast-moving, menacing clouds had given way to an ominous evening, and Mrs. Lloyd glanced out the window before closing the curtains against the darkness. The lamps in her sitting room cast a cozy, comforting light, and she turned on the radio, choosing a station playing soft background music. She lit several candles and grouped them on the coffee table. She stood back and surveyed the room. Deciding that it looked welcoming and attractive but not too obviously seductive, she headed to the dining room to check on the table. Florence had left everything very nice indeed, Mrs. Lloyd had to admit. The silver shone, the dishes were carefully set out, and a centrepiece of white roses gave everything a serene but somehow seasonal look. Satisfied with all the arrangements, she entered the kitchen to see to the dinner.

At ten minutes to seven she put the fish pie in the oven to heat and then returned to the living room. She reached in her handbag for a lipstick and, using the little mirror in her compact, applied it carefully, smacking her lips together and giving them a little rub. She patted down her skirt and, after a quick glance around the room, sat down on the sofa and idly thumbed through the Christmas issue of *The Lady*. A few moments later she tossed the magazine aside.

Seven o'clock. He should be here any minute now, she thought, aching with delicious anticipation.

Fifteen minutes later, as the aroma of fish pie began to seep out from the kitchen, Mrs. Lloyd picked up her mobile phone and rang Harry. There was no answer. Had he forgotten? Had she been clear about the day and that she was expecting him tonight?

Mildly anxious, she fiddled with the dial on the radio until she heard a voice.

"That was Mary Hopkins and her wonderfully appropriate 'Snowed Under,' which is what we're going to be tonight with a low front moving in, bringing with it heavy snow for much of the northwest," said the radio announcer. The voice continued, "Police are advising motorists to take to the roads only if their journey is essential, as between four and eight inches of snow are expected to accumulate overnight." A whiteout in South Wales led to a twenty-six-mile tailback on the M4 during rush hour, the voice added.

Oh damn, thought Mrs. Lloyd, switching off the radio. That'll be what's keeping him. Of course, if he can just get here, he'll have to stay the night.

She strode over to the window, pulled back the curtain, and peered out into the empty street. Large flakes of snow were falling, swirling, and catching the sodium orange light from the streetlamp as they tumbled to earth. The snow was beginning to pile up on the window ledge and Mrs. Lloyd found the whole notion of being snowed in with Harry for a day or two unbearably romantic.

It had been so many years since the town, or the country for that matter, had experienced a really severe winter that she could barely remember the last one. Sometime in the 1980s, would be her best guess. Of course, back when she was a girl the winters had been much worse, but somehow everyone survived. Was there a possibility with a severe snowstorm that the electricity might go off, she wondered.

Or might it be better if the power did stay on so she and Harry could listen to the radio and dance? But, on the other hand, if the electricity did go off, that might not be so bad either, having to cuddle up together by candlelight . . .

Two hours later, the dripping candle wax had set into hard, pink puddles and their formerly cheerfully romantic appearance now seemed sad and pathetic. Over the past hour Mrs. Lloyd had reluctantly and gradually realized that Harry would not be coming. She had pulled the fish pie from the oven and, after taking one look at its charred, dry edges, had scraped it into the rubbish bin and left the pan to soak in the sink. After one last monitoring of the snow piling up outside, she yawned, accepted defeat, and plodded upstairs to bed. As she settled under the covers, she ran her hand longingly over the empty half of her bed. With a heavy sigh, she rolled over onto her side, turning her back on the spot where she had imagined Harry, arms outstretched and eager to hold her and smother her with tender kisses. She turned off the bedside lamp, pulled the duvet up around her ears, and closed her eyes.

I hope nothing bad's happened to him, she thought. Still, he could have telephoned me. I hope he's all right. Why didn't he ring me? He might have known I'd be worried. As anxious little thoughts nibbled away at the edge of her consciousness, she pushed them away and slipped into an uneasy, restless sleep.

A few streets away, bundled up against the snow, Penny Brannigan said good night to Victoria and stepped out into the pathway that led to the road. Framed in the doorway, Victoria peered out into the shadowy night. She could just make out the River Conwy, its dark waters shifting like moving slate.

"I guess we should have paid more attention to the weather," Victoria said, "and not worked so late so you could have been away earlier."

"Well, there's lots to do and it needed doing," Penny replied. "Anyway, I don't have far to go and I'm going to enjoy this." She gestured at the snow and then, picking up a handful, threw it at Victoria who squealed, ducked for cover, and then with one last good night and a little flap of her hand, shut the door behind her.

Penny knew snow.

Growing up in Nova Scotia she had seen plenty of it during long, white winters filled with blinding storms. And, of course, according to elderly relatives, it had been even worse in their day. She recalled an aunt describing winters so severe the snow reached the top of the telephone poles and hardy folk who took the weather in their stride would cheerfully ski to church. Penny had left Canada behind decades ago and had made a good life for herself in this small Welsh town, safe and happy among its warm, welcoming people. Until recently, she'd thought that her life was in a pretty good place but now gratefully recognized it was in a much better one.

She was letting herself become increasingly attached to Detective Chief Inspector Davies and she knew he cared deeply for her. Unsure of just where she wanted the relationship to go, she was secure enough in herself to let it become what it was meant to be. She was smart enough to appreciate what she had while she was lucky enough to have it, and the thought of her warm, peaceful cottage waiting for her cheered her on.

The snow was blowing across the street and it was becoming increasingly difficult to see through the cascading flakes. She clutched her collar tightly and pressed on toward the cobbled town square. There was no traffic and the streets were eerily quiet. Lights glowed behind curtained windows, and for a moment she envied the people who lived there, snug and warm in their homes. But just a few more streets to plow through and she, too, would be home.

As she passed the churchyard, a small movement caught her eye and she stopped. Edging along the side of the rectory, she recognized the dim outline of two figures in the doorway of the church, caught in a tight embrace. She smiled to herself and prepared to move on, but something about the pair held her attention. She placed a hand against the rectory wall to steady herself and watched as the couple stepped back a few inches from each other. They were too far away and it was too dark to make out who they were, but something about them seemed familiar.

She watched as they held hands, looking at each other. As the smaller figure, whom she assumed to be a woman, turned to leave, the larger one pulled her back. They embraced again, obviously reluctant to part. The woman reached up and brushed a few flakes of snow off the man's jacket. Penny watched for a few more moments, and then, starting to feel the cold seeping through her gloves and beginning to shiver, she turned and slipped silently into the night.

She arrived home a few minutes later, and after taking off her boots and hanging her coat and wet gloves to dry in the hall, she turned on the light in her sitting room and then passed through the dining area to her kitchen. She opened the fridge and pulled out a bottle of milk. If there was ever a night for a comforting mug of cocoa, this was it. She placed a small saucepan on the cooker, poured some milk into it, and turned on the element. While the milk heated, she took down a large mug, put in some cocoa powder, sugar, and a little milk, and stirred it all up to make a smooth brown paste.

When the milk was almost at the boiling point, she added it to the mug, gave it a good stir, and took her mug back to the living room. She settled on the sofa, tucked her legs under her, picked up her telephone, and dialed the code to listen to her voice mail messages.

"Hi, Penny, this is Alwynne. Do you think because of the storm we could postpone our lunch and sketching at Conwy Castle to Tuesday? I can't make Monday and the roads should be clear by Tuesday. Let me know. Thanks."

The Stretch and Sketch Club had planned to hold its annual Christmas lunch at a popular restaurant in Conwy on Sunday, and combine that with some sketching, if the weather permitted, at the castle. If it was too cold, the members would take photographs and paint from them later.

Tuesday it is, then, Penny thought. She looked at the clock on the mantel and, deciding it was too late to ring Alwynne, made a note to telephone her the next day. She drained the last of her cocoa and, licking her lips, suddenly realized how tired she was.

Half an hour later, settled in her new bed, and enjoying the tranquility of her stylish bedroom that overlooked the garden at the back of the house, she picked up her library book. A few moments later, realizing she had read the same paragraph three times without any recollection of it, she put the book down and switched off the light.

She lay there in the dark thinking about the courting couple she had seen in the churchyard.

But were they courting, she asked herself. Something about their body language, the way they couldn't seem to resist each other, the way he pulled her back to him, suggested something different. There had been an unfulfilled eagerness there, a reluctant yearning. She closed her eyes and visualized the scene. And a moment later it came to her.

At least one of them, she thought, is married to someone else. What she had seen was the excitement, the furtiveness of forbidden passion.

She'd had a classmate at university who had been swept up in a mad affair with a married professor. She'd come upon them one morning during Reading Week, when the campus was relatively deserted, kissing passionately in an empty classroom, unable to keep their hands off each other. They'd had that same look about them, except that pair had noticed her. They'd jumped apart, their faces filled with guilt and, in his case, fear. The professor had gathered up his briefcase and, avoiding Penny's eyes, had hurried out of the room. That relationship had ended badly, as most relationships built on the sandy foundation of deceit tend to do. By the next September a new intake of impressionable female students had provided the professor with lots of new girls to choose from, and her former classmate did not return to school.

She wondered what lies the married one she'd seen earlier that evening had told his or her partner to get out of the house in the middle of a snowstorm. And then she realized it didn't matter. There would always be enough lies to cover up an affair. At the beginning, anyway. But only for a while.

Ten

And still it snowed. Tree branches bowed under the weight of the snow and deep drifts made the rural roads almost impassable. On the hill farms above the valley the sheep had sensed the approaching storm and taken shelter in the hollows. But there lay danger, so the shepherds, helped by their trained and eager dogs, moved the ewes and rams onto more exposed land so the drifting snow would not bury them. The flocks huddled together beside the stone fences, vague silhouettes, almost invisible against the cold landscape of endless snow.

In the town, the primary school was closed, shelves in the food stores had been stripped bare, and travel was almost at a standstill.

Many were forced to stay home from work, but those who could, plowed bravely through the snow to open their businesses. Among this hardy group was Huw Bowen, who held the keys to the bank. And not only did the bank open as usual, it opened on time.

At ten past ten his assistant knocked on the door to his office. "Come."

"Morning, Mr. Bowen. Just wanted to let you know that there's been a request from the branch in Chester to transfer funds out of an account that was recently opened with us. It's a large sum." She glanced down at the slip of paper in her hand. "Yes, quite large, actually. Twenty thousand pounds. It all seems in order, but I thought you'd like to know."

"Quite right, too, Gaynor." He let out a long sigh. "Now don't tell me. We're talking about the Lloyd–Saunders joint account."

"Yes, Mr. Bowen, that's right. That's the one."

"Right. Chester, you say. Thanks very much."

He waited until she closed the door behind her and then reached for the telephone.

Mrs. Lloyd put the phone down and stood in the hall, unseeing. She had been ringing Saunders on his mobile for two days and had not reached him. At first she had been able to push back the rising tide of anxiety that kept creeping into her awareness, but as the days and nights passed, the mild anxiety had turned into a dawning realization, with an undercurrent of disbelief, desperation, and cold, gripping fear that clawed at the very centre of her.

And just now, Huw Bowen had called from the bank to tell her that the bank had released twenty thousand pounds to Saunders. Well, they'd had to, hadn't they? It was a joint account with his name on it and only one signature had been required to make a withdrawal. He was entitled to what was essentially his money because she had given it to him. Everything had been done by the book. Oh, if only she'd listened to Huw.

She tried to reassure herself for the thousandth time that

Saunders had been trapped in the storm over the weekend and today had taken out the money to invest, just as he'd said he would. But the little voice inside her, that she was wishing she'd paid more attention to earlier, would not be silenced. And it was telling her something different.

When the phone rang again, she picked it up eagerly. Oh please be him, she breathed.

"Hello? Is that you, Harry?"

Her shoulders sagged.

"Yes, I figured you were trapped in the storm, so I wasn't worried about you at all, Florence." She listened. "Oh, meant to clear up, is it? You're taking the train. Yes, well, I'll see you some-time tomorrow then. Thank you for ringing. Must get on. Good-bye, now."

She replaced the telephone receiver and then immediately headed to the drinks table in the sitting room to do something she had done only once before in her life at ten o'clock in the morning. She poured two fingers of whisky into a glass, hesitated, then added another two. She took a small sip, then a large gulp. A moment later she set the empty glass on the tray and, fueled by a surge of alcohol-laced adrenaline and anger, strode back to the hallway and opened the closet door. She pulled out her warmest coat and scrabbled around in the back of the cupboard to see if she could find her old pair of winter boots. She found one boot, covered in dust with a broken lace, but it would have to do. She dove back in, tossing out pairs of shoes, a lost glove, a long-forgotten dog lead, and a hairbrush, until she found the mate to the boot she held in her hand.

She shook the dust out of them and, hoping no spiders or mice were living inside, put them on. She pulled on a warm hat and let herself out of the house. As she plowed along Rosemary

Lane, clamping her hat to her head with one hand, her wind-bitten face was taut with distress.

She wasn't sure if there was anything to be done, if anything could be done, but she desperately needed to speak to Huw Bowen. As she turned the corner into the town square, she glimpsed a patch of blue sky over the church tower and realized it had finally stopped snowing. Maybe now, she thought, maybe now he'll be able to get here and everything will be fine. It'll all have been much ado about nothing.

A half hour later, she left the bank. She took her time walking home, knowing there was nothing more she could do, except wait to see if Saunders, as she was beginning to think of him, would contact her. Her conversation with Huw Bowen had not gone well. There had been no hearty reassurance, no attempt to comfort her, just a hard cold dose of reality. Yes, he'd had his suspicions. Yes, he had tried to talk her out of it. Yes, he had recommended two signatures on the joint account. But it was too late to put that right, the question was what could she do now.

But the worst part had been when she had asked Huw what he thought had happened.

"May I speak frankly?" he had asked, and when she nodded, he had said, "I think he's gone for good, Evelyn, and he's taken your money with him." Along with my self-respect and position in this town, Mrs. Lloyd thought.

"And what's more," Huw had added, "I think it's time we called in the police and I am advising you to do that."

But why, Mrs. Lloyd had asked. He hadn't done anything illegal, and besides, she didn't want the whole town knowing about this.

"That's exactly how these men operate," Huw had replied. "They work quickly to build trust and then trick sensible, intelligent women into giving them money, and they count on the fact that their victims, for one reason or another, usually shame and embarrassment, will not go public with it. And it's that silence that allows them to move on to their next victim. And the one after that."

But Mrs. Lloyd was not ready to call in the police and told her financial advisor that she wanted to give it another day or two, just in case there was a simple explanation.

But still, hoping against hope that everything might yet turn out all right, in her own mind she feared the worst. And she had another long day, filled with stomach-churning dread, to get through. She needed to talk to someone, someone she could trust.

As she turned into Rosemary Lane, she decided that as soon as she took her coat off, she would call her longtime friend Bunny from the old post office days and see if she was free for lunch tomorrow. Somewhere different, Conwy, maybe. It wasn't far. And while she didn't think she'd be in the mood for Christmas shopping, a look round the shops might be nice. She might pop into that kitchen-supply place and buy Florence something for the kitchen as a Christmas present, since she liked cooking and baking so much. Looking forward to a little outing always made things seem brighter, Mrs. Lloyd told herself. Taking charge of the situation was the thing to do. And besides, Bunny would not only understand but, being a practical person, might be able to suggest something. Anything.

But the first call she made when she got home was to Saunders. He didn't answer, but how could he? The ringer on his mobile phone had been switched off and the device lay at the bottom of a rubbish bin on a platform of the Chester railway station covered with a banana peel, a couple of sandwich wrappers, a dirty nappy, and a half-empty can of ginger ale.

Eleven

*T*he next morning, as the sun tried valiantly to assert itself through a pale battalion of dense, grey clouds, Penny and Alwynne Gwilt set off on the twenty-minute drive up the valley to Conwy where the Stretch and Sketch Club had been able to change their reservations at a local restaurant for the group's Christmas lunch. The narrow rural road wound on, bordered on each side by stone fences, hedges, and the occasional cluster of holly bushes bearing bright red berries. Fields, green just a few days ago but now blanketed in snow, sloped away into the distance.

"It's nice that our two new members were able to come today," Alynne remarked as she slowed down to take a sharp turn. "Brian and Glynnis."

"I've been meaning to ask you about her," Penny replied. "I don't know her very well, but she seems, well, I'm not sure if sad is the right word but down in the dumps."

"She didn't used to be like that," Alwynne replied. "She used to be quite lively and great fun. But I think living with Huw Bowen would take it out of most women. He's a good man in many ways, I guess, but he can be domineering and demanding. Maybe it's the banker in him, but everything's got to be done just so. I think that would be very hard on any woman, living with that day after day. Still, I expect they have no more of the ups and downs of married life than the rest of us."

"Why did she marry him, do you think?"

Alwynne gave a little shrug and glanced at her companion in the passenger seat. "Why does anyone marry someone? Maybe she thought he was her last chance. She was in her late thirties when they married. She gave up her job—used to be a teacher at the high school."

She pointed out the window as the battlemented outline of Conwy Castle came into view.

"I've seen that view all my life and it never fails to amaze me, the sheer size and strength of it," said Alwynne. "It gives a whole new meaning to the word intimidating."

The little car squeezed through the upper gate, the main landward entry into the town and one of only three arched gateways in the well-preserved stone walls that encircled the town. They inched along narrow one-way streets until they reached the restaurant, located in the looming shadow of the great medieval fortress.

Built in the thirteenth century by King Edward I as one of a series of castles across North Wales, Conwy Castle sits in an authoritative position on a rocky outcrop on the banks of the River Conwy, set against the mountains of Snowdonia. Roughly rectangular in shape, with four massive towers along each long side, the castle has no equal for visual impact.

Alwynne parked her car, and the two women entered the restaurant where eight other members of the Stretch and Sketch Club, including the two latest additions to the group, Glynnis Bowen and Brian Kenley, the photographer from Yorkshire, soon joined them.

"We'll have about an hour and a half for lunch," Penny told them, looking down the table. "The castle closes at four and we want to have plenty of time to look around, sketch, and take some photographs before we start to lose the light." A waiter in a jaunty red jacket brought menus to the table, and the group began to discuss their orders. Two hours later, lunch over and the account settled, they walked to the castle visitor's centre and prepared to buy their admission tickets.

"Oh, a group, is it?" asked the ticket seller. "I'll give you the special rate, as it's getting late in the day." Money paid in and tickets distributed, the artists set off to explore the castle.

"The castle closes at four," the ticket taker reminded them as they disappeared through the modern glass door and stepped back seven hundred years into the ruins of a fearsome, dark-stoned fortress that had not lost its power to cast a magical spell.

Florence Semble trudged along the platform of the Chester Station. She glanced up at the electronic announcement board and was happy to see that the Llandudno train was on time and due in eight minutes. She sat down on a bench to wait.

Ten minutes later, the turquoise train approached the station, and as it slowed down, Florence picked up her suitcase and shuffled forward with the other passengers preparing to board. When the train had come to a complete stop, the doors opened and she stood to one side as two hooded teenagers jumped down and slouched off toward the exit.

Holding the handrail with one hand and her suitcase with the other, she hauled herself on board as quickly as she could. The carriage was quite full, and she was relieved to see an aisle seat about halfway down. As she struggled to lift her case into the overhead compartment, a young man came to her rescue, shifting it easily and quickly into place. She smiled her thanks and sat down just as the doors closed and the engine started making the huffing noises that signaled the train was about to depart.

Moments later, it gathered up speed and soon had crossed the invisible border into Wales, leaving England behind. Something about the rhythmic movement of a train always made her want to go to sleep, so wrapping her arms around her handbag, she leaned back in her seat, rested her head against the headrest, and closed her eyes.

Her eyes opened wide a few moments later when the man in the seat directly behind hers began to speak in an accent and a voice she recognized.

Florence pushed her woolly hat up over her ears so she could hear better and scrunched down in her seat, which was tall enough to shield her from the view of the passengers behind. She turned her body slightly, ignoring the glare from her seatmate, so her ear was up against the narrow divide between her seat and the one next to it.

"Yes, I do come from America, as you call it," the man behind her was saying. "California. I work for an electronics firm. Just over here on business. Arrived a couple of days ago."

The woman said something that Florence couldn't quite catch.

"Well, my firm does sensitive work for a certain United States government agency, but I can't really talk about it. Let's just say

I travel the world on top-secret missions." He gave a little chuckle. "I've already said too much. Tell me about you. Where are you headed?"

Florence thought the woman said Deganwy, but she spoke so softly Florence wasn't sure she had heard correctly.

"And will your husband be meeting you at the station? It looks as if we might get more snow. Hope you don't have far to go?"

The woman murmured something.

"Oh, live near the school, do you? My mother was a teacher. I have such admiration for teachers."

You lying bastard, thought Florence. Her brain was racing at warp speed as she tried to figure out what to do. Should she make herself known and let him know she'd overheard everything and that she was going to expose him for the fraud he was? But something told her better not, as least not yet. She shrank farther down in her seat and listened to his patter as the woman sitting beside him became increasingly quiet. Finally, overcome by boredom and lack of interest, Florence surmised, she no longer responded to him. Florence couldn't see if she was looking out the window, reading, or pretending to be asleep, but she had certainly managed to send a message that as far as she was concerned, the conversation was over.

Florence smiled to herself. Nice try, old son. You win some, you lose some, eh, Harry?

The train rolled on to Llandudno, slowing as it approached the next station.

"Well, this is where I get off," Saunders was saying. "It was nice meeting you."

This can't be Llandudno, Florence thought, checking her watch, and sure enough the signs on the station platform read Conwy. Why was Saunders getting off here? Surely it would make more sense for him to go to Llandudno and make his way from there to Llanelen or wherever he was going.

In an instant she made her decision. She rose out of her seat, slid into the aisle, and careful to keep her head turned away from Saunders, reached into the overhead bin and tugged at her suitcase. She followed him down the aisle, her suitcase bumping against her leg.

As the station announcer intoned, "Anyone alighting from the train should take extreme care as the platform is slippery," Florence stepped cautiously onto the platform just behind him.

He made his way to the station exit and then, once he was on the street, paused for a moment to get his bearings and then turned in the direction of the castle.

Where on earth is he off to, Florence wondered, as she walked a little way behind him, keeping a steady eye on the back of his green anorak. She was not bothered that he would recognize her even if he did turn around. He hadn't paid much attention to her when they'd met in Evelyn Lloyd's home, today she was wearing a hat, and as she had learned a long time ago, women her age are almost invisible to the rest of the world. Florence had long ago accepted that no one takes any notice of an elderly woman, except for the occasional well-brought-up person who might, say, offer some assistance with a suitcase on a train.

Florence watched as Saunders entered the castle visitor's centre. She crept after him and once inside busied herself picking through a selection of Welsh dragon key chains, playing cards with pictures of the castle on their backs, pencils, and bookmarks. She heard Saunders ask for a single admission ticket and waited until he had taken it, stepped away from the counter, and followed the arrow.

"The castle closes at four," the woman told him.

Florence rummaged about in her bag for some change and approached the counter.

"How much is a senior's ticket?" she asked. "That much?" She winced when told the cost.

"Well," said the kindly clerk, "as it's getting a bit late in the day, I'll let you in for a pound, but don't tell anybody."

Florence slid a coin across the counter and accepted her ticket.

"Thank you. I appreciate this."

"No problem," the clerk replied, pulling out a notepad from under her counter. "The castle closes at four o'clock."

Mrs. Lloyd finished telling her story to an astonished Bunny, who didn't know whether to be upset because her friend had been hurt or because of the amount of money involved and was feeling pained for both in equal measure.

"Oh, Evelyn," she said, her voice filled with warm concern. "How could you have been so . . ."

"It's all right, Bunny. You can say it. Stupid."

The two old friends looked at each other, and Bunny reached out to give Evelyn a comforting hug. At the tenderness of the gesture, Mrs. Lloyd's eyes filled with tears.

"Oh, Bunny. I know I've been such a fool. But he was so charming and he made me feel like I was the only woman on earth. Special, like. I remembered things I hadn't experienced in years. How good it felt to have a man admire me, tell me that I looked nice, open a door for me, give me a nice dinner. I enjoyed being seen out and about with a man. I liked being thought of as half of a couple. And he seemed so sophisticated, not like the men you get around here."

Bunny inclined her head as she listened. "But what did you

really know about him, Evelyn? You'd only known him for, what, a few weeks?" She shook her head and winced. "And to give him so much money. How could you? What came over you? What on earth were you thinking? How did all this happen so quickly?"

"I trusted him," Mrs. Lloyd said simply, as if that explained everything. They remained looking at each other for a few moments, and then Mrs. Lloyd gave a little shrug and broke eye contact.

"It's still early and I don't feel like going home yet. Shall we walk on for a bit, maybe stroll past the castle?"

"I'd like to go in," replied Bunny, "if you're up to it. I haven't been inside for years and I've never seen it in winter. Let's just have a wander round, shall we? When I was a child, I used to try to imagine what it must have looked like when it was built. I pictured the queen sewing in her apartment all hung with tapestries, with her ladies gathered about her while the king was busy planning his war with his military advisors, or whoever he would have planned wars with. Of course, there would have been huge fireplaces with Irish wolfhounds or some such gigantic dog lying in front of them."

Mrs. Lloyd managed a tight smile.

"Oh, Bunny, you always did have such a wonderful imagination. I can almost picture it. Yes, all right, let's go in. Anyway, the views from the wall walks are lovely. You can see for miles."

"The castle closes at four," advised the attendant as the two women moved toward the glass doors that opened to a wooden walkway that led to the modern, upward path that would bring them to the castle entrance.

Twelve

.

Mrs. Lloyd and Bunny entered a narrow enclosure, or barbican, and then continued on into the ruins of the castle proper. The roof and floors had disappeared centuries ago, leaving the dark grey stone walls, green with lichen in places, standing open to the sky.

The women talked quietly as they walked slowly through the outer ward, referring to the guidebook Bunny had bought in the gift shop, until they reached what Bunny said was the hall range.

She pointed to their right.

"Although it now appears as one long room, the interior was divided into at least two sections—the chapel and the great hall," she read. As they prepared to move toward the middle gate, the cross wall that divided the castle into what had been its public and private areas, they spotted Penny Brannigan seated on a low stone wall, making rapid, sweeping marks in her field sketchbook. She looked up as they approached.

"Oh, Mrs. Lloyd, imagine seeing you here," she said as she looked from one to the other. "Hello, Bunny." A slight frown creased her brow. "I think I just saw Harry Saunders. Were you meant to be meeting up with him?"

Mrs. Lloyd exchanged a quick glance with Bunny, and both of them took a step toward her.

"Did you, Penny? How long ago? Where was he going? I mean, what direction was he headed?"

Penny waved her hand in the direction of the stone wall that ran across the width of the castle. "I think he went through there," she said. "I didn't have a chance to speak to him."

Mrs. Lloyd put a hand on Bunny's arm.

"Wait here. I need to speak to him on my own." She hurried off in the direction Penny had indicated, leaving Penny and Bunny staring after her.

"I hope she catches him up," Bunny said.

"Well, when she finds him, he may not be alone," Penny replied. "Just after he passed me, Florence came along. I thought at the time something was up, but she hurried right past me. Took no notice. I'm not even sure she saw me." After a moment she added, "Is everything all right? What's going on?"

"Evelyn has something important she needs to discuss with him. She's been ringing him for days, trying to get in touch." She peered at Penny's sketch. "Do you mind if people look at your work while you're doing it?"

"I don't mind if they take a quick look at it, but I don't really like someone watching over my shoulder while I'm trying to concentrate," Penny said.

"Oh, right," said Bunny, stepping back. "Look, I'll just go

and sit on that bench over there and wait for Evelyn to return."
Bunny looked up at the towering castle walls.

"This place is so massive, she could be anywhere."

"It's not really as big as it seems, once you understand how it's all laid out," Penny replied, making a shading motion on her sketchbook. "Of course, we're really just seeing its footprint. When it was built, with all the different levels, then, it would have been enormous." She rubbed her hands. "And busy, too, with everyone running up and down the stairs all day long."

"Here on your own, are you?" asked Bunny.

"No, I'm with some members of my sketching club, but we're all over the place. I haven't seen any of them, but they'll be around, somewhere. Some of them could be back there, I suppose, looking at the remains of the royal apartments," she said, gesturing toward the inner ward.

She had just returned to her work, as Bunny settled down on the nearby bench to study her guidebook, when a primal sound ripped through the peace and stillness of the vast space. Penny dropped her pencil and turned toward the source of what had now become an urgent scream. At that moment a man emerged, waving his arms, through the entranceway to the Great Hall opposite her. Although he was some distance away, she could hear him clearly.

"Ring 999! Someone's fallen from the wall walk!"

Bunny jumped up, her face white with fear and confusion. Penny snapped her sketchbook closed and, telling Bunny to stay where she was, reached into her handbag for her mobile. After a few words with the emergency operator, she rushed over to Bunny.

"Can you go and see who it is," Bunny wailed. "Oh dear God, please let it not be her." Penny thrust her sketchbook into Bunny's arms and bolted.

She raced across the wooden bridge that led to the narrow circular staircase of the prison tower that would take her to the wall walk high above. Holding on to the rope hand railing, she clambered up the stone steps as fast as she could until, panting slightly, she reached the top and stepped out into the fading afternoon light. A strong gust of icy wind greeted her, and she clung to the cold stones of the ancient tower for support. A small group had gathered a short distance away, and one of them was pointing over the low wall to the frozen ground below.

She inched along the narrow wall walk, fighting back vertigo, and leaned over the outer wall as far as she dared. She could make out what looked like a man in a green anorak, lying on his side facing away from the castle, his left leg crumpled and bent outward at a terrible angle. He did not move.

"The police and ambulance are on their way," she told the small crowd. "I think you should all just stay where you are until they arrive." She noted a few members of the Stretch and Sketch Club in the group, including Alwynne Gwilt, who was clutching photographer Brian Kenley's arm. His camera dangled from a strap around his neck. She made a mental note; he might have captured something important and the police will certainly want to examine the digital photos he had taken.

Down the road from the castle, in the two-storey grey stone police station that faced Lancaster Square, Detective Sergeant Bethan Morgan was wrapping up a crime prevention presentation to a group of seniors.

"So, ladies, remember when you go to the supermarket, to leave your handbag at home. Just take as much money as you think you'll need or a debit or credit card and keep them in your pocket. Because while you're turned this way"—Bethan twisted away from the old leather handbag she had placed on a table—"looking at the mince on sale and your handbag is behind you in your shopping trolley, it's an open invitation to a thief."

She stopped as a police officer entered the room, smiled at the pensioners, and signaled he wanted a word with her.

Bethan listened and then nodded.

"Well, ladies and gentlemen, PC Jones tells me I've been called out, so we're going to have to leave it there for today," Bethan told her grey-haired audience. "Just remember, thieves are opportunists and if you don't give them an opportunity, they can't take what's yours." She gave them a reassuring smile. "Sorry, I've got to run, but Constable Jones here will see you out."

As she prepared to leave, Jones called after her, "The detective chief inspector said to tell you he'll get there as soon as he can." Bethan held up a hand to show she'd heard him and was gone.

Pulling on her fluorescent-yellow high-visibility jacket as she went, she walked quickly across the paving stones of Lancaster Square and sprinted down Rose Hill Street, rounding the corner at the Guildhall, and burst into the castle's visitor centre. After flashing her warrant card to the woman at the ticket sales desk, who had just been told that someone had fallen off the wall walk, Bethan prepared to enter the castle.

"The castle closes at four o'clock," the woman called after her.

"Not tonight it probably doesn't, love," Bethan shot back over her shoulder as she sped through glass doors that would take her to the wooden bridge that gave access to the castle ramp.

A few more curious onlookers had joined the crowd gathered on the wall walk peering down at the body, and one or two were pointing at it.

"Would have been interesting if he'd gone over the side at the western end near those two towers," said a man holding a guidebook and pointing off to his right. Stunned faces turned toward him.

"Those things, those stone structures projecting beyond the parapet of the main curtain wall between the two western towers. They're called machicolations. Murder holes."

"Who said anything about murder?"

The small crowd that had gathered to peer over the parapet turned around to see a young policewoman, dark curls tucked into her bowler-style hat with its distinctive navy-blue-and-white-checkered band and a North Wales Police silver cap badge, holding a notebook in one hand and a pen in the other. She looked from one cold, pale face to another.

"Who said anything about murder?" Bethan repeated.

"I was just saying that those things are called murder holes," the man with the guidebook said defensively. "It says here that those defending the castle could pour boiling water or large stones down them to kill the invaders below."

"Right, well, never mind that now. Was anyone here when it happened? Did anyone see anything? If you did, I'll need your names and we'll want to interview you," Bethan said.

The crowd started to speak all at once and Bethan held up her hand.

"If anybody saw anything, please go and stand over there and do not talk to each other," she ordered, pointing a little way down the wall walk. "If you did not see anything and cannot help with our inquiry, then you are free to leave and I would ask you to do so."

Nobody moved.

"Who was the first one here?"

The man with the guidebook raised his hand. "Right," Bethan said. "What's your name?"

"Huw Bowen."

"Good. Now then, Mr. Bowen, can you tell us what you saw? Did you see someone go over the wall walk?"

"No," Bowen replied. "But I arrived soon after it happened. I was the first one to spot the body and I raised the alarm." Bethan noted this. "Anything else you can tell me?"

He shook his head. "I was looking for my wife. I wonder where she's got to."

As he spoke, police officers on the ground began erecting a screen with a roof on it around the body to hide it from public view and cordoning off the area with blue-and-white crime-scene tape.

Thirteen

*T*ell me everything that happened," Victoria said that evening, reaching for the glass of red wine Penny was holding out to her. "From the beginning and don't leave anything out."

At first, Victoria hadn't been too keen on the idea of Penny's taking off the best part of a weekday to attend the Stretch and Sketch Club Christmas party but had agreed when Penny pointed out that most of the club members were either customers or potential customers, so it would be good if she went. Victoria had then suggested that Penny take business cards with her and be sure to hand them out.

Victoria had dropped in on Penny on the pretext of a few documents that needed signing, but they both knew the papers could have waited until the next day and that the real reason for Victoria's visit was to hear all about the events at Conwy Castle.

"Well, I didn't really see much," Penny replied. "I was at ground level sketching, and the other members of the group were roaming all over the castle. I have no idea where they were. In fact, some of them might even have gone home, for all I know. Anyway, a few people were wandering about, and then I saw Harry Saunders stroll past. A few minutes later Florence hurried after him, and then Mrs. Lloyd and her friend Bunny showed up, and then Mrs. Lloyd rushed after Saunders, hoping to catch him up, I think. She seemed very determined and quite agitated. I didn't get a sense that she knew that Florence was there. And a few minutes after that, the commotion started. A scream came from somewhere"—she raised her arm and made a fluttering motion— "and then the next thing I knew, a man came running out of the Great Hall area shouting that someone had fallen. I didn't realize until I got up there that it was Huw Bowen. Anyway, I called the police and then I climbed up the prison tower stairs." She winced. "They were very slippery, by the way, those stairs were. I hate heights and I really had to force myself to keep going up those terrible, narrow stairs."

After a sip of wine and a moment spent gathering her thoughts, she continued.

"Let me see. Where was I? Oh yes, and then Bethan arrived and joined us up on the wall walk and more police arrived and started taping off the scene on the ground. People had to be very careful coming down those awful stairs. So slippery. I was terrified on them. And besides, everyone was quite shaken up, as you'd imagine."

"But you didn't actually see anything?" Victoria asked. "You didn't see him go over the side or anything like that?"

"No, I wasn't anywhere near." She shifted in her chair. "I don't even know who it was, but I have my suspicions."

A knock on the front door halted the conversation. As Penny went to answer it, Victoria set her wineglass down on a side table and waited. A few moments later she heard voices at the front door and Detective Chief Inspector Gareth Davies entered the room, with Penny following, holding his coat.

"Evening, Victoria. How are you?"

She smiled at him. "Good, thanks. You?"

"Fine." He looked around a little uncertainly.

"Bethan not with you?"

Davies shook his head. "No, she's just gone to get something to eat, but we'll be meeting up in about, oh"—he consulted his watch—"half an hour."

Penny draped his coat over a chair, and they sat down close to each other on the sofa.

"Can we get you anything?" Penny asked. "We've just opened a bottle of wine, but somehow I doubt that's what you came for."

"No, no wine, thanks, but it's been a long day and I could murder a cup of coffee."

Victoria jumped up. "I'll get that. I know you came here to speak to Penny."

Gareth nodded gratefully as Victoria disappeared into the kitchen, and then he called after her, "And a couple of biscuits if there are any going."

"Right."

"I can't tell you very much," Penny said, and then recounted what she had told Victoria.

"Well, it's early days yet, of course," Gareth replied, "and I expect it'll get complicated, this case. Outdoor ones often do, with so many people milling about.

"And then there's the business with the witnesses. Everyone talking to everyone else and pretty soon people don't recall what they actually saw, they start repeating what someone else told them as the way they remember it."

He sighed and settled back into the sofa, stretching his legs out in front of him. "Oh, yes, there have been lots of studies done on that."

His face looked drawn and tired. The corners of his mouth were turned down, making him look older.

"You look knackered," Penny said.

Davies nodded. "I am, a bit," he agreed. "But it's more than that. It's bad enough when people die at Christmastime, but now we've got a major investigation to run and, frankly, the timing is terrible. If we don't get this sorted by Christmas, I'll have to assign young officers to this case—ask them to give up time that they should be spending at home with their wives and children." He glanced at Penny beside him, her face glowing from an afternoon spent in the fresh air doing something she enjoyed.

"And of course, there's my own agenda here, too. I was hoping to take some time off and that maybe we, that is, you and I, could go away somewhere nice for a few days. I've been on the Internet . . . there are hotels in Chester or Bath that do lovely Christmas breaks and I thought perhaps this would be something you'd enjoy. We'd arrive the afternoon of Christmas Eve, warm mince pies and a glass of mulled wine in front of a crackling fire . . ."

He stopped as Victoria entered bearing a small tray with a mug of coffee and a couple of digestive biscuits on a small, violet-patterned plate.

"I think I got the milk and sugar the way you like it."

"If it's warm and wet, it'll do." He took a grateful sip and told her it was just fine. Sensing that she had interrupted something, Victoria gave an apologetic shrug.

"It's all right, Victoria," Penny said. "We were just discussing Christmas, and Gareth was saying what with all this business at the castle that he might not be able to take any time off."

Gareth took a bite of his biscuit and smiled at her. "I'm sure we'll all sort out something nice for Christmas."

"Of course we will," Penny said brightly. "You and Bethan will come to us here—Victoria and me." She looked at Victoria, who nodded. "Right, now that that's all settled," Penny began eagerly, "let's move on. You must know more by now about what happened at Conwy Castle. What else can you tell us? Do you know who the victim is?"

"Ah," said Gareth, "that's a bit tricky, and the answer, I guess is yes and no."

The two women leaned forward.

"We'll need formal identification, of course, and I have no idea who will be able to do that. But I saw the body myself and I recognized the man I met at Mrs. Lloyd's open house, who was calling himself Harry Saunders. But he had no papers on him and we don't know yet where he was living. So we don't know for sure if Harry Saunders was even his real name. I doubt it was. It was likely one of many. The body will be fingerprinted and we'll get on to the American embassy and see if they know who he is. We'll also try dental records and DNA, if we have to."

"Yes, I remember you had your suspicions about him," Penny said. "That'll be that policeman's instinct we hear so much about."

Davies tapped his nose. "Sometimes things just don't smell right. And I've been doing this a long time, remember."

"Well, you'll be speaking to Mrs. Lloyd, of course," said Victoria. "She knew him better than anyone and was becoming very fond of him, by all accounts. I think she had high hopes there."

Davies groaned. "I haven't spoken to her yet, but that's what brings me to Llanelen tonight. I just wanted to have a word with you first, to see if you'd remembered anything else that you didn't think at the time worth mentioning to Bethan."

Penny shook her head. "No, sorry. Just what I told her."

"Then that's going to be a problem, I'm afraid. No one really saw anything." He set down his mug. "But someone certainly saw something." He started to rise from the sofa, but Penny laid a hand on his shoulder. As he glanced over at her, she tilted her head and raised an eyebrow.

"What do you mean 'someone saw something'? How do you know? The stairs were really slippery and I'm sure it was just as bad up there on the wall walks. Signs were posted everywhere warning people to be careful. And you know those open spots in the wall are really low. I thought how easy it would be for someone to fall over the side. You just lean over a little too far . . . He could have slipped over the side."

Davies nodded.

"Well, nine times out of ten a fall is just a fall. But not this time. Unfortunately for him, he had some help going off that wall. In fact, until we get the results of the postmortem, we won't know for sure, but it may not even have been the fall that killed him."

The room became still. Penny was aware of Victoria's quiet breathing.

"Are you saying he was pushed?" Victoria asked. "How can you tell that?"

"Pushed? Well, maybe, but certainly he was given a helping hand over the side." He looked from one to the other.

"When the officers on site got a closer look at the body, they found something pretty nasty in his back. A letter opener that had once apparently belonged to one Arthur Lloyd."

Penny gasped.

"No! Surely you're not suggesting that Mrs. Lloyd had anything to do with this!"

"I'm not suggesting anything," Davies replied smoothly. "We're just following up and going where the investigation leads, and the letter opener is certainly leading us in a certain direction. For now, at any rate."

He drained the last of his coffee, handed the empty mug to Victoria, and stood up.

"Right, well, thanks for the coffee, and I'm sure you'll let me know if anything else comes to mind. Sometimes we remember things later. Every little bit of information helps, remember, no matter how trivial it might seem to you."

"You're on your way to Mrs. Lloyd's house now, aren't you?" Penny asked, handing him his coat. "You're meeting Bethan there."

Davies put on his coat and headed for the door.

"I have to speak to her, yes. And Bethan will be present."

Penny closed the door quietly behind him and then, frowning, returned to Victoria. The two women looked at each other.

"There must be an explanation," said Victoria. "Mrs. Lloyd? That can't be right."

"Never in a million years," agreed Penny.

Fourteen

"Oh, it's you. You'd better come in, then."

Florence stood aside as Davies and Bethan Morgan crowded into Mrs. Lloyd's hallway.

"Give me your coats," she instructed. "And from the look of your boots, best if you took them off. If you don't mind," she added. The two visitors dutifully bent over, removed their boots, and set them down neatly, side by side, on a plastic tray.

"I expect you'll be wanting a word with Evelyn. She's in the sitting room, but she's pretty shaken up. Come through."

Mrs. Lloyd, her face creased with anxiety, stood up as the two police officers entered the sitting room. A cheerful fire blazing away did its best to dispel the gloom that seemed to hover around her. She waved her hand in the general direction of the sofa and the two officers sat down. As Bethan took out her notebook,

Davies addressed Mrs. Lloyd in a neutral, calm voice, as Florence remained standing in the doorway.

"Now, Mrs. Lloyd, I'm sorry to have to tell you this, but pending formal identification, we believe that your, um, friend, Harry Saunders, died at Conwy Castle this afternoon." Before he could continue, Mrs. Lloyd's shoulders sagged as she held her hand over her mouth, trying to stifle the sobs desperate to escape. Bethan reached out to pat her hand, and the two police officers waited for a few moments as Mrs. Lloyd struggled to control herself.

"I know this comes as unpleasant news," Davies continued, "but I'm afraid I have to ask you about your whereabouts at the castle this afternoon."

Mrs. Lloyd said nothing. Florence disappeared and returned a few moments later holding out a box of tissues. Mrs. Lloyd gave her a weak smile, pulled two or three from the box, and dabbed at her eyes.

"I had gone to the castle with my friend, Bunny," she said. "I had hoped to see Harry over the weekend, but he never arrived, because of the weather, you see. You know what the roads were like. It was your lot advising everyone to stay off them." She looked from one to the other. "So when Penny said she had just seen him heading toward the rear part of the castle, the inner ward I believe it's called, naturally I hurried after him. I needed a word with him. But when I got there, he was not to be seen."

"I need to be very clear about this. You didn't see him on the lower level," Bethan repeated. "Is that correct?"

"No, he was not there."

"So what did you do then?"

"Well, I thought maybe he had gone up on the wall walk, so I went up there. They had signs posted about how slippery the stairs and walkways were, so I took my time going up there I can tell you, clinging onto that rope railing for dear life, and when I didn't see him at the top of the stairs, I came down again. It was very windy up there. I didn't want to risk walking along the wall walk. It's all right in summer, I suppose, but not this time of year. Not for me. I'm very frightened of falling, and looking back on it now, I was daft to go up those stairs in the first place."

The two police officers had discussed whether this would be the right time to ask Mrs. Lloyd about the letter opener and had decided to take a wait-and-see approach, depending on how the interview went.

Davies was thinking about introducing it into the conversation when Bethan's eyes turned to Florence, who was now perched on a small chair beside the door just inside the room.

"And you, Florence, what about you? Did you see anything?"

Mrs. Lloyd turned sharply and looked at her companion.

"You were there, Florence? Whatever for?"

Florence straightened the collar of her blouse.

"How do you know I was there?"

"I recognized you at the edge of the crowd that had gathered on the wall walk, Florence," said Bethan. "But you left before I could speak to you."

"Well, yes, I was there," Florence admitted. "I spotted him on the train coming from Chester, and when he got off at Conwy, I decided to follow him to see what he was up to. I managed to keep him in my sights as far as the castle, but by the time I had bought my ticket and found my way inside, he was quite far ahead of me. I thought I spotted him going down the length of the place, but he just seemed to disappear. I don't see as well as I used to, to be honest, and I didn't know where he'd got to, so I thought I'd just take a wander round, and look for him. I was trying to work out what business he had there because he certainly didn't seem like the sightseeing type to me." And then she added, "But I guess he could have fancied visiting an old monument. There's no accounting for taste, is there?"

Mrs. Lloyd glared at her and started to speak, but Bethan raised her hand, silencing her before she could say anything.

It was now Davies' turn to speak.

"Mrs. Lloyd, do you own a gold-coloured letter opener with the name Arthur Lloyd engraved on it?"

"Why, yes, I do! It was given to Arthur as his Pineapple Award by the fruit and veg vendors association back in the 1980s. How do you know about it? Has it turned up? We misplaced it, oh, what Florence, a couple of weeks ago? I can't remember exactly, but one day we went to open the post and it was nowhere to be found." A puzzled look crossed her face. "But why do you ask? Where is it?"

She stood up and walked over to the little desk where she kept her bills, thank-you notes, and other small bits and pieces of correspondence. She pointed to a small, blue, glass jar that held pens and pencils. "It used to live right there in that blue jar, but we haven't seen it for a while. I thought maybe Florence had stuck it in a drawer or something when she was dusting. Odd that it never turned up, but now that I think about it, we never really looked for it, did we, Florence? Not properly, I mean."

Florence nodded glumly.

Mrs. Lloyd returned to her seat.

"Florence, do you know where the letter opener is?" Davies asked.

She shook her head. Her eyes betrayed a dawning fear.

Watching her intently, Davies told the two women that the letter opener had been found and then, his eyes moving quickly from one to the other, told them where. In Harry Saunders's back.

Mrs. Lloyd touched her hand to her cheek and recoiled. She looked as if she had been slapped.

"I don't think I can take that in," she said. "Harry stabbed with my letter opener? O dear Lord." Across the room, Florence rose from her chair, hesitated, and then sat down again.

"I'm sorry, Mrs. Lloyd," Davies continued, "but at some point, we're going to have to show you the letter opener, just so we can be sure we're talking about the same one. We'll need you to confirm that it is, in fact, yours."

Mrs. Lloyd nodded.

"I expect I'll have to go to the station to do that, will I, Inspector?"

"Yes."

"But not tonight, surely? It's getting a bit late and I don't feel up to looking at something like that, knowing that it . . ."

"No, Mrs. Lloyd, not tonight. We've covered enough for now."

"Well, I'll say good night, then. Florence will show you out."

As the three of them turned toward the door, Mrs. Lloyd spoke.

"Inspector, there's something I need to ask you."

Davies gave her his full attention.

Mrs. Lloyd hesitated. "No, it's all right. It doesn't matter. It can wait." The detective chief inspector turned his head slightly. "No, really," Mrs. Lloyd said. "It's nothing."

"Mrs. Lloyd, if you know something, you must tell us what it is. Did you see something? If you have information and you're not sure if it's important or not, tell us and we'll decide if it's relevant."

She pinched her lips together.

"No, I was just going to ask you something, that's all."

Davies put on his coat. "I don't need to tell you two that this situation is very serious, and we haven't finished with either of you yet. You have confirmed that the murder weapon belongs to you, Mrs. Lloyd, you were unable to account for its whereabouts, you were both at the castle, and neither of you seems to have an alibi."

He cleared his throat.

"But because of your standing in the town"—and here Florence raised an eyebrow as Mrs. Lloyd pinched her lips together—"we won't take you into custody tonight. But neither of you is to leave town without letting us know."

The police officers said good night and Florence closed the door behind them and returned to the sitting room.

"What was that all about, then?" Florence demanded when they were sitting down.

"Oh, Florence, I've gone and done the most terrible, stupid thing." Her face seemed to have aged years since Florence had last seen her. Deep worry lines had formed where none were before, dark circles had developed under her eyes, and her cheeks appeared sunken.

Florence leaned forward, her practical, work-worn hands braced on her knees.

"You can tell me, Evelyn," she said. "In fact, you might feel better if you did tell me. Maybe I can help."

"I was going to ask those police officers if they had found a cheque or something like that in Harry's pockets when they found the body."

"A cheque?" Florence processed this information and then, as she seemed to realize the implication, gave a little gasp.

"Oh, you didn't, Evelyn! You loaned that awful man money?

140

Oh, I hope it wasn't a lot. How much? Five hundred pounds? Was it as much as that?"

Mrs. Lloyd shook her head. "Much more than that. I'm not sure I can bring myself to tell you."

"Tell me. How much?" Florence said in a low voice.

"Twenty thousand pounds."

Florence gave a little gasp with her next intake of breath.

"I don't believe it. How could you? What were you thinking?"

"It gets worse, Florence. I didn't lend it to him. I have no memo of understanding or anything like that." She looked down at her hands. "I pretty much gave it to him. He was going to invest it, you see. And as my savings weren't earning very much interest at the bank, it seemed like a good idea."

Florence looked as if she were about to cry.

"Oh, Evelyn, you foolish woman."

Mrs. Lloyd nodded. "Oh, Lord, I know that. You don't need to tell me." She looked at her hands and then raised her eyes to her companion.

"Maybe I should tell the police about it. Huw Bowen, at the bank, he suggested I should go to the police."

Florence thought about that for a moment.

"But if you go to the police, and tell them about the money, they might think that gave you a good reason to kill Saunders. Oh, what do they call that? You see it on the television shows all the time."

"Motive," said Mrs. Lloyd. "They might think I had a motive."

"Motive, that's it."

"But speaking of motive, Florence, maybe you had a motive, too."

"Me?"

"Yes. You were settled and comfortable here in my home and maybe you thought if Harry moved in, as he and I had been discussing, you'd have to leave. As you would have."

Mrs. Lloyd sat back and folded her arms. "So maybe you had a motive, too."

Florence gave a little chuckle. "Pfft. Why would I waste my time and energy killing that man? I had no reason to."

A curtain of coolness had begun to descend between the two women.

"And not only that," Mrs. Lloyd continued, "but you could have taken the letter opener yourself to try to make the police think I did it. Well, I know I didn't kill him," she said with edgy emphasis. "And if I didn't, and you had a motive, then maybe it was you."

"Ha! Funny you should say that. I was just thinking the very same thing about you."

The two women glared at each other as the temperature dropped another few degrees.

A few minutes later Mrs. Lloyd glanced at her companion and remarked, "Well, there's one thing I should thank you for, I guess, Florence."

"What's that, then, Evelyn?"

Expecting her response to refer to the baking, tidying up, or all the other ways Florence had made herself useful around the house, Florence almost cracked a smile when Mrs. Lloyd replied, "Well, a few minutes ago when you called me a foolish woman at least you didn't call me a foolish, old woman." She choked back a sob and then covered her face with her hands as the tears began. Florence held out the box of tissues to Mrs. Lloyd and in that small gesture the two friends seemed to understand that some kind of silent apology had been offered on one side and accepted on the other.

"Here. You'll feel better after you've had a good cry. When you're up to it, we'll talk. I've had an idea. I'm going to put the kettle on now and I'll be back in a few minutes. I'll make us some nice herbal tea."

Mrs. Lloyd gulped and nodded. Florence busied herself in the kitchen, and when she heard the sobbing start to subside, she returned to the living room with a tea tray. She poured Mrs. Lloyd a cup of steaming camomile tea and handed it to her.

"Now listen to me, Evelyn. You need to buck up. When the police find out about the money, as they're bound to, you could find yourself in serious trouble. They might very well regard that as a motive, and they'll figure out that's what you wanted to talk to him about. Come to think of it, I'm surprised that policewoman didn't ask you tonight what you wanted to talk to Harry about. They'll ferret out every detail of your life, the police will. They have to. That's what they do. They leave no stone unturned."

She lifted her teacup to her lips while Mrs. Lloyd gazed anxiously at the fire.

"And you were right, you know, I do like living here and I did think that if Harry moved in I'd have to leave. So I could be in trouble, too, if the police see that as a motive for murder, except for one thing. Because, as it happens, I had no motive. It wouldn't have mattered to me if Harry had moved in."

Mrs. Lloyd took a tentative sip of her hot herbal tea.

"What are you trying to say, exactly, Florence? What are you getting at?"

"When I was away in Liverpool, I went for a job interview

with the head housekeeper at the Adelphi Hotel. I told her what all I'd been doing here for you and she was impressed. She said young women today don't know the first thing about keeping house, and she offered me a job right then and there to train the maids. With live-in accommodation. I'd have my very own room right in the hotel! And I'd decided to accept it. So I was coming back here to tell you that I'd seen the writing on the wall and I was leaving and you and Harry Saunders could have the house all to yourselves. Then I would have collected my belongings and been on my way and good luck to the pair of you."

Mrs. Lloyd looked aghast.

"So, you see, Evelyn, I know for a fact that I didn't kill Harry Saunders. And what's more, I don't think you did, either. You don't have it in you."

Mrs. Lloyd shook her head. "Of course I didn't kill him."

"But the police might see things differently. So if you didn't do it, and I didn't do it, I think we should ask that Penny Brannigan to help us find out who did."

Mrs. Lloyd took another sip of her tea and nodded, thought for a moment longer, and then moved her head up and down with a little more certainty.

"Well, it wouldn't hurt, I suppose, although I'm not convinced she's quite as good a detective as she might think she is."

"Evelyn! She's your best hope!"

"Well, I suppose it can't hurt." Mrs. Lloyd brightened. "Wouldn't it be wonderful if she could somehow get my money back?"

"We don't even know yet if she'll help. And as for the money, miracles do happen, but don't hold your breath. Now, come on, it's getting late. Drink up so I can tidy things away." Florence set her cup on the tray and walked over to switch off the gas fireplace. As the flames died away and long shadows crept into the corners of the room, Mrs. Lloyd sighed, handed her half-full cup to Florence, and got heavily to her feet.

"Well, so much for us being amateur sleuths. I'm so confused by all this I wouldn't know where to begin," Mrs. Lloyd said.

"Well, we'd better try to get some sleep. We'll talk some more in the morning. Things might seem clearer to us then."

It had been some time since Florence had felt in command of a situation and she was enjoying it.

Victoria set her bag down beside Penny's front door and slipped into her warm boots. They had just about exhausted the topic of Saunders's death and then moved on to the business of the spa, which would be opening in two days. Every service was ready except the hair salon. They'd had several applications from local hairdressers, but none of them seemed quite the right fit. "It's a man you should be looking for, even if he's gay," Eirlys had told them. "Ladies love the idea of a man touching them, running his fingers through their hair."

After a quick exchange of amused glances, Victoria had given Eirlys a broad smile.

"You just might be on to something there, Eirlys," she had said, adding she would see what she could do.

"Now listen, Penny," said Victoria, giving her a friendly shake of her index finger, "you're not going to get us involved in this Harry Saunders investigation, are you? We're going to leave it to the police, aren't we?"

"Yes, Victoria, we are. It's got nothing to do with us, and we've got to stay focused on the spa and get it up and running smoothly."

"Good. I'm glad we agree on that. We've also got that window display judging to sort out. We need to get on with that."

"Are you all right to walk home?"

Victoria peered out the door. "Yes, there's not much snow now and I'll be fine. Good night!"

Penny closed and locked the door behind her and returned to her living room. She switched off the lights, made sure the door leading from the kitchen to the garden was locked, and by the light of the hall walked up the stairs to her freshly painted bedroom with its comfortable bed and soft, puffy duvet.

After a quick glance at the frozen garden sleeping in the darkness below her window, she closed the drapes against the night and began undressing.

I wonder if Mrs. Lloyd will sleep tonight, she thought as she tossed her shirt in the laundry basket. And then, as she sat on the edge of her bed and reached under her pillow for her nightdress, she allowed herself to contemplate the question that had been nagging at her all evening.

What was Saunders doing at the castle? What, or who, had brought him there?

Fifteen

I know it might have seemed like a good idea last night, Florence, but now, in the cold light of morning, I'm just not sure."

Mrs. Lloyd spread a generous dollop of ginger marmalade on her whole-grain toast and then sliced the bread in half.

Florence's eyes narrowed slightly, giving her a no-nonsense look and Mrs. Lloyd immediately backtracked.

"What I meant to say is, I'm still thinking about it. I don't know what Penny can do that the police can't."

"Well, from what you've told me about her, she'll get to the bottom of it," said Florence. "I think you should go and see her this morning. In fact, maybe we both should." As the carriage clock on the mantel chimed the half hour, the two women turned to each other. They had both been dreading the arrival of the morning post with its unfortunate reminder of the late Arthur Lloyd's letter opener.

Mrs. Lloyd shuddered.

"When all this is over, if they were to return that letter opener to me, I could never, ever use it again to open my letters." She took a crunchy bite of toast and brushed a few rather large bits of crust off her bosom.

"And in all this, Florence, I can't help thinking how I've let my poor Arthur down. I know he would have wanted me to be happy, and if I had found someone nice to marry, I don't think Arthur would have minded too much. But when I think about the money and how Arthur scrimped and saved every year of our married life so I would be provided for. Do you know, he never had a holiday abroad? 'What do I want with all that foreign muck?' he used to say. I tried to talk him into going to Spain, telling him it would be good for him to experience the oranges firsthand, so to speak, but he wouldn't have it." She punctuated the last few sentences with a little series of sighs.

She wiped her lips and then folded her napkin and tossed it beside her plate.

"Oh! I can't bear to think of it."

"Well, I've made my opinion very clear, Evelyn, and I'll not say it again. But I will say this. I'm going to see Penny this morning and I'd like it very much if you would come with me."

Before Mrs. Lloyd could reply, the soft, shuffling sound of the morning post landing on the hall carpet caught their attention. As their eyes met, Florence tilted her head in the direction of the front door.

"I'll go," she said, standing up and leaning on the table with her hands in front of her. "And here's a thought. I know you hate opening your mail with your fingers, so while we're in town, why don't we stop in at the charity shop and see if they've got a letter opener? There's all kinds of nice things in there and you never know what you'll find." She took a step away from the table and folded her arms. "Makes you wonder at the things people give away or throw out, it really does."

She took a few steps toward the hall and turned back to remark to Mrs. Lloyd, "I'm so glad to see you haven't lost your appetite over all this, Evelyn."

At the rectory, Reverend Thomas Evans and his wife were finishing their coffee. They liked to read their morning post over breakfast, and the rector often read aloud interesting bits from the various magazines he subscribed to.

This morning, however, he was reading the account of the death of Harry Saunders in the morning newspaper.

"Oh, my," said Bronwyn. "How dreadful. But I wonder what will happen to the dancing lessons. I believe people were really enjoying his classes. Do you think someone else will take it on?"

"I doubt it," replied the rector as he turned the pages to the national news section. "I don't think we have anyone else around here who could give dancing lessons or he'd have been doing so by now."

He paused as an item caught his attention. He read a few lines and then looked at his wife, who was scraping crumbs from one plate onto another.

"The bishop isn't going to like this," the rector said, clearing his throat.

"What's that, dear?"

"The headline says, 'Gay vicar, 65, to "marry" Nigerian male model half his age.'"

Today was the last day Eirlys would be doing manicures in the old salon, and Penny was filled with mixed emotions. She had loved the little shop she had started all those years ago and was grateful for the modest income it had provided her. But she recognized she had outgrown it and was eager and excited to move on to the new challenges that awaited her. She trusted Victoria's business acumen and was confident the new enterprise would thrive, just as her old one had. She also trusted her own ability to handle whatever obstacles or setbacks the new venture might bring, and she knew there would be plenty of those.

This evening a couple of local lads would move all the stock out of the old shop, and among her other tasks for the morning, Penny wanted to dust shelves at the spa in preparation for the arrival of the best of the old stock. The rest would be donated to a local women's shelter.

She had taken her time over her coffee this morning, sipping it while she got dressed and mulling over what she thought the day would bring, making a rather lengthy list of all the things she needed to do. One of the items on this list was to take the snowflake brooch Gareth had given her on the night of the spa party to the jeweler's for an insurance appraisal. So after breakfast she unpinned the brooch from the red dress she had worn to the spa launch party and, before replacing it in its little red leather box, had taken a few moments to admire it. She loved the way the brooch felt in her palm, cool and glittering with its intricate six-point pattern. She thought about each snowflake being unique and wondered if that's how Gareth saw her.

She had been surprised when Victoria had asked if she had had it appraised for insurance purposes. That seems like trying to find out how much he paid for it, Penny had said. Victoria shrugged. If it's valuable, you need to insure it. Seeing the logic in that, Penny planned to take the brooch to the jeweler's later that morning, after she dropped into the salon to see how Eirlys was getting on.

Although the spa would not be providing services until tomorrow, Rhian, the newly hired receptionist, was in place at the front desk, busily answering the phone, responding to e-mails, and taking bookings. The door was open and several women had come in just for a look round. It's that irresistible fresh paint smell, Victoria had suggested. Just had to see what's happening, and once they were inside, several young women who had peered in "just looking" had booked a manicure or a facial.

Arriving just before ten, Penny set a small stack of file folders down on the front desk, along with her handbag, and flipped through the appointments book. Although Rhian had wanted to manage the bookings electronically, Victoria, who preferred paper, had insisted that she do it two ways, on her computer but with backup in an appointments book with a smart cover splashed with pale pink peonies.

Penny smiled when she saw who was down for the first manicure of the day tomorrow. Well, it was Thursday, after all. She decided that as a special gesture, which she knew would be appreciated, the manicure would be complimentary. She turned around as the door opened.

"Hello, Mrs. Lloyd," she said with a welcoming smile. "I was just thinking about you. I'm really happy to see that you're going to be our very first customer tomorrow." Mrs. Lloyd shifted from one foot to the other and, unusual for her, said nothing.

Penny turned to her other visitor. "Hello, Florence. How are you?"

The two women exchanged a charged glance, and then Florence turned to Penny.

"We were wondering if you had a few minutes to talk to us. You must be very busy, getting ready for tomorrow, we know that, and we wouldn't bother you now if it wasn't important."

She took a small step closer and lowered her voice.

"It's about that nasty business at Conwy Castle. Evelyn wants a word with you."

Penny glanced down the hall. "Right. Let me just see where Rhian has got to." She walked down the hall and stuck her head into a room adjacent to the reception area.

"Rhian, I'll just be in the quiet room for a few minutes if you need me." Penny then returned to the reception area and gathered up the two visitors.

"We'll just step in here." She led them to the small sitting area, where she and Florence had spent a few minutes on the night of the spa launch party discussing her concern over Mrs. Lloyd's increasing fondness for Harry Saunders.

"Here we are," she said, gesturing toward the chairs and then seating herself, facing them. She clasped her hands together and leaned forward. When Florence began to speak, without any hesitation or glancing at Mrs. Lloyd for unspoken permission, Penny realized they had talked this conversation through, probably in detail, before they arrived. Who would say what and how much would be said.

"It's like this," Florence began. "That police officer you're friendly with came to see us last night about the death of that awful man. Harry Saunders. There are things he doesn't know yet, your police officer, but he'll probably find them out. And when he does, we're afraid that one or both of us might come under suspicion."

Florence stopped and rubbed her nose with the back of her hand.

"Go on, Florence," Mrs. Lloyd prompted.

"You see, the police might think I wanted Saunders out of the way because if he moved in with Evelyn, I'd have to leave. I sold the few bits and pieces I had in Liverpool, and, well, to be honest, if I did have to go, I'd be very hard pressed, on my pension, to find any kind of decent accommodation. You know all about that. We talked about the situation in this very room on the night of your spa party."

Penny nodded as Florence glanced at Mrs. Lloyd. "Even though I've had a rather attractive offer of employment, I have it very good at Evelyn's and I know how lucky I am. I like it there. It suits me. Well, suits both of us, I think."

Mrs. Lloyd gave her hand a friendly, reassuring pat and Penny smiled.

"So you think the police might think having to move out of Mrs. Lloyd's house gave you a motive for murder?"

"Well, from what you read in the papers, people get killed for less than that all the time. There was that story about the man who killed his dad because he ordered the wrong kind of toppings on a pizza."

She shrugged. "But I'd had an offer of employment before Harry was killed, so I didn't really have any reason to wish him dead. No, it's Evelyn here we're worried about." She turned to her. "Do you want to tell or shall I?"

"You."

Florence squared her shoulders.

"If you'll remember, Penny, I knew that man was up to no

good. He tricked Evelyn into giving him some money. An awful lot of money, I'm afraid, and it might look to the police like she killed him to get her money back. Or because she was angry with him."

"Oh, let me tell her," Mrs. Lloyd cut in, suddenly coming back to life.

"Well, if you're going to tell her, then if you don't mind, Penny, I'm just going to go along to the loo. I can't bear to hear this all over again. It's too painful."

"Down the hall, past reception, on the left," Penny said, and then turned her attention back to Mrs. Lloyd.

"You met Harry," Mrs. Lloyd began. "You must have seen for yourself how he could charm the birds out of the trees." She explained how Saunders had suggested they set up a joint account so he could invest her money and how she had waited all that snowy weekend to hear from him but he never arrived.

"And I know I've been a foolish woman, so please don't ask me how I could have been so gullible because I don't know. What's done cannot be undone, as they say. And as you can imagine, I'm dreading all this getting out, so I hope you'll keep this to yourself."

Penny groaned.

"What's the matter?"

"Oh, Mrs. Lloyd, Mrs. Lloyd. I don't know if I can keep this to myself. You're right that the police are bound to find out about the money during the investigation, and when they do, and they then find out that I knew about it and didn't tell them, well, I'm not sure what my legal status would be, but I expect it could be considered obstruction of justice or perverting the course of justice or something."

"Nonsense!" snorted Mrs. Lloyd. "You've been watching too many of those American crime shows, you have."

Penny grimaced. "I'm sorry, but I really don't know what I can do to help. The police are going to investigate every aspect of this case, anyway, you must realize that. It's murder, after all."

"Well, what we're afraid of is that they'll sort it out to their satisfaction but not to ours. I know you're just an amateur sleuth with no credentials and not much experience, but Florence and I want you to look into it so you can get to the bottom of it. Find out the truth, like."

"That's right," said Florence, who had returned in time to catch the end of Mrs. Lloyd's account. "We know we didn't do it. We want you to find out who did."

Penny gave a big sigh. "Well, I must admit I have been rather wondering about it. What particularly puzzles me is what he was doing at the castle in the first place. Do you have any idea?"

She sat back in her chair as they shook their heads.

"I'll have to think about this. With the spa just opening, the timing couldn't be worse. So much going on. I won't have a lot of time, you do realize that? I can't promise anything."

She turned her attention to Mrs. Lloyd.

"I think the best thing you can do is tell DCI Davies yourself. About the money." She looked from one to the other. "And I don't know much about these things, but you might also want to consult a solicitor." She stood up.

"I'm sorry, I know this is very important to you, but you'll have to forgive me. I do have to go. I've got errands to run and we've got simply masses to do before tomorrow."

"Yes, of course, we understand," said Florence, picking up

her handbag. "Come on, then, Evelyn, we'll find something nice for our elevenses, and then maybe we should think about going to the police about the, you know." She lowered her voice. "The money." The women walked down the hall, thanking Penny as they went.

She watched them walk slowly out the door, unsure what to make of them, and then spoke to the receptionist who had just emerged from the storage room.

"Where are those files and my bag, Rhian? I left them right here on your desk."

"Oh, sorry, hope you don't mind, but I moved them out of the way. I put them on your desk in your office."

Penny hurried up the street, past the Red Dragon Hotel, through the cobbled town square and turned right down a narrow side street. She passed the butcher's shop with its signs urging customers to order a fresh Norfolk turkey now to arrive in time for Christmas, and stopped for a moment at the bakery, its irresistible window display filled with mince pies dusted with icing sugar, mince slices, brandy butter tarts, Eccles cakes, scones, sugar cookies shaped like pigs with bits of glacé cherries for eyes, Christmas cakes with marzipan icing, gingerbread men, custard tarts, and shortbread treats shaped like bells and tiny reindeer. Thinking how wonderfully inviting and creative most of the shop windows looked this year, carefully and lovingly decorated to compete in the local merchants window dressing competition that she and Victoria had yet to judge, she moved on and pushed open the door to the jewelry store.

The bell attached to the door tinkled as she entered, and the jeweler, who was working behind a glassed-in enclosure, stood up, removed a loupe from his right eye, and came out to greet her, taking his place behind the display counter. A short man, he was dressed in an old-fashioned but well-pressed suit with a white shirt and striped tie. His hair was brushed back from his face, revealing deep lines running across his forehead. Something about his round face and deep-set dark eyes suggested an Eastern European heritage.

"Hello," Penny began. "I wonder if you can do an appraisal for me. It's a little embarrassing, really, but a friend of mine gave me a brooch as a present, and another friend suggested I should have it appraised, in case it needs to be insured. I'm afraid I don't know if it's valuable or not. I don't even know where he bought it." She gave a little laugh. "Or even if he bought it."

The jeweler raised an impressive set of bushy eyebrows.

"Oh, heavens no, I certainly didn't mean that it might be stolen, no, nothing like that, in fact my friend, the man who gave it to me is a police officer. I simply meant it might have belonged to his mother, or . . ."

"Oh, right," said the jeweler. "Would you by any chance be Penny Brannigan?"

"Yes, I am," said Penny, somewhat surprised that he should know her name. "Have we met before? I'm sorry, I know in a small town our paths have probably crossed, but . . ."

"No, it's just that I remember now. Your piece'll be the snowflake brooch with the rose-cut centre stone, surrounded by six heart-shaped settings, each holding two smaller stones, and six emerald cuts forming a—"

Penny laughed and held up her hand. "You're familiar with it, I see."

"Familiar with it? I made it!" said the jeweler, opening a drawer and removing an envelope. "He was going to give this to you, but it took me a few days to write it up, so you can have it now. He called to say he was going to suggest you come in and get it. He just didn't want to give the appraisal to you at the same time as he gave you your gift." He handed over the envelope and leaned on the counter.

"So tell me, how do you like it?"

"I love it," Penny said. "It's beautiful, and I will treasure it all the more knowing that you made it." The jeweler came around from behind the counter and gave Penny a shy smile. "The police officer knew exactly what he wanted for you," he said, "so it wasn't too difficult. Between us we worked out something he thought you might like.

"I told your friend that if he ever needed any other fine jewelry for you"—he gave a little open-handed gesture—"a ring, for example, to come and see me. I would create something very beautiful."

Penny felt the beginning of an uncomfortable blush begin to creep up her neck.

"I don't know about that!"

The jeweler smiled as he held the door open for her, and as she stepped out into the street, she tucked the envelope he had given her into an outside pocket of her bag, snapped it shut, and after a longing glance in the bakery window, set off on the short walk back to the spa.

The morning was mild, but dark clouds were gathering once again to settle on the tops of the hills and she could sense the coming of rain.

A few minutes later, in the privacy of her office, she pulled out the envelope, opened it, and unfolded the document it contained. A little smile played at the corner of her lips at the sight of the colour digital photo of her brooch, displayed to sparkling advantage against a black velvet cloth, stapled to the piece of paper. She glanced over a detailed description of the brooch, the cut and positioning of the stones, the total carat weight, the white gold setting until she arrived at the insured value at the bottom. Her mouth opened slightly and her head jutted forward. That much, she thought. He spent that much on a brooch for me? She picked up her bag, unzipped it, and reached inside to pull out the little red box containing her brooch. It was not on top where she was sure she had placed it just before leaving home, so thinking it might have settled or shifted within the bag as it had been carried about all morning, she scrabbled around inside the bag. An icy sense of panic began to creep into her chest when she did not feel it. She touched the familiar shape of her wallet, her diary, and a small makeup bag. With her heart beginning to pound, she picked up the bag, dumped its contents on her desk, and spread them out. The box was not there. She felt in the four side pockets, hoping against hope but knowing that the smooth leather box she longed to touch would not be there. As waves of disbelief tinged with fear began to wash over her, she rushed down the hall to the reception area.

"Rhian," she croaked, barely able to speak because her mouth was so dry, "did you see a small red leather jewelry box this morning? It was in my bag and now it's not there. Is it on your desk?"

"No, I didn't see any jewelry box," Rhian said, looking up from her computer and then shifting her coffee mug and a few pieces of paper around on her desk. "I'll have a look, though."

"Where's Victoria?"

"She's, ah, let me see, did she tell me where she was going? She was here about half an hour ago and then, I think she . . ." Rhian held her hand to her face.

"Rhian! Where is she? Tell me!"

Not waiting for an answer, Penny ran back to her office and picked up her mobile.

It seemed an age until Victoria answered.

"Where are you? I need to see you."

"Why? What's the matter? You sound terrible."

"Where are you?"

"I'm at the salon with Eirlys packing up the rest of the nail varnishes. Where did you think I would be?"

"Victoria, come back, please, now. Don't ask any questions. Just come back."

Penny pressed the button to end the call and with a dreadful desperation began turning over the things on her desk. Why is it, she wondered vaguely, when you've lost or misplaced something you keep looking for it in the same place? If it wasn't there the first time you looked, why would you expect it to be there the second time? Or the third? Or the fourth?

She checked the floor around her desk and then hurried down the hall to Rhian's reception desk.

"Rhian, stop what you're doing and help me look for that jewelry box. Clear everything off your desk right now, please."

Rhian did as she was told, but as Penny dreaded, the box was nowhere to be seen. She stepped back from Rhian's desk just as a breathless Victoria burst through the door.

Penny gestured toward her office and the two women walked quickly down the hall.

"For God's sake, Penny, what is it? What's happened? I've been imagining all kinds of awful things on my way here. Tell me what's happened."

"You know that snowflake brooch Gareth gave me? It's gone missing. I've looked everywhere and I can't find it."

"It'll turn up, surely," Victoria said. "You probably set it down somewhere where it didn't belong, and when you least expect to see it, there it'll be."

Penny shook her head and whispered, "No. The brooch was in its little box, and I remember very clearly putting it in my bag this morning and then closing the zipper. I came here, set the bag down on the reception desk, went to the jeweler's, came back here, and when I looked for it, it was gone. Rhian and I have looked everywhere."

"Right. Well, before we panic, call the jeweler and see if you left it there."

"No," said Penny emphatically. "I didn't take it out of my bag. He had already done the appraisal, so he didn't need to see the brooch. In fact, he made it."

"Oh, right. OK, well then, go home and look for it there. Perhaps you only think you put it in your bag, and it's sitting on the table or counter or wherever you had your bag. Is that possible?"

Penny pursed her lips and closed her eyes. "I suppose it might be possible if I didn't remember so clearly setting it in my bag. I will look at home, though, just in case."

Victoria made an apologetic little gesture that included a shrug and something approaching a grimace.

"Was it very valuable, or dare I ask?"

Penny handed Victoria the appraisal document. Victoria's lower jaw dropped and she breathed in sharply.

"The awful thing is I know I should call the police, but I can't bear to tell him I lost it," Penny said. She hesitated. "One thing, though, did cross my mind, and that is that the jeweler who did the evaluation told me he had made the brooch. I was thinking maybe I could ask him to make a duplicate, and then I wouldn't have to tell Gareth."

"No," said Victoria. "You don't want to do that. You know you don't."

"No, I guess I don't. But I really don't want to tell him, either."

Victoria brightened. "Look, how about this? Go home and see if it's there. I really hope it is, but if it isn't, then call Bethan, and ask her to come and see you. You can talk to her about it. She'll know what to do and how to handle this."

Penny considered the suggestion.

"Here's the thing, Penny. It's an expensive piece of jewelry. If it's been stolen, the police need to know that. There may be others. And besides, telling them is probably the only way you'll get it back."

Seeing the wisdom in that, Penny agreed and reached for her coat and then gave a little start.

"Oh, no," she said. "I've just remembered something. Mrs. Lloyd and Florence came in for a chat. We were in the quiet room, and at one point, Florence excused herself to go the loo. If Rhian was away from her desk and Florence spotted the bag just sitting there, she might have . . ."

"Don't jump to conclusions. Go home, and if it's not there, call Bethan." She started to leave and then turned back.

"And contact Jimmy. He's got connections that might be useful."

A few months ago, at a seniors' home in Llandudno, Penny had met an elderly man who, in his younger days, had been one of the best break-and-enter artists in the area. If anyone could find out quickly who was trying to fence a stolen diamond brooch, it would be Jimmy.

Sixteen

Sergeant Bethan Morgan closed her notebook and leaned forward.

"All right, Penny. Have you told me everything that happened since you unpinned the brooch from your dress this morning? You're sure you didn't leave anything out? Even the smallest detail can be important."

"Yep. That's everything that happened." Penny unclasped her hands. "As you can imagine, I've gone over and over it in my mind. I haven't been able to think about anything else." She took a moment to collect her thoughts while Bethan waited to see what she would say next.

"What about Florence? I guess you'll have to speak to her," Penny said.

"Yes, I will. But that's not necessarily a bad thing. Florence may have seen someone when she was out in the hall."

"I didn't think of that. But, tell me, do you think she could have taken it?"

"Penny, I don't think anything at this point. One of the first things you learn in this job is not to assume or make quick judgments. We'll keep an open mind, investigate, and see what turns up. Now then, when Florence returned from the loo, did you notice any change in her demeanor? Was she fidgety? Seem uneasy? Anxious to leave?"

Penny thought for a moment. "No, I don't think she was any different."

Bethan wrote a few words in her notebook.

"And what about Gareth? Will you tell him?" Penny asked.

Bethan gave her a wry look. "You know I have to. He'd be very annoyed when he finds out later and he didn't hear it from us. And of course, he will find out. There'll be a report and he'll read it. But for now, let's see what happens, shall we?" She gave Penny a soft, reassuring look. "I can tell you he'll be very understanding, not to mention extremely motivated to find the brooch and the person who took it."

Bethan looked at her watch. "Right, well, I'd best get on it. But I'm really glad you told me. We've had a few incidents of theft reported and, you never know, this might tie in with those."

"Thefts? What kind of thefts?"

"Little things taken from shops. Nothing nearly as valuable as this."

She stood up. "Thefts like this are crimes of opportunity," she explained. "Someone saw your unattended bag, unzipped it, saw the little box on top, and just snatched it. It was all over in seconds. The receptionist pops out for a moment, the coast is clear, the thief is in and out. And he counts on the theft not being discovered for a while, and in the meantime all kinds of people have come and gone. And you might have even forgotten the details of when you last had it."

"Those other thefts," said Penny, "I don't suppose you could tell me about them. Or let me have a look at the file?"

"Have a look at a confidential police file? Absolutely not," replied Bethan with a smile. "That would be completely against proper police procedure. But I don't suppose anyone would notice if I happened to take a photocopy."

She took the evaluation form Penny offered her, glanced at it, and then tucked her notebook in her pocket as they made their way to the front door.

"We've been that busy with the opening of the new spa that Christmas has completely slipped my mind," said Penny. "But it's almost upon us. We'd love to have you join us, if you can."

"I thought you'd never ask! I'm on duty so I can't get away to my parents in Porthmadog. I'd love to come."

She stood in the doorway breathing the cold, clean air and then lifted her eyes toward the top of the hills that encircled the town. The dark clouds shrouding the tops of the hills had become more ominous.

"I'm off to have a word with Florence now. I'll let you know how we get on. And try not to worry too much."

"I hope you're not suggesting that I took the brooch!" Florence's eyes flashed with indignation. She met Bethan's eyes and then gestured at Mrs. Lloyd, who was seated on the sofa. "Now, Evelyn, I've been here with you for weeks now and have you noticed anything missing?" Realizing what she had just said, Florence tried to backtrack. "Well, not the letter opener; I didn't have anything to do with that, either."

"No, I'm not suggesting you took the brooch. I'm asking if you took it. There's a difference," said Bethan calmly. "And suggesting that if you did take it, or if you know anything at all about its disappearance, that things will go better for you if you tell me everything you know. But you are not under caution or anything else. I'm investigating a missing piece of jewelry and I have to ask questions."

"Well, I most certainly did not take it," Florence replied in a softer tone, "and I guess I can see why you have to ask. You think I had the opportunity because I stepped out of the little room for a bit on my own."

Bethan nodded. "That's right. Now, if you didn't take it, let me ask you if you saw anything while you were out in the hall that can help us get Penny's brooch back."

Florence pondered the question and then shook her head slowly.

"No, I didn't see anything, but now that I think about it, I felt something. It was cooler, as if the door had just been opened and a blast of cold air had come in. But it didn't really register at the time and I went back to that little room where Evelyn and Penny were."

"OK," said Bethan, offering Florence her business card. "Call me if you think of anything else, no matter how unimportant or trivial it might seem. Let me be the judge of what's important."

"Yes, Officer, I will." Florence looked at the card and then gave Bethan an honest, level look. "I like that Penny Brannigan. I wish I could help. If I could help her get her brooch back, I would."

"Well, I believe you, Florence," said Bethan, adding, "Don't get up. "I'll show myself out."

A few moments later, while the front door was quietly being opened and then closed, Mrs. Lloyd turned to Florence.

"Well, Florence, I expect you'll have had enough of us here in Llanelen and you'll be more than ready to take up that offer at the Adelphi Hotel in Liverpool. I've practically accused you of murder, and now the police are here suspecting you of stealing a valuable brooch."

Florence almost smiled. "Leave? I haven't seen so much excitement in years. How could I possibly leave until I see how all this turns out? It did seem a bit strange, though. I felt I was being grilled harder over the stolen brooch than I was over the murder." She stood up and retied her apron. "Now, should we have a little chat about what we are going to do about Christmas? I expect we'll be having a quiet little dinner here, just the two of us, unless you have some friends you'd like to invite. And I saw a poster in a shop window about a presentation of *A Child's Christmas in Wales* and I'd very much like to go. I've seen that on the telly, but it would be a proper treat to see it for real. With proper Welsh voices as the poet intended."

"Yes, we should go," agreed Mrs. Lloyd. "Everyone will be there. And no doubt there'll be refreshments afterward."

"It's good to see you getting back to being your old self, Evelyn."

"Well, what choice is there, really? We must keep calm and carry on, as they used to say during the war." She reached for the latest copy of *Cheshire Life* magazine. "I'd love a cup of tea, Florence, if you were thinking of putting the kettle on, and do you know, I believe I could do justice to one of those lovely scones you baked this morning."

This time Florence cracked a small, brief smile.

For the second time that day Penny walked from her home to the spa, this time quickly and deep in thought. Surprisingly and suddenly, the sun had come out, adding a warm, welcoming touch to the day and, for the moment at least, pushing the rain clouds to one side. Although most of the snow had disappeared from the streets, some remained, brown and crusted, pushed up against the sides of the buildings. But the pavement was bare and dry, and quite a few people were out and about.

As she passed the old manicure salon, she glanced in the window and saw Eirlys, the young manicurist who had been hired a few months ago and who had done so much to bring in younger customers, bent over a large packing crate. Penny pushed open the door. The shelves were now bare, the furniture was gone, and the room held surprisingly few memories. Eirlys straightened up and ran her hands down the sides of her jeans.

"Hi, Penny. I'm almost done. Victoria was here for a while, but after you called, she rushed off to the spa and hasn't come back."

"That's fine, Eirlys." Penny looked around. "You've done a great job here with all this."

"There were just a lot of small items to pack up, and Victoria helped with some of it," Eirlys said as she put the lid on the last box. "Are you feeling sad to be leaving your salon?"

"No, surprisingly I'm not, considering how many years I spent building up the business and working here. I'm really looking forward to all the exciting things we're going to do in the spa." She smiled at her young assistant. "Well, you're almost finished here, so let's lock up. Have you taken a break today?"

Eirlys shook her head.

"Right, well, tell you what. Take the rest of the afternoon off, and we'll see you at the spa bright and early tomorrow, all ready for our first day. Mrs. Lloyd is your first customer, and you know she'll expect everything to be just so."

Eirlys grinned. "What I'd like to do, if it's all right with you, Penny, is eat a little something, take a bit of time to get cleaned up, and then come to the spa this evening and help you set up the new manicure space. I'll need to know where everything is in the morning anyway, and Mrs. Lloyd isn't the only one who likes everything just so."

"Eirlys, that sounds like a wonderful idea. Shall we say seven P.M.? I don't know where we'd be without you."

"Lost?"

"That's exactly the word I was looking for. Couldn't have said it better myself."

As Penny pushed open the door to the spa, a trim woman in a bright red hat who had been speaking to Rhian, the receptionist, turned around and gave her a warm smile.

"Oh, there's Penny that I was telling you about, one of the owners," Rhian said. "She'll be able to help you."

The woman thanked Rhian and took a step closer to Penny.

"Hello," she said. "My name's Dorothy Martin, and I just dropped in on the off chance I might be able to get a manicure. I've never had one in my life and I thought it'd be fun. But I didn't realize that you haven't opened yet, so I'll just be on my way."

"No, wait," said Penny, intrigued by her soft midwestern

American accent. "It's true we aren't really open until tomorrow, but if you don't mind a bit of chaos, I can do you now, if you like. Most of our nail polishes won't be arriving until later this evening, but I have a few colours here that might suit you, as long as you're not too fussy."

"I'm certainly not fussy, and I'd appreciate that very much," Dorothy said.

"Well then," said Penny. "Come through and we'll get started."

The two women conversed for about fifteen minutes on their shared experiences as North American expatriates living in the U.K. Penny admitted she'd never really acquired a taste for curry, and Dorothy said that even after all these years she was still quite shocked by the strange ingenuity of British crime.

"In the States, people just tend to shoot each other and get it over with, but here they'll fiddle with the electricity so the missus will electrocute herself while she's trimming the hedge."

"Yes!" Penny said. "I've noticed that myself. In fact, we've just had a murder here at Conwy Castle that you might have heard about. A man, an American in fact, went off the wall walk with a letter opener in his back. Two ladies who might have connections to the case have asked me to see if I can find out anything."

"I've solved a few murders myself, oddly enough," said Dorothy. "Why don't you fill me in and I'll see if anything comes to mind."

After listening carefully while Penny described the events at the castle and mentioned Detective Chief Inspector Davies' role, Dorothy thought for a moment. Then: "This is really going to be a difficult one. Open space and everyone coming and going. But, you know, I've always found in our kind of murder that often the important thing is not what's present at the scene but what isn't there. Or sometimes your lead will come from someone whom you would expect to behave in a certain way but instead does something that's really out of character."

As Penny applied the finishing top coat, Dorothy smiled at her.

"I don't know if you're aware of this, Penny, but your eyes lit up when you mentioned that policeman of yours. I married mine, and it was absolutely the right thing to do. We're very happy, Alan and I."

"That's the second time today someone has hinted at that."

"Well, no pressure then!"

Penny helped Dorothy gather up her belongings and then showed her out.

"Let me know how you get on, Penny," she said. "Alan and I are heading home to Shderebury for Christmas, but if you're ever out our way, we'd love to see you. You and Gareth, too, of course."

Penny thanked her and waved as Dorothy went on her way. She spent a few moments organizing her office, thinking about her brooch, and for the hundredth time regretting the momentary carelessness of leaving her handbag unattended on the reception desk. She was now paying dearly for that.

Somehow she managed to get through the day with her missing brooch always lurking just beneath her thoughts, waiting to surface again the moment a crack in her concentration appeared. In the evening, grateful for an enthusiastic Eirlys who had taken great care in arranging the nail varnishes on their display shelves, they had finished the final preparations for the new manicure salon. The job done, Penny saw Eirlys safely home and then continued on to her own cottage.

As she pushed open the door, something jammed under it caught her attention. She bent over and picked up a plain beige envelope which she carried through to the kitchen. Setting her bag down on the countertop, she noticed the envelope was not addressed to anyone. She ripped it open and pulled out two sheets of paper, stapled together, with a yellow Post-it note stuck on the first page.

She read the message on the Post-it note.

Told him about brooch, he was upset <u>for you</u>, he'll be in touch.
Here's photocopy of the report on recent thefts.
Bethan

Penny smiled at the underlined *for you*. She hadn't thought for a moment that Gareth would be angry at her, but he must be disappointed.

She peeled off the Post-it note and sat on the sofa to read the report. Written in official police language, the gist of it was that various items had been reported missing from several Llanelen stores, including a charity shop and two or three private residences.

She looked at the list of missing items: a plate with a daffodil pattern; a biography of John Lennon; a small Royal Doulton figurine in the shape of a shepherdess in a blue dress; one candlestick, part of a pair; a small framed print of Lloyd George's cottage . . .

The list went on for about eight more items.

These are all things that people have lying about in their sitting rooms, Penny thought. Ordinary household things without much real value. My brooch doesn't fit this list.

She left the papers on a side table and went through to the kitchen. She looked in the fridge to see what she had, and after realizing there was not much there except an elderly tomato, some cheese with a bit of mold on the rind, and a few other sad items, she checked the freezer, hoping for a ready meal.

In luck, she found a chicken breast with a side of vegetables, so she put that in the microwave and set the timer.

While she waited for it to heat up, she returned to the sitting room and looked at the list again.

I'm sure the police have thought of this, she thought, but one item that might belong on this list is Mrs. Lloyd's letter opener.

She looked at her watch, and as it had just gone nine, she decided it would not be too late to ring.

A few moments later Florence picked up the telephone, answering in the old-fashioned way of giving the number.

"Florence, it's Penny, here. Yes, sorry to bother you so late, but I've just had a thought. Could you and Mrs. Lloyd put your heads together and try to figure out exactly when your letter opener went missing?"

After Florence reassured her they would have another go at trying to remember the last time they'd seen it, Penny rang off, and just as the bell on the microwave signaled her meal was cooked, the telephone rang.

It was Gareth, hoping she was all right and telling her not to worry about the snowflake brooch. We will get it back, he said confidently. Just a matter of time. In reply to her question about the Conwy Castle case, he told her he was going to issue an appeal to the public to see if anyone would come forward with information that could help confirm the identity of Harry Saunders or provide information on his movements on the day he died.

"What do you think he was doing at the castle?" Penny had asked.

"I think he had arranged to meet someone. To me, that's the only thing that makes sense."

They talked for a few more minutes, and then Penny raised the subject that was never far from her thoughts.

"I've been thinking about the skeleton of the woman's body that was found in our spa," she said. "Anything new there?"

And then she answered her own question.

"Of course not. If there had been, you would have told me."

Seventeen

*E*very year the Stretch and Sketch Club put on an event to raise funds. The money might be used to pay an honorarium to a special guest speaker, provide group entry fees to a local exhibit, or take out an advertisement in the local paper announcing an exhibit of their own work.

For this year's fund-raiser, the group had teamed up with the Llanelen Players, the local amateur dramatics society, to give a reading of Dylan Thomas's much-loved *A Child's Christmas in Wales*. The Stretch and Sketch Club had agreed to handle the logistics of the performance, including booking the community centre, ticket sales, and refreshments while the actors took care of the performance, and both groups would share the profits.

At seven fifteen the community centre doors opened and a small but steady queue offered five-pound notes to the ticket sellers, Penny Brannigan and Alwynne Gwilt, seated at a small table.

"Looks like a very good turnout despite the weather," Alwynne said to Reverend Thomas Evans as she accepted the ten-pound note he handed her. "Indeed," he said, "Bronwyn and I prefer staying home with Robbie on rainy nights, but we wouldn't have missed this for anything."

"So glad you could come." Penny smiled at them.

"Well, we're here to support you, Penny, you know that," Bronwyn said, giving her a warm, affectionate look. "And it's been some time since we've been out to see the Players, so it's high time we did."

"I think there are still some good seats over there on the left," Penny said, pointing down the hall. "Enjoy the performance."

By eight o'clock, when the performance was scheduled to begin, all but one or two seats had been filled and eager chatter and laughter filled the room. Chairs had been placed to one side for Stretch and Sketch volunteers, although Penny and Alwynne remained seated at the ticket table in case any latecomers arrived. The community centre did not have a formal stage with curtains, but a raised platform at one end served the purpose.

The crowd rustled as it settled, obscuring the opening sentences of the piece and then there was stillness as the actor's clear voice emerged:

"I can never remember whether it snowed for six days and six nights when I was twelve or whether it snowed for twelve days and twelve nights when I was six."

The audience members looked at one another and smiled at the beauty of the words and all the rest to come, so familiar and dear to them.

As the prose poem neared its end, Penny slipped out of her seat and crept into the kitchen where Stretch and Sketch Club newcomers, Glynnis Bowen and photographer Brian Kenley were setting out food and drink. There were bowls of walnuts and glasses of sherry, just as in the poem, and plates of mince pies and slices of rich, dark, brandy-soaked Christmas cake with marzipan icing, a traditional Welsh cake known as Bara Brith, and fancy cheeses and oat cakes and cream crackers.

"The refreshments look wonderful," Penny said to Glynnis, who had organized them. "The play's almost finished, so they'll be here any minute." Glynnis handed Brian a large stack of napkins and a tray. "Well, we're ready"—she smiled—"aren't we, Brian?"

"We are indeed."

"Huw not here with you tonight?" Penny asked.

"He said he had a few things to attend to and that he'd be along in time to close up," Glynnis said. "I'm expecting him any minute."

"Right, well, I'll leave you to it," said Penny, who then slid into her seat beside Alwynne just as the play came to its conclusion.

"Looking through my bedroom window, out into the moonlight and the unending smoke-colored snow, I could see the lights in the windows of all the other houses on our hill and hear the music rising from them up the long, steady falling night. I turned the gas down, I got into bed. I said some words to the close and holy darkness, and then I slept."

After a moment's silence the room filled with wild, enthusiastic applause as Mrs. Lloyd got to her feet to lead a standing ovation.

"Wasn't that wonderful!" she exclaimed to Florence. "Now you'll not be getting entertainment like that in Liverpool."

"Certainly not," agreed Florence, "nothing like it."

If Mrs. Lloyd was not shy about leading the ovation, she was also not shy about leading the audience to the space around the kitchen's serving hatch where the refreshment tables had been set up. The audience was encouraged to help themselves to refreshments while Brian Kenley circulated in a gentlemanly way, holding a half-full plate of mince pies in one hand and a half-full plate of Christmas cake in the other. He approached Penny, who was talking to Victoria. "I'm just going to set these down for a minute, Penny," he said, "and put everything on one plate. They'll look better that way."

"Well, let me help you," said Victoria with a smile, helping herself to a mince pie. Here's one less you'll have to shift."

As Victoria lifted the mince pie from the centre of the plate revealing a bright yellow daffodil, Penny let out a little gasp. Recovering quickly, she took a pie herself and signaled to Victoria that she needed a word.

Holding a small paper plate under her mince pie, Victoria allowed herself to be led off to one side of the hall.

"What is it?" she said as she took a bite. "You look as if you've seen a ghost."

"That plate, the one with the daffodil on it. Bethan showed me the list of things that have been stolen from around here recently, and that plate is on the list."

"Mprgh," said Victoria through a mouthful of mince pie, which she then swallowed. "Penny, you've got to be joking. Do you have any idea how many plates there must be around here with daffodils on them? Everybody's got one. I'll bet you anything"—she looked around the room for a familiar face—"I'll bet you Bronwyn over there's got one. Or Mrs. Lloyd, she'll have one for sure. So what are you saying?"

"Well, the plate belongs to someone in our Stretch and Sketch Club," said Penny, "because we organized the refreshments. So I'm going to stick around and see who that plate belongs to. See who it goes home with. Come on."

Victoria groaned.

"Do we have to? We've just opened the spa and I'm really tired. We've had a couple of long, tiring days and another big day coming up tomorrow. Those display windows aren't going to judge themselves, you know. Mrs. Lloyd loved her manicure, by the way. She was well chuffed to be the first client and was in heaven when she learned her manicure was free. Nice one, there."

Thinking back to the manicure she had given Dorothy Martin, Penny realized that Mrs. Lloyd hadn't technically been the first customer, but close enough.

"Well, if you won't wait with me, that's fine, you go. But I'm staying here until I find out who owns that plate."

"Oh, all right," said Victoria, stifling a yawn. "I guess I can find something to do while I wait."

"Wait? We're going to go in the kitchen to help with the washing up so we can keep an eye on that plate."

"I've just thought of something," said Victoria. "Did you actually touch the plate?"

"No," said Penny. "I didn't. Why?"

"Because when I was a girl if my mother was bringing squares or cakes to a church social, say, she always put a piece of tape on the bottom of the plate with her name on it. That way, she'd know which one was hers."

"Did she have trouble recognizing her own plate?" Penny asked as they walked back toward the refreshment area.

"No, but there was another woman who used to have trouble recognizing that the plates belonged to other people. With the tape on the bottom, my mum could say to her, 'Oh I'm so sorry, but I'm afraid you've mistaken my plate for yours. See here, there's a little piece of tape on the bottom with my name on it.' So easy to mix up . . . one plate looks so much like another."

179

Penny laughed. "Oh, right. My plate has violets on it and yours has daffodils. I can barely tell them apart!"

Victoria smiled at her and shrugged. "Well, it's all about saving face, isn't it? And there's no accounting for plate envy."

As the crowd began to thin out, thanking their hosts for a lovely evening before heading out the door, Penny and Victoria entered the kitchen. Huw Bowen, who had arrived soon after the performance ended, was sipping a glass of sherry while he talked to Brian Kenley. Glynnis Bowen, up to her elbows in the washing-up bowl, had her back to them. She turned around and said to Kenley, with the slightest hint of sharpness, "Have you brought in all the dishes that need washing up, Brian?"

"I'll go," volunteered Penny. "No problem, Brian, you're all right." With a slight nod at Victoria to keep an eye on things in the kitchen, Penny returned to the refreshment area. A few audience members, apparently working on their second sherry, lingered to talk to neighbours they hadn't seen for a few days or to make arrangements to get together soon with a friend for cake and coffee. Mrs. Lloyd and Florence, Penny noticed, seemed to have left.

Several half-empty trays and plates remained on the serving table, so she piled the food on three plates and set three empty ones aside. As she handled the daffodil plate, she ran her hand underneath it and felt a sticky little tab. Turning the plate over and pretending to look at the manufacturer's label, she noticed what looked like a small strip of white adhesive medical tape, and just as Victoria had suggested, there seemed to be some writing on it. She held it up to the light, closer to her eyes, and tried to read it. The letters were blurred, probably from having been washed a few times, but she managed to decipher something that looked like Rhys Hughes. Who's she when she's at home, Penny wondered. Or he. I suppose a man can own a plate.

She put the three plates together, carried them into the kitchen, and set them down beside Glynnis Bowen.

"Thank you, Penny," said Glynnis, as she slid the plates into the sudsy wash water.

Penny gave Victoria a meaningful glance and a slight nod.

"Well done," she said softly. "You were right. There was a name on the bottom, but I didn't recognize it. Now we just have to wait and see who collects the plate."

"And how long's that going take?" Victoria whispered back. "And what are we supposed to do in the meantime? Just stand here?"

"You're right," said Penny. "I'll speed things up."

She joined Glynnis at the sink and, after picking up a dish towel that was sitting beside the draining rack, selected a plate from the rack, dried it, and then carried it over to the table and set it down carefully. She repeated this with two more plates.

When the daffodil plate arrived in the rack, Penny picked it up and gave it a brief swipe with the drying cloth and then turned toward the table. With a quick glance at Victoria, she let the plate slip from the towel. It crashed to the floor, shattering into several pieces. At the instantly recognizable sound of kitchen breakage, all conversation stopped and everyone turned in surprise toward the source of the sound. As Victoria knelt down and began picking up the broken shards, Penny turned to the others in the kitchen.

"Oh, how clumsy of me!" she exclaimed. "I'm so sorry. Of course I'll replace it. Do we know who owns it?"

"It's mine, but don't worry about it. These things happen."

But Brian Kenley's words did not match his facial expression. He looked almost as shattered as his plate.

Eighteen

The little group stood for a moment in the kitchen and then, as the sound of rain began to rattle the windowpanes, resumed their work. Alwynne arrived in the kitchen carrying plates of leftover food and empty glasses on a tray. She set everything down on the counter near Glynnis.

"Everyone's left," she said. "And this is the last of the food. Not sure what to do with the rest of these mince pies," she said. "Don't know who brought them. Would someone like to wrap them up and take them home?"

"Why don't you have them?" Glynnis said. "There's a box of plastic wrap just over there."

"Well, if no one else wants them, I'd be glad to have them," Alwynne said, looking around the room. "Or my husband will be glad to have them, I should say. Have to wrap them up well to get them home in this rain, though."

The group worked quickly to finish the cleanup to Huw Bowen's satisfaction and then trooped out, with him bringing up the rear so he could lock up behind them.

A cold, sharp rain assaulted them as they emerged into the dark street. Brief good nights were said as everyone went their separate ways, the Bowens hurrying off toward the car park; Alwynne gratefully accepting a lift from Brian Kenley; and Penny and Victoria, seen as two bobbing umbrellas, setting off at a fast pace to walk to Victoria's flat in the spa by the river.

The rain bounced off the pavement, finding its way into the small stream that gurgled along the side of the road toward the drains.

"Don't say anything until we get to yours," Penny said. "I have to concentrate on keeping my feet dry and I can only think about one thing at a time."

Victoria did not reply and the two walked steadily but quickly past silent shops through the dark, deserted streets. The rain, large, heavy drops against the orange glow of the streetlamps, did not let up, and occasionally they had to lower their umbrellas in front of them to protect their faces from the steady, driving downpour. Every few minutes a car splashed by, causing them to leap into a doorway or huddle against the side of a building to avoid being sprayed. After about ten minutes of hard, steady slogging, hunched against the rain, they reached the River Walk and turned toward the spa.

Crouched in darkness on the bank of the rapidly rising River Conwy, the spa loomed out of the darkness to greet the two women as they pressed on for the last moments of their sodden walk. Victoria led the way up the path and then to a side door that bypassed the front reception area and opened near the kitchen and back storeroom. She fumbled about in her bag, put the key in the lock, pushed the door open, and switched on the light. Shaking the rain off their umbrellas before entering, the two stepped out of the night and into the welcoming warmth just as the rain began to transition into icy pellets of sleet.

"Let's just leave all our wet things down here," Victoria said. "We can hang them overnight in the reception area and keep all the wet in one place. We'd better take our shoes off, as well."

"Right," said Penny. "Here, give me your coat and I'll hang it up. The umbrellas, too." She padded down the corridor, hung up the coats, left the umbrellas open to dry on the doormat, ducked into the supply room, and then returned to Victoria, who was unlacing her shoes. "Let's get upstairs and get dry," she said to Victoria, handing her a fluffy white towel she had picked up in the supply room. "My feet are soaked. Hope you've got a spare pair of socks you can lend me."

A few moments later, their hair towel dried and feet in warm, dry socks, they settled into the new flat Victoria had created on the top floor of the spa building. During the day it was filled with light and gave wonderful views over the River Conwy to the green hills beyond.

"Right, let's see where we're at," said Penny. "Let's go over what we know so far."

"Which isn't very much," said Victoria, handing Penny a glass of white wine and setting down a small plate with cheese and oat crackers on it. "I must say, I was really surprised when you deliberately broke that plate. That was the last thing I expected you to do."

"Yeah, I felt bad about it," replied Penny. "But I'm pretty sure it was on the stolen list and I wanted to see who owned it." She shrugged and held up her hands in an open gesture.

"Well, it's done now," said Victoria. "Do you want anything more to eat?"

Penny shook her head. "No, thanks, I'm fine."

She looked around her.

"I haven't been up here in your flat for a while. You've done a great job. Very smart and comfortable."

"Glad you like it. But I can see now that I'm going to keep you away from my crockery. I was so shocked when you broke that plate. And poor Brian Kenley. Did you see the look on his face? I think he was really upset that his plate got broken." She took a sip of wine and then cut a sliver of Brie and balanced it on a biscuit.

"What do we really know about him? He's new to the area. Did I hear someone say he's from Yorkshire?"

"He is," Penny said, "but you wouldn't really know it from his accent. He joined the Stretch and Sketch Club, oh, I don't know, about six months ago, I guess. I asked him once why he joined our group and not the photography club, since he's a photographer, after all, and he told me he had joined both, but he likes our group for the rambles and outings we go on."

Victoria nodded. "Keep talking. Maybe it will help if you just throw out everything you know about him. Something might come to mind."

"Well, he seems a very quiet, decent kind of man. I can't really picture him as a thief, or a murderer, come to that, although he was there when Harry Saunders was killed. That reminds me, I wonder if he's shown his photos to Gareth yet."

She gave a little start.

"That's what I'm going to do! I was trying to think of a reason to pay him a visit so I could look around his place . . ."

"Snoop around, you mean," said Victoria.

"Well, call it what you like, but have a good shufty. Bethan gave me a list of some of the stolen things and I'd really like to see if any of them are in his place."

"If he's been nicking things from the local shops, he's hardly likely to leave them out in full view, is he?"

"You wouldn't think so, but people do strange things. He'll probably figure no one will know. And really, why should they? He lives alone and maybe he doesn't have too many visitors."

"Anyway," said Victoria, "if you're looking for an excuse to call on him, you created the perfect one for yourself tonight."

Penny raised an eyebrow.

"Penny, you broke his plate! You have to replace it with something at least as good." Victoria set down her wineglass, walked over to the window, and pulled back the curtain.

"It's got very nasty out there," she said, peering out the window into the dark night and leaning a little to her right so her cheek almost touched the glass. "I can't even see the bridge." She dropped the curtain and turned to Penny. "Is there any particular reason why you need to go home tonight? I think you should stop here in my spare room. I've got one of those five-pack of toothbrushes so you can have one. I can lend you a nightdress."

"You're right as usual," agreed Penny. "I couldn't bear to put on those awful wet shoes. It wasn't until I moved to Wales that I developed the wet feet theory."

"And what's that, exactly?" asked Victoria, placing the now-empty cheese plate on a tray.

"It's like this. You can walk around in wet shoes and socks if you have to, but once you take them off, you can't put them on again whilst they're still wet. They're too cold and uncomfortable. You have to put on clean, dry shoes and socks. So I couldn't possibly put those wet things on again and walk home in them.

So either you have to lend me dry socks and boots or I have to stop here." She spread her arms against the back of the sofa and gave Victoria an amused look.

"So I'm stopping right where I am."

"Well, that's settled, then," said Victoria. "Means you can get to work on time tomorrow."

"Ah, yes, I was going to mention that to you. I'm going to be just a little bit late. I have to go and see a woman in the charity shop about a plate."

Victoria groaned. "Oh, here we go."

"Well, I won't be that long," Penny protested. "I'll be quick about it."

"And there's something else you should do tomorrow," said Victoria.

"And what's that?" said Penny, getting up off the sofa as Victoria switched off the lamp.

"You need to call Gwennie and see if she can come to yours and do the Christmas dinner. You know how hopeless you are in the kitchen, and I'm not doing it. You're the one who started inviting people. How many have you invited, anyway?"

"Let me see. There's Bethan, and you, and Gareth, of course. And they're going to bring Jimmy with them from Llandudno . . ." Their voices trailed off as they drifted down the hallway to their beds.

The rain, driven by heavy wind, continued to lash furiously against the building, turning its dark grey stone black and glistening. But its deep walls had stood strong and sheltering for almost two hundred years, and after this night's storm had passed, and all the storms to come, the building would go on for another two hundred years.

In the morning, Penny drank a quick cup of coffee with Victoria and then left for the charity shop that had reported the stolen items.

Last night's storm had blown itself out and the frosty morning air felt crisp and fresh on her face. Her breath condensed into tiny clouds ahead of her, and she was just starting to feel the benefit of starting the day with a brisk walk when she arrived at her destination.

"Good morning," she said to the woman behind the charity shop counter. "I'm wondering if you can help me. Do you happen to know if someone called Rhys Hughes, I think it was, donated a plate with a daffodil pattern?"

The woman behind the counter called to her colleague in the back to join her.

"Now that's a very odd question," the first woman said. "Why do you ask?"

"It's just that I came across a plate with that name on the bottom, and I wondered if it had come from your shop, that's all."

The two women exchanged glances.

"Well, it wasn't Rhys, but Rose Hughes. She might have had her Welsh name, Rhosyn, on the plate that you saw, so it could have looked like Rhys. She died recently and her family brought in a few boxes of her things."

The second woman joined the conversation. "Where exactly did you see the plate? Do you know who owns it?"

Penny smiled at them.

"Unfortunately, the plate got broken. Well, truth be told, I broke it. I'm trying to figure out where it came from so I can

189

replace it. Do you have anything else available that would be similar, I wonder?"

"Actually, you're in luck," said the second woman. "That plate had a companion from the ones in the Rhosyn Hughes donation. Not quite the same, mind you, but close enough. It's on this shelf over here. Let me get it for you."

"About the owner," said the first woman, somewhat anxiously, "if you find out who owned the plate, would you mind letting us know? It could be important."

"Yes, I will," said Penny, taking out her wallet to pay for the plate that the second woman was wrapping up. "Do you mind putting an extra bit of cushioning on that?" Penny asked her. "I can be a little clumsy at times and we wouldn't want anything to happen to this one." She gave each of the women a bright, conspiratorial smile. "Wasn't it lucky for me that you had a similar plate? Thank you very much."

The two women waited until she had left the shop, and then the first one asked, "Do you think we should call the police? She knows more about that plate than she's letting on."

"Not sure what we'd say to the police, exactly," the second one replied. "Let's think about it. I'll slip out and get a couple of Bakewell slices. You put the kettle on and we'll discuss what to do over a cup of coffee."

"See, I told you I wouldn't be long," Penny said, popping her head round the door of Victoria's office. She held up the well-wrapped plate. "Got a replacement."

"Good." Victoria looked up from her computer. "I need you to go through those invoices, and Eirlys wants a word in the manicure salon. Oh, and I've had an interesting résumé come in for the hairdresser's position. A man, so we need to discuss that. I'm thinking we should get him in for an interview. Goes by one name only, like Madonna or Cher. Calls himself Alberto."

"Right, I've just got some phone calls to make, but I'll check in with Eirlys and then get on with things."

Victoria took a closer look at her friend. "You look excited. What's up? You're on to something. Tell me."

"I'm going to ring Brian Kenley and see if I can pop in and see him this morning." She shrugged. "I don't know if he's got anything to do with the theft of my brooch, but you can understand how much I want it back."

Victoria nodded. "I do understand, but don't forget Gareth and Bethan will have made it their top priority, so why not just leave it to them? They'll find it. Gareth told you they would and they will."

"Well, let's just say I'm helping them with their inquiries, in a good way. Anyway, I'll get Brian's number from the Stretch and Sketch membership list and see what happens."

She ducked out into the hall and returned in a few minutes, holding a modest but charming spray of pale pink roses that she had picked up at the florist on the way over and set down outside Victoria's office.

"These are for you for putting me up last night."

"Just plain putting up with you, more like." Victoria laughed. "Right, I'll hold the fort. Off you go."

Penny left for the second time and then reentered, and this time she sat down in the visitor's chair that faced Victoria's desk.

"It's just a theory, and it might be half-baked, but I think Mrs. Lloyd's letter opener was stolen, and whoever stole it used it to kill Saunders. I don't think Florence or Mrs. Lloyd would have had the strength to do it—Saunders might have put up a struggle up there on the parapet—so it had to have been some-one else."

"But Brian Kenley? Surely not. I can't picture it." Victoria's eyes widened. "Are you mad? If you think he killed Saunders, why would you be going over there by yourself to confront him, deliberately putting yourself in harm's way?"

"Because I can't picture it myself, either, but I think some-how he's linked to both the thefts and the murder, through the plate." She thought for a moment. "It may be that he just doesn't know it. I'd really like to talk to him. And, of course, look at the photos he took that day at the castle."

"The police have probably seen those photos."

"Right, but they don't know the people in the photographs. I do. I might spot something that they missed because it didn't mean anything to them. Something that might be significant, but they just didn't see it." She thought back to what Dorothy Martin had said to her during her manicure. "Something or someone who should have been there who wasn't, or just some-thing out of place . . . not quite right."

"Well, be careful, and good luck," Victoria said. "You can tell me later how you got on." She held up the local newspaper. "Oh, and we've got to get on with that window judging. There's a piece in here about us doing it. Great publicity for the spa."

Nineteen

*J*ust after eleven Penny walked slowly up the path that led to the front door of Brian Kenley's pebbledash bungalow a few streets from the town centre. The small garden, filled with dead black roses, had been damaged by the wind and rain of the previous night, and several hydrangea bushes were lying crushed and broken on the dark, damp earth.

Just as she was about to knock, the door opened and Brian Kenley invited her in.

Tall and thin, with an almost gaunt look about him, Kenley gave her a thin, superficial smile. He cleared his throat and gave a wheezy chuckle.

"Hello, Penny. Do come in."

He tapped his chest. "Sorry, I have a touch of bronchitis and this damp weather isn't helping."

He led Penny down a short, narrow passageway that opened

into a small sitting room and gestured toward a chair that faced the front door. As she sat down, holding her package on her lap, Penny noticed a small suitcase leaning against the wall.

"Going somewhere nice, Brian?" she asked.

"Yes, I'm leaving on Monday for Yorkshire. Spending the holidays there with family. My brother and his wife and their sons, actually. They're the only family I have left."

"Oh, that will be nice." Penny smiled. "I hope the weather will be good for the journey. Driving, are you?"

Kenley nodded as Penny shifted forward in her seat.

"I wanted to see you, Brian," she began, "to apologize for the breakage last night. Your daffodil plate. But fortunately I was able to get a pretty good replacement at the St. David's Charity Shop." She held the package out to him. "Is that where you got yours?"

Kenley reached out to accept the package. "This was very kind of you, Penny, and much appreciated, but you didn't need to go to all that bother. The plate wasn't worth much, I don't think, and anyway, I hadn't had it very long. Still, very good of you. Thank you."

Penny groaned inwardly. He hadn't answered her question and she couldn't think how to ask it again.

"The ladies at the charity shop told me that the plates had once belonged to Rhosyn Hughes," Penny said desperately. "Did you know her?"

"No, I never heard of her."

A heavy, awkward silence descended. Penny smiled at Kenley, then took in her surroundings. The room was neat and well kept. The surfaces were free of clutter and appeared to have been recently dusted. A built-in set of shelves stood floor to ceiling near an arched opening that led to the kitchen. Realizing that

Kenley wasn't going to offer her a cup of coffee and sensing that he wanted her to leave, Penny tried one last time.

"We're really glad you decided to join our Stretch and Sketch Club, Brian. Your photographs are wonderful. We'll be organizing an exhibit in the spring and I do hope you'll consider showing some of your photos." At this, Kenley's face lit up.

"I was wondering, Brian, if you'd consider letting me have copies of the photos you took that day at Conwy Castle? With all the commotion, I didn't even get my quick sketches finished. I don't have the perspective or the details nearly right. And we'd love to have a couple for our Stretch and Sketch newsletter."

Kenley hesitated. "I didn't know there was a Stretch and Sketch newsletter. I've never seen one. Still, I guess that would be all right. Perhaps I could e-mail them to you?"

Penny pulled a computer memory stick out of her pocket.

"Do you think you could put them on here? That would be easier. Sometimes the files get too big and the e-mails don't arrive."

"Oh, right. My computer's in the spare bedroom. Won't be a minute." As Kenley disappeared down the hall toward the back of the bungalow, Penny jumped up and reached the bookshelves in two long strides. She ran her fingers over the titles on the spines but saw only popular fiction paperbacks and several expensive-looking nature and photography books. Displayed amongst the books were several thriving plants in copper pots and photos of smiling boys with their happy parents. Hearing Kenley's footsteps in the hall, she pulled out a book on Bodnant Garden and was leafing through it when he reappeared, holding out her memory stick.

"Here you go. They're all here."

"Oh, thanks very much, Brian. These will be really helpful."

Now that the two of them were standing, the timing seemed natural for her to leave.

"Well, again, I'm sorry about the plate, but I hope you'll enjoy the new one."

"Yes, I'm sure I will," Kenley said politely, looking somewhere over her shoulder. "It was very kind of you to bring it, although, really, you needn't have bothered." He gave another wheezy chuckle. "I was a bit shocked when it got broken, but honestly, it's fine."

He showed her out and she returned to the spa where Victoria was waiting for her. They reviewed the most recent applicant for the hairdresser's position, and Penny agreed that Alberto was definitely someone they should interview. With Christmas coming up so quickly, though, it might not be possible to get the position filled. The name seemed vaguely familiar, but she couldn't place him. She smiled at his confidence in calling himself by just one name: Alberto.

The day passed quickly, filled with small things that needed crossing off the to-do list and other things that popped up and needed her attention right away. As she responded to yet another e-mail, she wondered how business ever got done without it. She had just about cleared her electronic in-basket when a direct message popped up. Seeing who it was from, she read it immediately.

Have dinner with me tomorrow night? it read.

She thought for a moment, then typed. *Early? 5 P.M. Conwy?*

Where? came the reply.

Meet you police station?

Right!

A few minutes later another message arrived from Gareth. *Doing TV appeal tonight Harry Saunders.*

It was getting on for four, so Penny checked on Eirlys in the salon and, after reassuring herself that everything was fine, gave Eirlys a grateful pat on the shoulder and went off in search of Victoria.

She found her in the photocopy room, bending over, feeding paper into the machine. "I'm not sure where all the paper goes, but we're going through reams of the stuff," she muttered as Penny walked in. "What did we do before we had our own photocopier?" she asked as she stood up, and then answered her own question. "Got by just fine, thank you very much."

Penny looked at her with a raised eyebrow. "Just coming to tell you that I'm ready to go now. I'm tired. Oh, and I'm having dinner with Gareth tomorrow night. Seems ages since I've seen him."

"Right," said Victoria. "And thanks again for the flowers. They're lovely. I'll take them upstairs." As the photocopier resumed its printing job, she tossed a couple of wrinkled bits of paper into the recycling box. "Did you get in touch with Gwennie? Have you asked her to do the cooking for Christmas yet?"

"Yikes, thanks for the reminder. I'll call her now."

A few moments later she put down the phone in her office. Gwennie had cheerfully agreed to do all the cooking for Penny's Christmas lunch and, indeed, had said she welcomed the opportunity to get away from her bossy, controlling sister's home for a few hours. Gwennie had said she would bring Penny a shopping list of everything she must get in for the meal, and she, Gwennie, would take care of the rest. Oh, and there was just one other thing. Would Penny mind if she brought Trixxi? Penny had assured her Trixxi, an adorable black Lab, would be most welcome.

Gwennie had worked for many years as housekeeper to the

Gruffydd family, owners of the charming Ty Brith Hall, situated high above Llanelen with spectacular views over the valley to the hills beyond. But with the murder earlier in the year of Emyr Gruffydd's posh bride, and the death soon after of his father, Emyr was now spending much of his time at the family's estate in Cornwall. Ty Brith Hall, the family home in North Wales, remained silent and shuttered. Gwennie, who adored Trixxi, was happy to look after her, especially as this meant living in at the Hall as her house-proud sister would not allow an animal in her tidy home in Llanelen.

Satisfied that most of her Christmas arrangements were taken care of, Penny set off for the short walk home. On the way, her thoughts turned to her visit to Brian Kenley's home. Was it odd that he was leaving for Yorkshire? Not really. A man living alone would naturally seek out his family at Christmas, and the pictures on the bookshelves, probably taken by Brian himself, indicated a strong family bond. But something about the way he had responded to her giving him the replacement plate began to bother her. Something was not quite right; his behavior had been odd. Something was missing, but she couldn't put her finger on what exactly it was. Except, maybe, he had seemed uninterested. Detached. And yet he'd seemed quite upset when the daffodil plate had got broken.

Deep in thought, she approached the darkened charity shop and paused for a moment to study the window display. It was filled with the best the shop had on offer, but everything in it, from a small milk jug to a souvenir bell marking the wedding of Prince Charles and Lady Diana Spencer, was a castoff, no longer wanted or needed. She liked the idea that people could donate unwanted articles to help fund a good cause and that everything in the window had been kept out of the landfill. As she turned to go, a small artificial Christmas tree, tilted a little to one side, caught her attention. Its little red and green lights winked cheerfully on and off, illuminating its small ornaments. Her eyes moved upward, expecting to see an angel at the top. But, instead, she saw what looked like a six-point snowflake and as her heart began to beat faster, she realized with a flush of joy that she was looking at her snowflake brooch. She tried the door, but it was locked, and the sign listing the shop's opening and closing hours indicated it closed at four on Saturdays. She banged on the door, hoping one of the women who ran the shop might still be on the premises, but when no one came to see who was knocking, she accepted that the shop was empty.

She fumbled about in her bag for her mobile and was disappointed to get Detective Inspector Gareth Davies' voice mail.

"I think I've just spotted my brooch," she said. "Call me."

A few minutes later she let herself into her cottage and once again, finding nothing in the refrigerator that looked as if it might make a decent dinner, pulled a ready-made meal out of the freezer, telling herself as it heated in the microwave that she really needed to do a better job of getting in proper food.

After looking over a few documents Victoria had asked her to check, she switched on the television and waited for the news. At the sight of a familiar face on the first news clip leading off the broadcast, she set down her mug and leaned forward.

Wearing a dark overcoat and standing outside the floodlit walls of Conwy Castle, Detective Inspector Gareth Davies conveyed sincerity and concern as he spoke directly into the camera.

"The case of Harry Saunders remains a complex, unexplained death inquiry," he began. "We are appealing to anyone who may have seen or had contact with Mr. Saunders, in the period between about the first of December until his death, to come forward and speak with us. We believe he was an American and we'd like to know if he has family in the area or what business dealings might have brought him here. We are asking for swift public help in reconstructing events leading to his death."

Penny was impressed by his apparent ease in front of the camera and then remembered he had mentioned that all senior officers had been sent on a media training course. It's paying off, she thought. He's confident someone's going to come forward, and I won't be the least bit surprised when someone does.

A few moments after he went off the air he rang her.

The police will try to contact the store manager in the morning, he said, and told her to keep the evaluation handy.

Twenty

*O*f all the police stations in North Wales, the grey, two-storey pebbledash Victorian building in Conwy was Detective Chief Inspector Gareth Davies' favourite. He liked its location overlooking Lancaster Square, the way it seemed to keep a benevolent watch on the town, and he especially liked its bright red door. If you ignored for a moment the signage on the front of the building advising visitors to ring for assistance, or if you somehow failed to notice the police cars parked alongside, you might think it the home of a prosperous businessman or solicitor.

On Sunday afternoon Penny sat on a bench to one side of the police station and made a few simple sketches that she would work with later. From years spent drawing she intuitively understood the importance of getting the proportion and perspective absolutely right. The deepening shadows added depth and interest to her drawing, and when she was satisfied that she had captured the feel of the building, she tucked her papers and pencils into her carrier bag and rang the bell of the police station. A few moments later the door opened.

"Penny? Hi, please come in. I'm Chris Jones, the local beat manager."

Penny smiled at him. "Didn't you used to be known as the local bobby? Is it just me or . . ."

Jones gave her a little sheepish grin. "I think a lot of people round here agree with you. But come through."

While the outside of the building suggested gentility, its interior was completely given over to police business. Penny entered a reception area whose walls were covered in posters of missing persons. High-visibility vests hung on a row of hooks and a teetering pile of bright orange traffic cones leaned into the corner. Jones led her down a long hall painted a pale, institutional yellow and past a darkened room filled with high-tech electronic equipment, including sophisticated computers and scanners. A couple of officers looked up as Penny passed and then turned their attention back to their keyboards.

Davies was waiting for her at the end of the hall, holding his coat over his arm. He nodded his thanks at Jones, who gave Penny a friendly wave and then disappeared through a door marked COMMUNICATIONS.

"Hello," Davies said.

"Hello, yourself," Penny replied. They smiled at each other as Davies put his coat on and then reached behind him to switch off the light.

"I am so sorry about the brooch," Penny began, but Davies held up both hands.

"It wasn't your fault," Davies said. "We knew there'd been no attempt to sell it and now we know where it is. We tried to contact the store manager today but weren't able to reach her. We'll be there first thing tomorrow morning."

He put his arm around her. "We'll get the paperwork sorted, and you'll have it back in a day or two. You'll just have to sign something saying you agree to produce it if it's needed as an exhibit in a court case." Seeing her skeptical look, he repeated, "You will have it back in a day or two. I can make that happen." They walked down the hall together, their footsteps making soft padding noises on the tiled floor.

"Good-bye, sir," called a voice. Davies raised his hand and a few moments later they entered the reception area. He opened the door, and Penny brushed past him into the cold evening air. Together, they walked silently down the stairs into the square.

They'd agreed to have dinner in a cheerful bistro that Davies liked for its good food and easy walk from the police station. Noted for its uncomplicated meals, made from fresh, local ingredients, the small restaurant was at the height of dinner service when Penny and Davies arrived. They hung up their coats and then wedged their way through the dining room to a table for two at the back of the room. After they squeezed into their chairs and accepted menus from the server, Davies raised an eyebrow and Penny smiled at him.

"Soup!" they both said at the same time.

The server returned and they ordered. They talked about their Christmas plans, how the spa was doing, and other small matters until their starter arrived. As they tucked into steaming bowls of a delicate mushroom soup, their talk lightly turned to murder.

"I couldn't really get it out of him," Penny said. "I know Brian Kenley took photos at Conwy Castle the day Saunders died, but I wasn't sure if he had passed them on to you. I've been meaning to mention that."

"No, he didn't," Davies said. "I wonder why not." He thought for a moment and then consulted his watch. "Sorry, I hope I'm not too late to catch her. I'll call Bethan and send her round for a word with him." He spoke quickly to his sergeant, then, in response to a question from her, inclined his head toward Penny and asked if she remembered Kenley's address. She told him and he repeated it back to Bethan.

"Right," he said, ending the call. "Let's hope she comes up with something." Penny held her spoon carefully and pushed it away from her through the soup. "This is delicious."

Davies pulled a bread roll apart. "We heard from a woman in response to the appeal last night," he said. "Lives in Chester. Apparently she and Saunders had been courting, as she put it. She was wondering why she hadn't heard from him lately." He added a dab of butter to the bit of bread roll in his hand. "She was pretty upset."

"Harry'd been putting himself about, then," said Penny. "Why am I not surprised?"

"It always amazes me when intelligent women fall for a guy like that," Davies agreed. "And they usually pay a very steep price. A smart, independent woman meets a man on holiday, a waiter, in Tangiers or Morocco or some such place. She's at least twenty years older than he is, and you'd think she'd hear those alarm bells ringing, but—" From his pocket came the sound of a a buzzing cell phone. He glanced at it, then pointed at it and said, "Bethan. Sorry, better take it. She knows I'm with you and she'd only be ringing if it's important."

He pressed the green button.

"Yes, Bethan."

He listened for a moment, his gaze slowly leaving Penny's face until he was looking at the sugar bowl. Although he displayed no emotion, Penny's stomach began to churn and she felt her appetite disappearing.

"Right. On our way." He ended the call.

"What's happened?"

"It's Brian Kenley. He's dead."

Davies pulled a few bills out of his wallet and set them down on the table. "Sorry, love, looks like our dinner's over." He signaled to the waiter, who hurried over. "Sorry, but we have to leave. I've left enough here to cover it, I think," he said.

The waiter looked flustered for a moment and then, looking from one to the other, asked, "Would you like us to wrap it up for you? It's ready and I was just about to bring it to you."

As Davies hesitated, Penny replied, "Yes, but hurry." The waiter turned immediately and headed toward the kitchen while Davies called the station. He spoke to the duty sergeant and then led Penny to the front of the restaurant. As they scrambled into their coats, the waiter held out a paper takeaway bag to her.

She smiled her thanks, and she and Davies opened the door to find a police car waiting for them. Davies helped her into the backseat and then went round and eased himself into the front passenger seat.

"Llanelen, is it, sir?" Davies nodded and gave him Kenley's address. "But first we'll be dropping this lady off at her home. It's on the way."

"Like hell!" came a determined voice from the backseat.

They arrived to find a small knot of curious neighbours clustered outside Kenley's house, attracted by the flashing lights of

Bethan's police car. With a stern warning to Penny to stay where she was, and telling their driver to see to the gathering crowd, Davies got out of the car and walked up the path to the front door where Bethan was waiting for him.

"Forensics are on their way and the pathologist, too," she said.

"How did you get in?" Davies asked.

"I knocked, but there was no answer, so I went round the back and looked in the kitchen window. Saw him lying on the floor, so I tried the back door and it was unlocked. Went in and there he was. Looks as if he's been hit on the head. There's some trauma there but not a lot of blood."

Davies nodded slowly and tucked his hands in his pocket. "Right, well, let's not touch anything until the scene-of-crime boys get here." And then remembering that he had to be mindful of gender and wasn't allowed to refer to team members as boys or men, he corrected himself. "The scene-of-crime team."

He looked around the kitchen and then peered down the hall.

"Nothing seems disturbed in here." He inclined his head toward the back of the bungalow. "Have you had a chance to look down there?"

Bethan nodded.

"I think that's where our motive is."

A few minutes later Davies returned to the police car and opened the back door. Penny shifted her bag of sketching materials and put the bag of takeway food on her lap to make room for him as he slid onto the seat.

"What happened to Brian?" Penny asked.

"We don't know yet. But somebody was after something."

He reached into his pocket for his notebook. "His computer's been smashed to smithereens." He nodded at her. "Yeah.

People have figured out that just deleting something doesn't get rid of it. Anything that's ever been on a hard drive can easily be recovered."

Penny thought for a moment and then patted Davies on the arm. "Right," she said decisively, swinging her legs to one side. "I'm off. You'll be here for ages, so I'm going to go now."

"Well, the sergeant here can drive you home," Davies said.

"I'm not going home," said Penny. "I'm going to Victoria's." She gestured toward the bag of takeaway dinner containers. "If she hasn't eaten, we'll just heat this up. You don't mind, do you? By the time you get around to it, it'll be well past it. And I don't need a ride, thanks. It's not far and I want to walk."

Davies got out of the car and reached back to take a couple of bags from Penny.

He looked longingly at the bag of takeaway. "I was so looking forward to that," he said, "but you're right, it looks as if we're going to be here for a good while. I don't know how long we'll be."

"Well, let me know what you find out." She looked past him to where Bethan stood on the front steps making a waving, summoning gesture.

"DCI Davies, I think you're needed."

He bent over and gave her a brief kiss and pulled her closer to him for a moment. Then, releasing her, he returned to the bungalow. Penny pulled on her gloves and, as she did so, felt the memory stick Kenley had given her yesterday in her pocket. She wrapped her fingers around it and was about to call out to Davies but changed her mind. He wouldn't be able to deal with this right now. She stood for a moment watching as Davies re-entered the house and then, gathering up her bags, headed off in the direction of the bridge.

Skeletal trees with boney, bare branches stood starkly silhouetted against the night sky, as the River Conwy flowed darkly by. She heard it splashing beneath the bridge as she hurried across. A few moments later she was on Victoria's doorstep, ringing the bell to be let in and shifting from one foot to the other as she waited for the sound of approaching footsteps as her friend came to let her in.

Twenty-one

A few moments later the door opened, casting a pool of pale light onto the front step. Penny handed Victoria the bags of takeaway food and stepped inside. "I've just left Brian Kenley's place," she said. "He's dead and it looks suspicious. His computer's been all smashed up. We were just starting our meal when Gareth got called out, and we didn't have time to eat, so I thought I'd bring the dinner over here."

"What?" exclaimed Victoria. "Slow down. This is terrible. Brian Kenley's dead? But you just saw him, when, yesterday, wasn't it?"

She hung up Penny's coat. "You haven't eaten yet, have you?" Penny asked. Victoria shook her head. "Right, well, let's heat that lot up, and while that's happening, we can check out these photos."

She reached round Victoria and into her coat pocket, producing the memory stick containing the photos that Brian Kenley had taken at Conwy Castle on the afternoon of the art group's outing.

"He loaded some photos on here yesterday, and I know you'll find this hard to believe, but I haven't looked at them yet. It didn't seem urgent before, but now it does."

"Let's get upstairs to the flat," Victoria said

They reached the top of the stairs and entered Victoria's sitting room. Victoria disappeared into the kitchen and returned a few minutes later.

"That food looks delicious, Penny. I'm glad you brought it. I'll bet Gareth was disappointed, though."

"Disappointed and hungry, that's for sure. Anyway, let's get these photos on your laptop and see what we've got." Victoria pointed to her computer on the coffee table, and Penny switched it on and inserted the memory stick while Victoria cleared a few books and papers off her dining table. She laid out two placemats, set a couple of dinner plates on them, added some cutlery and napkins, and then joined Penny on the sofa. She leaned in to her slightly. Penny turned the computer screen toward her so they could both see. They stared at a series of carefully framed images.

"This is so sad," said Victoria, "I can hardly bear to look at them. It's hard to believe that the man who took these photographs has just died."

Penny nodded as she leaned forward to get a closer look.

"Who's that?" she said, pointing at a blurry figure disappearing through an entranceway to one of the staircases that led to the wall walk. "It could be anybody, and I can't really tell which stair set this is."

She sat back and gestured at the computer. "It probably doesn't matter, anyway. The stairs all lead upto the wall walk, and we know who was up there at the time. I can't see how these photos are going to help."

"When did Brian give them to you?" Victoria asked.

"Yesterday. Why?"

"Well, maybe somebody else thinks there's something in the photos that could help solve Harry Saunders's murder. After all, you said Kenley's computer was all smashed up."

"Hmm." Penny opened a new file and began copying all the images from the memory stick onto the computer's hard drive.

"Just to be on the safe side, we'll copy the pictures onto your computer, and then I'll make sure Gareth knows about them." She looked up. "That food's starting to smell really good. Do you think it's hot enough?"

Victoria stood up. "Should be. I'll see to it."

Penny followed her and stood in the doorway to the kitchen. "Why don't we go over our notes for the window display competition while we're eating and do the judging tomorrow so we can call in the results to the newspaper tomorrow evening? The shop owners will want that extra bit of publicity while there are still a few shopping days left."

"Good idea," said Victoria, handing her a pair of oven mitts. "You put the food on the table and I'll get the notes we've made so far."

Half an hour later, Penny set down her pen. "So we have our criteria?"

Victoria nodded. "Most creative, most beautiful, and best in show."

"Not everyone will be happy with our decisions," said Penny, "but I think we'll make the right choices."

Victoria picked up Penny's plate and put it on top of hers. "Tea?"

"Love some. And while you're doing that, I'll make a phone call."

Victoria returned from the kitchen with a tea tray that she set on the table. She gave Penny an inquiring look.

"Bethan'll be here any minute. To pick up the memory stick. The police have all kinds of high-tech enhancement capabilities, and they might be able to make something of them."

Victoria poured the tea. "Do you think she'll say anything to you about not giving the photos to them earlier?"

"I don't think so. I just got them myself yesterday, and I thought Brian had already given them to the police."

Victoria sipped her tea. "This case has really got me confused. So many bad things going on. Thefts, murders, I don't know what's important and what isn't," she said. "Or if things are meant to be connected to other things."

Penny nodded. "Me, too."

"Would it help if we go over what we know so far? I know you're determined to find out who stole your brooch."

"It's more than that," said Penny. "I think whoever stole my brooch killed Harry Saunders."

"Why on earth would you think that? I mean, you may be right, but it seems like an awfully big leap to me."

"Because Mrs. Lloyd's letter opener was the murder weapon. And we know there've been thefts from the charity shop. Things with not a lot of value being taken. I can't remember them all, but there was a John Lennon biography, I remember that, and a shepherdess figurine. That sort of thing. So Mrs. Lloyd's letter opener would fit right in with that lot. But my brooch is different. It's valuable."

"Unless whoever took it didn't know it was valuable. Just thought it was costume jewelry."

Penny leaned forward. "I suppose," she said slowly, "but it was in its case, so whoever took it knew it came from a proper jeweler, so must have known that it had some value." She ran her fingers through her hair, shaking her head slightly and giving out a little groan. "But what are the chances that a town this size would have two thieves at work?

"I've just had an idea. Have you got a calendar?"

"There's one on my laptop."

"No, not that kind. A paper kind. Even better, go get your appointment book. You know, that little black one you can't live without. There's something we need to check."

Victoria rose and picked up her handbag from the table near the door. She brought it over to the sofa, opened it, and handed Penny a thin black diary. "Here you go."

"Right," said Penny. "Let's see. Saunders was killed on the Tuesday . . ." She ran her finger backward over the dates. "This was the big snowstorm, and here"—her finger came to rest on the Sunday of the weekend before—"this was the day Mrs. Lloyd had her open house. So anyone who was there could have taken the letter opener."

She looked triumphantly at Victoria.

"And a day or two after the open house Florence notices the letter opener is missing. So, I think the letter opener was stolen by someone who attended that open house." She handed the diary back to Victoria. "What do you think?"

"Maybe," Victoria replied slowly. "Unless of course it's Florence. Do you think . . ."

"Funny you should say that. I asked her a little while ago to try to remember the last time they saw the letter opener, and she never got back to me. You don't suppose . . ."

As they looked at each other, the sound of the doorbell ringing downstairs startled them.

"Oh, that'll be Bethan, come for the memory stick."

Victoria returned a few minutes later and showed Bethan into the room.

"Hi, Penny," she said with a broad smile.

"You're looking awfully chipper for someone who's just come from a murder scene," Penny said. "What's up?"

"We've just had the DNA results back from the lab on Harry Saunders," Bethan said. "We ran his results against all others on file. It's routine, just in case. And the lab team found a match."

"Really?" said Penny.

"With who?" asked Victoria, almost at the same time.

Bethan shook her head slightly. "You'll not believe this, but to the skeletonized remains of the woman found in the ductwork of your spa. And to a ninety-nine-point-eight percent certainty, that woman was none other than Harry Saunders's mother."

Penny and Victoria looked at each other in stunned silence.

"Could that explain what he was doing here?" asked Penny. "Was he looking for his long-lost mother?"

Twenty-two

*B*ut Penny, you can't," wailed Victoria. "We're that close to Christmas and the ladies want their manicures! You've got to come in. We need you here."

She listened for a few moments.

"Penny, you promised me you'd let the police handle this. All of it. Everything. You said you wouldn't let any of it interfere with the business, and we're going to lose at least an hour today judging those shop windows for the competition. We have to get that done today." She listened for a few more moments and then said in a softer tone, "Well, yes, I can see that. Of course, you do. OK, see you later. We'll do the rest of the windows this afternoon."

A minute later she rang off, put the phone down, and walked the short distance from her office to the reception desk.

"Rhian, Penny won't be coming in this morning. Can you

see if Eirlys has any openings and, if so, call Penny's clients to reschedule? She says she'd be happy to do evening appointments or later in the afternoon. She'll be in just after lunch."

The spa receptionist called up the appointments page on her computer screen. "Just three ladies," she said. "I'll call them now."

Victoria came around behind the desk and peered over Rhian's shoulder. "Like this booking program, do you?" she asked.

"Oh, it's great," said Rhian. "Once you've entered a client's information, you just have to enter the name again and the phone number pops right up. Like this." She clicked on one of the women's names and her phone number appeared. "Not only that, but watch this!" She clicked on the phone number, and the phone beside her desk lit up and rang a few moments later.

"Hello, Mrs. Bowen, it's Rhian here from the spa. I'm sorry, but I'm calling to ask if you would mind if Eirlys took your appointment this morning. She's very good." A few moments later Rhian replaced the receiver and turned to look at Victoria.

"She insisted on Penny, so she'll come in this afternoon instead. No problem."

Thinking about the practical applications of the software booking program, Victoria returned to her desk.

Shortly after nine, Penny paused at the window of the charity shop where she had bought the replacement plate for Brian Kenley and where she had spotted her brooch. Her heart began to beat faster when she saw it was no longer on top of the little Christmas tree that formed part of the window display. She pushed the door open.

"Hello," she said to the woman behind the counter. "The police were trying to reach you yesterday about the brooch that was on top of your Christmas tree. It was stolen. It belongs to me."

"Does it now?" the woman replied. "Well, as a matter of fact, they've already rung about it and I've just this minute taken it off the tree."

"Thank you," said Penny. "I'm that relieved I am to know it's safe." She smiled at the woman. "You know, something funny's been going on in this shop lately, and if it's all right with you, I'd like to spend an hour or two here to see how things work."

She gestured at the crowded shelves. "I wondered if you could use a volunteer."

"Carwyn," the woman called over her shoulder. "Come out here, please. You've got a helper this morning."

As a short, smiling woman emerged from the back room, the woman behind the desk turned to Penny. "Are you sure you can spare the time? Don't you have a fancy new massage parlour to be running?"

"It's not a massage parlour, it's a spa," said Penny, "although we can certainly do a healing, deep-heat massage. Might be just the thing for you after a long day here."

She groped around in her handbag.

"Here," she said, holding out two envelopes. "A gift certificate for each of you." The two women exchanged glances.

"Well, that's very nice of you, I'm sure," said the second woman, who seemed the friendlier of the two. "I'm Carwyn and it's nice to meet you."

"Penny Brannigan."

"Well, then, Carwyn, fetch Penny a duster or something!" said the first woman. "Let's get stuck in." She turned to Penny. "I told that policewoman who rang me that I have no idea who stuck that brooch on our Christmas tree. We didn't even realize it was there. I wrapped it up in a nice bit of silk and put it away for safekeeping. The policewoman said she would pick it up this morning and return it to the owner, so I'm afraid I've got to hold on to it, but I can show it to you if you'd like to see it."

"No, I don't think so," said Penny. "I'll wait until the police return it to me." Sensing that she was starting to build a rapport with the woman, she gave her an easy smile. "Now, why don't I make myself useful, and perhaps you could tell me who you think is behind those thefts you were experiencing. Do you have any regulars who've been acting suspiciously lately?"

As the overhead bell tinkled to announce someone entering the shop, three heads turned to see who it was.

"Here's a regular now," the woman said in a low voice. "She's only started coming in over the past month or so but comes in a lot now. Doesn't always buy something. Just browses."

"Morning, Florence," said Penny.

"Fancy seeing you here," said Florence, looking at Carwyn, then back to Penny. "Helping out, are you?"

"Just for the morning," said Penny.

"Well, I've come in to see if you've got such a thing as a letter opener," said Florence. "I want to get Evelyn one for Christmas. Cheap, if I can."

Carwyn motioned to a plastic box filled with odds and ends. "You might find something in there." She turned to the woman who seemed to be in charge of the shop. "Have you seen any letter openers? You don't see those around much anymore, do you, now that I come to think of it." She thought for a moment. "It'll be all that e-mail, I guess."

"Well, there is this one," said the woman, reaching behind the counter and pulling out one with a Plexiglas handle and silver-coloured blade. "We could let you have it for, oh, say, two pounds."

"Two pounds! You must be joking!" said Florence, reaching

out for it. She turned it over in her hand. "I'll give you fifty pence for it and not a penny more."

"Oh, very well."

The transaction complete, Florence tucked the letter opener in her handbag, thanked the staff, and reached for the door handle. "Let me get that for you," said Penny, adding, "I'll show you out.

"I'm glad you came in this morning," Penny said, pulling the door closed behind them. "I want to ask you to do something for me." Florence waited. "I need you to give me the guest list of everyone who was at Mrs. Lloyd's open house."

"Well, let's see. There was the Reverend Thomas Evans and his wife . . ."

"No," said Penny. "Not now. I need you to write down the names of everyone who was at the party. Even better would be the original guest list or a copy of it. Make sure no one's left out."

She folded her arms and hugged herself. "It's freezing out here. I've got to get back inside. But please put that list together for me. I'll be in touch."

She turned to go.

"Important, is it?" Florence asked.

"Could be very important, Florence."

"Right, then. I'm on it. See you later."

"Oh and, Florence, just one thing. Remember I asked you a little while ago to try to think of the last time you saw the letter opener? You didn't get back to me, so please get this list for me."

Florence looked surprised. "Did I not? I have to write every-thing down, me, or it just vanishes." She made a brushing gesture past the top of her head. "I thought I did. Anyway, as near as we could remember, the last time we saw the opener was just before the open house." She gave her cheek a little scratch with a gloved hand and nodded slowly. "Yes, because Evelyn remembered being somewhat annoyed that she didn't have the opener on the Monday for her Christmas cards." She shrugged. "Don't know how much help that'll be, though. Half the town was at the open house."

"And, Florence, Mrs. Lloyd has told the police about the twenty thousand pounds, hasn't she?"

Florence nodded. "She has, although she didn't want to. But she said afterward that when they told her that her coming forward might prevent the same thing happening to some other poor woman, she felt better. She thought maybe some good might come of it.

"But can you imagine giving up a sum like that? Twenty thousand pounds!"

Penny spent the rest of the morning sorting through boxes, straightening shelves, and doing a little dusting. A few people came in. A woman she did not recognize bought a small blue-and-white milk jug. Some of the pieces in the store were clearly old tat, but others, she had to admit, were rather nice. She was just thinking about buying a small figurine of a black-and-grey dog when the door opened and a large cardboard box presented itself, held by Huw Bowen.

"Morning, ladies," he said.

"Oh, it's almost noon," said Carwyn. "Morning, Mr. Bowen."

Bowen set the box down on the counter. "Would you like it here, or shall I carry it through to the back for you?"

"Well, if you wouldn't mind just carrying it through, that would be most kind," Carwyn said. "You can set it down anywhere."

Penny instinctively turned her back, hoping he wouldn't see her. For some reason that she didn't understand, she didn't want him to recognize her.

"Well, I'm meeting my good lady wife for lunch, so I must be off," Bowen said after setting down the box. "I hope you'll find a bit of profit in there."

"He brings us in all the bits and pieces from the bank's lost and found," Carwyn explained when Bowen had left. "Astonishing, really, the things people leave behind in the bank. Pens, books, children's toys, mobile phones, gloves. Gloves!"

Penny peered into the box.

"This lot will all be things left behind since the summer. The bank staff keep it around for about six months in case folks come looking for it, then donate it to us."

Penny reached into the box and pulled out a small bag from the local chemist and peered inside. A brand-new lipstick with the receipt. She pulled the top off the lipstick and wound it up. It was a nice colour, but she doubted the shop could sell it.

"Still, it's nice of Mr. Bowen to bring these things over to us," Carwyn said as Penny closed the lid on the box. "I'm a bit surprised to hear he's taking his wife for lunch, though. Rarely leaves the bank during the day." She shrugged. "Oh well, maybe the Christmas spirit is getting to him."

"Well," Penny said to Carwyn as she put on her coat, "thanks very much for letting me work with you this morning. I'd best be getting off to my own work now."

"Did you learn anything useful?" Carwyn asked.

"I don't know," Penny replied. "But I've got a few things to think about. I just don't know how important or useful they are. Yet."

Twenty-three

See, here's what I don't understand," Penny said to Victoria half an hour later as they had a cup of coffee in Victoria's office. "If Huw Bowen rarely leaves his office, what was he doing having a nice little outing on a business day at Conwy Castle on the afternoon Harry Saunders was killed? There's something not right there." She leaned back in her chair and crossed her legs.

"A little while ago I was talking to this American woman, Dorothy Martin, her name is, and mentioned the Saunders case to her. She's solved a few murders of her own, apparently, and she reminded me to look for something that was at the scene that shouldn't have been, or something that should have been there but wasn't. And maybe that's Huw Bowen. He shouldn't have been there, but he was."

Penny leaned forward and tapped her finger on the desk. "What if it's not a thing we're looking for? Not a some-thing, but a some-one?"

Victoria thought for a moment. "Well, maybe he was just there to pick up his wife?"

"Exactly!" said Penny. "If he'd just been there to pick up Glynnis, then he would've parked somewhere in town or met her outside the castle at a certain time. He wouldn't have been traipsing around the castle, himself. With a guidebook! It was meant to be a day out for her, and he was meant to be at work at the bank."

They looked at each other.

"So what was he doing there, then?"

Before Victoria could answer, Rhian, the spa receptionist, stuck her head in the door.

"Penny, your one o'clock appointment's here. We switched her from this morning, remember. Glynnis Bowen."

Victoria and Penny exchanged quick glances and Penny gave a small nod.

"Right, Rhian, here I come," she said and, with a raised eyebrow in Victoria's direction, added, "Now there's a coincidence for you."

"So, Glynnis, how are you?" Penny said as she picked up Glynnis's hand and began shaping her fingernails with an emery board.

"Good, thanks, Penny. Busy, you know, with Christmas and all."

"Going somewhere nice?"

"No, we stay in town for the holidays. Huw doesn't get much time off at the bank, and this is actually a busy time of year for him."

"Oh, I see," said Penny.

"And what about you?"

"Well, this is my first Christmas in the cottage, so I've invited a few friends round for Christmas lunch." She thought a moment as a new idea came to her. "We'll meet up in the morning for church, and after the service we'll go back to mine for a traditional Christmas lunch."

"That sounds lovely," said Glynnis. Penny detected a wistful note in her voice and was on the brink of suggesting that Huw and Glynnis might care to join them, when something held her back. Besides the fact that Huw was known to be a dreadful old bore, guaranteed to give the kiss of death to just about any social gathering, she was starting to have serious doubts about him.

"It was appalling what happened the day of our Stretch and Sketch Christmas luncheon, wasn't it?" Penny said. "And too bad really, as it was your first time with the group."

"Well, I don't think it had anything to do with the art group, though," said Glynnis. "But yes, it was terrible. Just terrible."

"I was surprised to see Huw there," said Penny. "At the castle, I mean. Had he come to pick you up?"

Glynnis gave her a sharp look. "Now why you would ask something like that?"

"Oh, no reason," said Penny, trying to gloss over it. "I was just wondering, that's all."

An awkward silence fell between them, and a few moments later Penny tried to put things right. "Anyway," she said, with false brightness, "have you thought what colour you might like?"

Glynnis let out a little sigh that Penny couldn't quite decipher. Despair? Despondence?

"Some women like the deep reds this time of year," Penny

suggested, showing a small sample to her client. "Do any of these appeal to you?"

"That one looks good," said Glynnis, pointing to one.

Penny applied two coats of the nail varnish as Glynnis watched silently. As she finished the top coat, Glynnis spoke in a low voice.

"I envy you, you know. You seem to have everything."

"I've had my ups and downs like everyone else," Penny replied, "but yes, my life is in a good place right now." She screwed the top back on the bottle of top coat. "There. All done. They'll take a few minutes to dry, if you want to make yourself comfortable in reception or in our quiet room. Just be very careful for the next hour or so." She helped Glynnis gather up her belongings, wished her a happy Christmas, and left her in the reception area.

That is one deeply unhappy woman, she thought as she returned to her manicure table. And that remark at the end, about having everything, what was that about?

Sergeant Bethan Morgan showed her warrant card to the woman behind the counter in the charity shop.

"Oh, you'll have come about that brooch, I expect," she said. "I'll just get it for you." She opened the cash register, lifted out the change drawer, and removed a small bundle of pale pink silk.

"Here it is," she said, handing it over. "Valuable, is it?"

"Very."

"Now, who would do such a thing, I wonder. Pin something like that to the top of our little Christmas tree."

"That's what we'd like to know," said Bethan. "Can you think of anyone who might have done it?"

The woman shook her head. "But before you go, Officer,

there's something else." She beckoned to Carwyn. "Carwyn, fetch that box that came in today from the bank."

Carwyn brought out the plastic box and set it down on the counter.

"Mr. Bowen himself from the bank brought this in earlier," she said. "We were sorting through it and noticed a camera at the bottom of the box. It looked expensive. We didn't know what to do, and as you were coming in anyway, we thought we'd ask you. Run it by you, like." Bethan leaned forward to look in the box just as the woman reached into it to pull out the camera.

"Don't touch it," Bethan said. "Have you handled it at all?"

"Well, just a little, so we could look at it, like, and then we put it right back."

Bethan flipped through her notebook and then pulled a plastic bag from her pocket and wrapped it around the camera.

"You did right to let me know about this. This camera was in the box brought in today by Mr. Bowen from the bank, you say. What time was that?"

"Oh, around noon, I think, wasn't it, Carwyn? At any rate, that Penny Brannigan was still here, and she left around one or a bit before, I think it was, so it was before that."

"Penny Brannigan was in here this morning, was she?" said Bethan.

"Oh, yes," said Carwyn. "Volunteering. Got quite a bit of dusting done, actually."

"Volunteering, is it now." Bethan smiled.

"Is there something the matter?" asked the woman behind the counter. "I thought there was something odd about her."

"No," said Bethan, "she's all right is Penny. You've no worries there."

She picked up the camera and silk-wrapped brooch, which she also placed in a small bag and prepared to leave. "One more thing," she said to the women. "You didn't happen to see the box for the brooch, did you? Red, with midnight-blue silk lining."

The women looked at each other and shook their heads.

"No, it was just the brooch. No box."

"Well, if it turns up somewhere, give me a call," said Bethan. "Here's my card."

The two women watched her go and then turned toward each other.

"There's something very wrong going on here, and we seem to be involved," said Carwyn.

"Yes," agreed her companion. "We'd better look sharp."

Twenty-four

*A*s the midafternoon sun bathed the town in a gentle golden light, Penny and Victoria set off from the spa to inspect the window displays of the half dozen or so shops that had entered the competition. Some of the shop windows they passed had been hastily hung with a bit of tinsel or paper chains, but the ones they were to judge had been carefully and creatively dressed with lavish attention to detail.

Victoria checked the list on her clipboard.

"Here we are," she said, stopping in front of a pale blue shopfront and giving her clipboard a quick glance. "Angharad Roberts, dressmaker and seamstress."

They leaned forward to study the display, which showed a tableau of a mouse family enjoying a quiet Christmas Eve. Three mouse children were tucked up in a bed, while their parents worked in front of a paper fireplace, the mother sewing a little skirt for her mouse daughter while the father assembled a small red fire engine.

Each character was made of satin, the coats a shiny grey and their large ears lined in pink. The expressions on their faces had been painstakingly embroidered to reflect the calm repose of the children, the quiet pride the mother took in her little family, and the father's apparent struggle to piece together the toy.

"Oh, look!" said Penny, pointing at the children. "The one in the middle . . . his eyes are slightly open. He's watching his dad try to put the toy together. There'll be questions about Father Christmas in the morning!"

Victoria smiled and jotted down a few notes. "Seen enough?" she asked Penny.

Penny nodded, and as they turned to go, the shop door opened and Mrs. Lloyd emerged, looking decidedly downcast.

"Hello," said Penny. "All right?"

"Oh, hello, Penny. Victoria." Mrs. Lloyd shifted her handbag to her other arm. "Yes, fine, thanks. How are you?"

"You don't look fine," said Penny, ignoring the question and gently touching Mrs. Lloyd's arm. "What is it?"

Mrs. Lloyd glanced across the street. "It's getting me down, all this. Everyone knows about Harry's death, and they think that I had something to do with it. People are avoiding me. I've tried to carry on as normal, but it's difficult when I know they're all whispering about me behind my back."

"Oh, surely not, Mrs. Lloyd," said Victoria. "Folk round here have been your friends for years. They know you couldn't possibly have had anything to do with it."

Mrs. Lloyd shook her head. "No, you should see them at the Over Sixties Club. Hardly anyone speaks to me, and if they do, they're only being polite. Then they move away as quickly as they can." She sighed. "About the only friend I have left is Florence." She shook her head. "That's what it's come to, I'm afraid."

Before Penny or Victoria could respond, Mrs. Lloyd pointed to a woman walking toward them. "Look," she said, "there's Ruth from the Over Sixties Club." As Mrs. Lloyd started to wave to her, the woman caught sight of the little group and quickly crossed the street.

"See what I mean?" said Mrs. Lloyd. "It's like that everywhere I go. I can hardly hold my head up anymore in this town." A sob caught in her throat and she turned to go.

"See," said Penny. "She's just gone into the bakery. She wasn't avoiding you."

Mrs. Lloyd gave her a sorrowful, pained look. "What are you two doing here anyway? Getting some alterations done?"

"No," said Victoria, "we're doing the window judging you volunteered us for."

"Oh, that," said Mrs. Lloyd, her voice dull and lifeless. "Well, I'll leave you to it."

Victoria and Penny watched her walk slowly away, her well-wrapped figure growing smaller, until she turned down the little street that led to the town square.

"She looks older, somehow," said Victoria. "This is really taking a toll on her. We've got to do something."

Penny nodded. "Yes, we need to get this sorted so she can get on with her life." She tapped Victoria's clipboard. "How many windows left on the list?"

"Let me see. There's the bakery and then the shoe store. The bakery has a distinct advantage, I'd say."

"Right, but we're not going in. And we don't have to spend much time looking at the display. I walk past that window every day and I've had my eye on every biscuit, pie, and cake."

Victoria laughed. "Isn't that the best thing about Christmas? We can give ourselves permission to be really naughty."

Half an hour later, as the afternoon sun began to cast long, slanting shadows, they stood on the pavement gazing through a window at the last entrant in the competition.

"I think we agree that it's down to this one and the dressmaker's mouse family," said Victoria.

Penny nodded. "They're both so charming." The window display of the shoe store, which also mended the townsfolk's shoes and boots, featured Santa Claus repairing the sole of an elf's pointy shoe. As Santa worked away, tiny hammer raised to strike the upturned shoe, the elf, seated on a small stool, used the time to check off items on the list he held on his lap.

Penny leaned closer and, breaking out in a sudden smile, pointed. "Oh look! That's just too adorable."

For the elf's green-and-white-striped stocking had a hole in the toe, which he was trying unsuccessfully to cover up with his other foot.

Victoria jotted down a few notes on her clipboard and then turned to Penny. "Right, well that's it, then. Shall we go back to mine and tally up the scores? The temperature is starting to drop and I'm getting cold."

The sky was becoming overcast, and as they made their way through the cobbled streets in the deepening gloom, the threat of snow hung over them.

"So we're decided?" asked Victoria, reaching for the telephone.

Penny nodded. "I think we did the right thing dropping the best-in-show category and replacing it with most delicious. The bakery was a no-brainer for that one."

"And," added Victoria, "I'm glad we were each able to assign a win to our favourites. The mouse family as most beautiful for me and Santa and his elf for the most creative for you."

"I can't get over that little hole in his sock," said Penny. "Absolutely delightful."

Over the next two days, an iron-cold, frozen fog settled over the valley, draping the hilltops in a misty shroud. And although winter held the town firmly in its grip, just about everyone had last-minute preparations for Christmas that needed seeing to, so bundled up against a bitterly cold wind, the townsfolk hurried from shop to shop, darting in and out of doorways, clutching overflowing bags.

Finally, as the late afternoon gave way to the deepening darkness that signaled the onset of Christmas Eve, they returned to their homes, bearing a last-minute gift, a remembered-just-in-time jar of cranberry sauce, or a few extra batteries to power the children's toys on Christmas morning.

In the warmth of Mrs. Lloyd's home on Rosemary Lane, as Florence closed the curtains against the encroaching night, Mrs. Lloyd looked up from her copy of *Country Life* magazine and frowned.

"I don't know why we should have to entertain an old lag like that Jimmy fellow tomorrow," she grumbled. "Just because Penny Branningan asked us to have him over doesn't mean we have to."

Florence switched on the Christmas tree lights and then sank gratefully into a wingback chair. With only an hour or so off for a nap, she had been busy all day preparing the sausage stuffing for the turkey, peeling vegetables, setting the table, creating an attractive centrepiece, and ensuring that every aspect of to-morrow's Christmas lunch would be perfect. She planned to attend church in the morning with Mrs. Lloyd, and then hurry home to see to all the last-minute details. Reverend Thomas Evans and his wife, Bronwyn, had accepted their invitation to join them for lunch, and Florence wanted everything to be exactly right.

"He's coming over for a couple of hours in the afternoon after lunch because he wants a little visit with us," Florence explained with exaggerated patience. "You know he lives in that dreadful senior's home in Llandudno, and according to Penny he's been looking forward enormously to this Christmas Day outing. It's a special day for him."

Florence took off her glasses and contemplated the smudged lenses. "Really, Evelyn, I'm surprised at you. You have a big, kind heart, and to begrudge an elderly man who's confined to a wheelchair a bit of pleasure on Christmas Day is just not like you." She put her glasses back on and peered at Mrs. Lloyd over the top of them.

"Yes, Florence, you're right. We must do everything we can to make him feel welcome. I wonder what he likes to drink."

Victoria tied a pale green bow around a small parcel covered in shiny paper and tucked it under the small tree in Penny's living room. "There," she said, "that's the last of them. Who's it for?"

"It's for you," Penny replied with a grin.

"You didn't!" Victoria exclaimed. "You've just had me wrap my own present? What kind of person does that?"

"It's just a little something for the flat. It's not your main present. You'll see tomorrow. And anyway, you offered to make yourself useful, and the wrapping needed doing, so . . ."

Victoria took a sip of wine, sighed, and sat back in her chair.

"I must say, I thought you'd be spending Christmas Eve with Gareth, not here on your own."

"I'm not on my own. You're here." She shrugged. "He did ask me if I fancied going away with him for Christmas, and then the murders happened, so we're staying in town. He's spending this evening with his son and daughter-in-law, and we'll see each other tomorrow."

She looked at her friend. "What about you? Do you miss having someone special in your life at this time of year?"

Victoria thought for a moment. "In a way, yes, I do. It can be difficult on your own. But you were alone for a few years before you met Gareth, so you'd know all about that."

Penny nodded. "There was someone once, a long time ago. Another policeman, in fact. Tim. I still think of him, but it doesn't hurt the way it used to." They fell silent, each remembering the lovers' ghosts of Christmases past. A few minutes later Victoria brought them back to the present.

"Are you all ready for the big day?"

"I think so. I've got everything in that Gwennie told me to get. She's coming over early in the morning to put the turkey in the oven and start on the vegetables. She said she'd be here about eight. I gave her a key so she could let herself in. She said it would be very helpful if I could peel and parboil the potatoes and set the table tonight." She raised a hopeful eyebrow.

"Right. You set the table, I'll start on the potatoes," Victoria said, hauling herself out of the chair and heading for the kitchen. "I hate these winter nights when it gets dark so early," she said a few minutes later as she picked up another potato. "It always feels so much later than it is."

Beside her, Penny reached into the cupboard and with her fingers counted out the number of plates she needed.

"How many?" Victoria asked.

"You, me, Gareth, Bethan, and Jimmy. Five."

"And Gwennie. Six."

"Gwennie said she'd walk to church with me but will sit with her sister and brother-in-law. And she said she won't eat with us. She prefers to eat afterward in the kitchen, by herself."

"Yes, I can see that. It'll be what she got used to at the Hall." Victoria dropped another peeled potato into the pot.

Penny awoke Christmas morning to the sound of someone moving about downstairs. At first panicked, thinking she was being burgled, she started up in bed. When she realized it must be Gwennie, who had let herself in with the key Penny had given her, arriving to start work on the lunch, she shrank back into her comforting bedclothes. She checked the time on her bedside clock. The luminescent numbers winked back at her: 7:34. She would enjoy a few more minutes in her warm bed, going over all the things that still needed doing, and then . . .

An hour later she groaned and sat up, just as Gwennie knocked on her door.

"You'd better think about getting up, Miss Penny, if you want to make morning service on time," she said, opening the door slightly. "I've just put the coffee on. Would you like a boiled egg?"

"That would be great, thanks, Gwennie," Penny replied, and then added, "Happy Christmas."

"And to you," called Gwennie from halfway down the stairs.

The damp fogginess of the last two days had dissipated, replaced by a crisp, sunlit morning.

Frost glittered on the stone fences and added sparkle to the holly bushes in the hedgerows, bursting with red bright berries displayed against their backdrop of glossy, pointed leaves. There had been an abundance of holly berries this year, and the townsfolk who had strolled along the country lanes over the past few days, taking small cuttings off the holly to adorn their Christmas puddings, had made not the slightest dent in their numbers.

Warmly dressed against the cold, Penny and Gwennie walked together through the quiet streets. Smoke from wood and coal fires curled from the chimneys, wafting skyward and drifting up and away, then disappearing into a bright blue sky. They parted company on the steps of the church, as Gwennie left to sit with her sister and brother-in-law and Penny, meeting Victoria, made her way to a pew on the right side of the church. At Penny's suggestion they chose a pew near the back, Penny turning occasionally to see if Davies and Bethan had arrived. She smiled as Mrs. Lloyd made her entrance, Florence trailing along behind her like a doleful bridesmaid.

She waved to Davies when she spotted him with Bethan and Jimmy at the entrance to the church and then slid along in her seat so they could squeeze in.

Everyone seemed to arrive at once, and soon the church was as full as Penny had ever seen it. Bronwyn Evans took her place in the front row and Reverend Thomas Evans appeared in front of them.

"*Bore da, bawb. Nadolig Llawen,*" he greeted them in Welsh. "Good morning, everyone. Merry Christmas."

The service began with voices raised in joyful song as the familiar words of a timeless carol rang through the church.

237

When the rustling of the congregation settling into their seats had subsided, Reverend Evans began his Christmas sermon.

"I was browsing the Internet the other day," Reverend Evans began, "and I came across a website that promised to help me write a Christmas sermon in just a few minutes that would sound as if I'd spent a lot of time on it. And that got me thinking about how we do things today. Everything has to be fast. We want a recipe for a five-minute meal made from three ingredients that looks as if it took a Cordon Bleu chef all day to prepare. If we can find the time to read at all, we are looking for a book with well-developed characters and a complicated plot that still promises to be a fast, easy read. We have learned to be multitaskers. We talk on the phone while we draft an e-mail. We eat and text while we drive.

"So I would ask you on this beautiful Christmas morning to consider those three wise men who made that journey to Bethlehem two thousand years ago and . . ."

Penny's attention drifted away. She shifted in her seat and gazed slowly around the church. I wonder if this person is here this morning, she thought, this person who killed two people. She spotted a few members of her art group, sitting with their husbands and grown-up children. One reached over to comfort a bored grandchild who struggled to get down out of his father's tight hold. Her eyes moved on to Huw Bowen, the bank manager, staring stiffly ahead while his wife, Glynnis, stifled a yawn behind a black-gloved hand. I wonder how her manicure's holding up, Penny thought. Behind the Bowens, her friend Alwynne reached over to pick up a hymnbook and began leafing through it, turning the pages slowly. When she reached the place she was looking for, she stuck a marker between the pages and returned the book to the rack in front of her. She smiled at her husband then turned her face toward the raised lecturn where Reverend Evans was wrapping up his sermon.

"I hope you will all take the time to reflect on the bounty and blessings of the season," he was saying. "And now, let us pray."

The light that had been streaming in through the multicoloured stained-glass windows had become muted and dimmed.

As the service drew to a close, the congregation rose for one last carol and then began to make their way slowly out of the church, stopping to exchange a few words with Reverend Evans as he shook everyone's hand. Friends greeted one another, wishing them all the joys of the season. Penny slipped her arm through Gareth's as they walked off a few paces to wait for Victoria, who had stayed behind to talk to Bronwyn. A few snowflakes drifted lazily down, and although the sky had clouded over, the snow felt temporary.

The Bowens emerged and stood off to one side turned slightly toward each other. As a few snowflakes settled on Huw's collar, Glynnis reached up and brushed them off. Something in the gesture startled Penny. It was at once intimate and yet somehow out of place. And then she remembered where she'd seen it before. On that very snowy night when she had spotted the couple in the churchyard. She had thought one of them was married and assumed it was the man. But it wasn't the man, it was Glynnis. And could the man have been . . . She struggled to bring the scene into focus, to imagine them as they were in that embrace.

"Penny, are you ready to go?"

"What? Sorry, I was thinking about something else. Sorry."

"We're heading back to your cottage now, Penny," said Victoria, tucking one end of her scarf through its loop as Gareth approached. "Are you ready? Gwennie left a few minutes ago.

Said she wanted to get the appetizers in the oven. And Bethan should have arrived with Jimmy by the time we get there." After exchanging greetings with those around them, the three set off for Penny's cottage.

Twenty-five

*A*fter shaking the hand of the last of his parishoners, Reverend Thomas Evans headed back into the church and, after stopping at one pew to pick up a hymnbook and replace it in the rack, entered the small office beside the vestry where he and his wife, Bronwyn, would count the morning's collection. Bronwyn, who had slipped over to the comfortable rectory to fetch their cairn terrier, Robbie, while her husband was seeing off the last of his flock, was beginning to sort the contributions placed in the collection plates during morning service. She placed the cash in one pile, and the small, white numbered envelopes preferred by regular members of the congregation in another, then set aside the collection plate. As Reverend Evans slipped off his surplice, Bronwyn removed a brown envelope from the second collection plate. She turned it over and then held it out to her husband.

"What do you suppose this is, Thomas?" she asked.

"Well, there's only one way to find out," he replied good-naturedly. "But first, I have a little something for us before we start the counting." He reached behind his desk and pulled out a bottle of sherry and two glasses. "What do you say, my dear? Just this once, because it's Christmas, shall we have a little libation while we count the takings?"

"Oh, go on then," said Bronwyn, laughing as Robbie wagged his tail enthusiastically. "But just a small one. We don't want to arrive at Mrs. Lloyd's stinking of sherry!"

She took a small sip and set down her glass.

As Reverend Evans reached for a pencil and a piece of scrap paper that he would use to help them count the morning offering, Bronwyn opened the envelope and peered inside. Then, turning the envelope upside down, she shook out its contents, revealing a small red box and a piece of ordinary lined notepaper.

She picked up the box as Reverend Evans stopped to watch.

She opened it, shrugged, and then showed it to her husband.

"Empty." He pointed at the folded piece of paper. "What does the note say?"

Bronwyn opened it slowly, read it to herself, then held it out to the rector.

"'Penny Brannigan—Feliz Navi-dead!'" he read, then looked at his wife. "What on earth does that mean? And how did that dreadful thing get in our collection plate?"

"Somebody put it there," said Bronwyn. "And it's Spanish for Merry Christmas, only it should be *Feliz Navidad*."

"Well, yes, but who could have put it there?"

"I don't know, dear. But we have to figure out what to do about it. It could be some kind of stupid joke, I suppose."

The rector drained the last of his sherry and looked long-ingly at the bottle on his desk.

"Thomas," his wife said sharply, "listen to me. If this is a threat, and it sounds like it to me, then there's only one thing we can do. We need to call the police."

"Yes, but it's Christmas Day. We wouldn't want to waste their time. Especially not today. Do you think this is important enough to warrant their attention? It might just be a sick joke of some kind."

"I think we should let them be the judge of that. From what I've heard, if Penny's in danger, that police inspector friend of hers, Gareth Davies, would want to be the first to know about it."

The rector reached for the telephone on his cluttered desk.

"Right you are as usual, Bronwyn dear."

"Everything looks beautiful, Gwennie!" exclaimed Penny as everyone admired the table setting before taking their seats. Victoria had arranged a small bouquet of red roses, their stems trimmed, in a setting of holly and tied it all together with a plaid ribbon. Penny and Gareth sat at the ends of the table, with Jimmy on one side and Victoria and Bethan across from him.

Jimmy beamed at everyone around the table and chuckled.

"If anyone had told me that one day I'd be having Christmas dinner with not one but two coppers, I would have said they were mad," he said.

Penny laughed. "I would have thought the same thing my-self not so long ago."

All eyes turned toward Gwennie, who emerged from the kitchen with a beautiful golden brown turkey on a large platter, which she set down in front of Davies. "Here you are, sir," she said. "It's been resting and ready for carving. I'll bring the vegetables through now."

She stopped, startled, as Bethan's phone rang. With an apologetic shrug at Penny, Bethan pulled the phone out of her pocket and glanced at the caller ID. "I'd better take this," she said, getting to her feet. "Excuse me." She walked a few steps away from the table and put the phone to her ear.

The conversation at the table continued as Davies picked up the carving knife and fork. He sliced off a piece of breast meat and set it down carefully, held between the sharp knife and large fork, onto a smaller platter.

"Is there any news of the identity of that body found in your spa?" Jimmy asked Penny.

"We know a little more than we did. We know who she was but not what happened to her." She provided a few more details and, with an anxious glance at Davies, finished up, "But of course, after all this time we may never know what happened to her."

Bethan ended the call and signaled to Davies. "A word, sir, please."

Trying to hide his annoyance, Davies set down the carving knife and fork and joined Bethan. They spoke together in urgent, low tones as Davies cast an anxious glance in Penny's direction.

"I'm sorry, everyone," Davies said, "but we're going to have to go out for a bit. A call's just come in that we need to follow up on. We'll be as quick as we can."

Penny started to rise from her chair, but Davies put a gentle hand on her shoulder.

"No, you carry on with your meal. We'll be back as soon as we can."

"If you're not back, we'll keep it warm for you."

"Let's hope it won't come to that."

"Can't you just tell us what's happened?" Penny asked.

"Later, when we know more."

Gwennie reentered the room carrying a large bowl of roasted potatoes and Brussels sprouts, which she set down beside Penny.

"Shall I carry on with the carving while you pass the vegetables?" she asked.

"Yes, thank you, Gwennie, I think that would be best."

"Don't worry, Miss Penny. We'll save some for them, and it'll be no bother to warm it up when they return."

"I'm so sorry about this, Gwennie. And everything looks so wonderful, too."

The others murmured their agreement.

"That's how it is, Miss Penny. At the Hall, back in the old days, dinners were often interrupted when one of the Labs decided that was a good time to have her puppies or it was lambing time or any number of things. But we just carried on, the way you do. Dinners can always be reheated. Now then, who's for a nice bit of drumstick?"

"So this woman's body in the spa, then," said Jimmy. "They found out she's related to that man who went over the wall at Conwy Castle, is that what you're saying?"

"That's right," said Victoria. "They think the woman's body had been there since the 1960s. And then all these years later, her son turns up dead, too."

A thoughtful look crossed Gwennie's face.

"If you'll excuse me now, I'll see to Trixxi in the kitchen." She hesitated. "Miss Penny, would it be all right if I used your telephone? I'd like to ring my sister."

"Yes, of course, Gwennie."

The two police officers entered the church office where the Evanses, who had finished counting the Christmas offering, were waiting for them.

"We're so very sorry to call you out today, of all days," Reverend Evans began, "we weren't really sure what to do, but we thought you'd want to see this." He pointed at the little red box.

Bethan pulled an evidence bag out of the kit she kept in her car and wrapped it around the box. "I'm assuming you touched this? If so, we'll need to get your fingerprints for elimination." She looked from one to the other.

Reverend Evans nodded. "Yes, I think we both touched it. At least, we might have." He looked at his wife. "Would you need us to do that today? It's just that we're meant to be having Christmas lunch with Mrs. Lloyd and Florence and we're already so late."

"No, that's all right," said Davies. "You can pop into the station tomorrow and they'll take your prints."

"But why are you so interested in the box?" Bronwyn asked. "There's nothing in it. We couldn't understand why someone would put that in the collection plate. It was the note we thought you should see." She reached out to pick up the note but then pulled back as if she had touched a hot stove.

"Sorry," she said. "Forgot I shouldn't touch it in case of fingerprints. But that note," she said, gesturing at it. "See what it says."

Using a pencil she had picked up from the rector's desk, Bethan unfolded the corners of the note. She and Davies read it, and then Davies looked at the rector.

"You did right to call us and we're very glad you did. Tell me how you came by this. It's very important."

Penny filled a cup with coffee, added a splash of cream, and handed the cup to Victoria, who took it over to Jimmy, seated on the sofa.

He took an appreciative sip and then set the cup down on the small table that had been placed in front of him.

"Very nice, thank you, Penny. Just the way I like it. And I enjoyed lunch very much."

"Well, when you've finished your coffee, Victoria and I'll drive you over to Mrs. Lloyd's. I hear Florence is looking forward to seeing you again."

Jimmy's face lit up.

"Well, I think we've taken up enough of your time," Davies said to the Evanses, as Bethan bent down to give Robbie a pat. "Shall we give you a lift over to Mrs. Lloyd's and then we'll all be able to get on with our dinners."

"Oh, that's very kind of you," said the rector. "I don't like taking the car out in winter, so if you'd be kind enough to drive us, that would be wonderful." He exchanged glances with his wife. "Then the three of us can easily walk home. I'll just ring Florence to let them know we're on our way."

"I don't think I've ever been in a police car before," Bronwyn remarked when she and the rector, with Robbie between them, were arranged in the backseat of the police car.

"I'm sure you'd remember if you had." Bethan smiled as she put the car in gear and drove off. The rector smiled and reached for his wife's hand.

Bronwyn laughed good-naturedly "Well, in any event, I know Robbie's never been in one."

"First time for everything, my dear," said the rector. "Now, I wonder if we should be hoping that no one we know will see us driving by, or just for the fun of it, should we hope that some-one we do know does see us?"

"And if we do see someone we know," replied Bronwyn, "do we stare straight ahead and look very worried or should we smile and wave?"

As they pulled up in front of Mrs. Lloyd's home on Rosemary Lane, Bethan spoke softly to Davies. He nodded, then turned to his passengers in the back.

"We're just going to pop in for a quick word with Mrs. Lloyd and Florence. They might have noticed something in the church this morning."

"No, I didn't see anyone put anything in the collection plate, ex-cept what you'd expect, regular collection envelopes and money," said Mrs. Lloyd. "Did you see anything untoward, Florence?"

Florence slung a tea towel over her shoulder and then held a hand up to her cheek. "Let me think."

The rector took off his coat and folded it over his arm as Bronwyn bent down and unclipped Robbie's leash.

"Would it be all right, Mrs. Lloyd, if he just had a little wan-der about to get his bearings?"

"Yes, of course. Florence has put down a bowl of water for him in the kitchen."

"Sorry to be taking so long," said Florence, glancing at Bethan. "I was just going over everything in my mind, like. I remember the sidesmen passing the collection plate, but there was nothing amiss when we were in our seats. On the way out, however, I took one last look at the altar decorations and noticed an envelope about this big"—she made a small square with her hands—"sitting on top of one of the collection plates. "Brown, it was. It wasn't a regular collection envelope, and I thought maybe someone had donated something special, it being Christmas and all. But I didn't think any more about it."

Bethan leaned forward slightly.

"Did you see who put it there?" she asked. "Think carefully now. You've been doing really well with this."

Florence's eyes shifted to the rector.

"It was just after the rector had left to go to the rear of the church to say good-bye to folks and some people had left their seats. There was a cluster of folk there, and I don't know many of them. The only person I saw that I recognized was Bowen, the bank manager."

She tipped her head to one side.

"And now that I think of it, that's a bit odd because he was sitting behind us, wasn't he, Evelyn?" Mrs. Lloyd nodded. "Yes, he was. We said good morning to him and his wife as we walked past them on the way in.

"So it does seem strange, now that I think of it," continued Florence, "that instead of making his way to the back of the church when the service was over, that he had gone to the front."

"Can you remember anyone else who was at the front of the church at that time?" asked Davies.

"Well, his wife was with him, I think, but she was talking to someone. The woman from the charity shop, I think. Having a good old natter, they were."

Davies shot Bethan a quick glance and thanked Florence. "You've been very helpful. We won't keep you away from your dinner any longer, and we do apologize for holding you up."

Something seemed to occur to Florence, and she leaned forward as if she was about to say something important. "Have you had your dinner yet, Inspector?" she asked.

Bethan and Davies shrugged.

"Just wait there a moment, Inspector," said Florence as she hurried into the kitchen.

She emerged a few minutes later and handed them a hefty packet wrapped in aluminum foil.

"From the look of things, it might be a while before you get to your dinner and there's nothing open today, so here's a couple of turkey sandwiches to take along with you." As a wide grin spread across Bethan's face, Florence brushed away her thanks. "I put a little cranberry sauce and stuffing in them. Not as good as the real thing, I know, but something to be going on with." She pulled two bottles of water from her apron pockets and solemnly handed them to Davies. "I expect you'll be wanting these, too."

"Well, thank you so much," Davies said. "And a very happy Christmas to all of you."

Twenty-six

*D*avies checked his watch as the car pulled up in front of the Bowens' two-storey home.

"The whole afternoon is disappearing," he grumbled. "I really didn't want to spend Christmas Day like this. Let's just hear what Bowen has to say, and then maybe we can salvage what's left of the day."

"There won't be much of it," said Bethan. "It'll be dark in an hour or so. But I'm starving. It was so good of Florence to think of sending those sandwiches with us. Should we take a few moments to eat them before we go in?"

"Yes, I think we should."

Huw Bowen answered the door, still wearing the shirt and tie he'd worn to church, but his suit jacket had been replaced by a frayed green cardigan with leather patches on the elbows.

"Oh, it's you," he said when he saw who it was. "You'd better come in, then." He stood aside to let them enter and then shuffled along behind them in worn slippers down a short hallway into an overheated, overdecorated sitting room whose predominant colour was beige. No Christmas decorations had been put up, and there was no Christmas tree. A few cards had been propped up on the mantelpiece, but one had fallen over and no one had bothered to set it upright. A small lamp in the corner of the room was losing its battle to dispel the gloom.

"This is my wife, Glynnis," he said, with a defeated wave in his wife's direction. "I don't know if you've met before." The two police officers nodded at her, then turned to Bowen.

"We're sorry to bother you on Christmas Day," Bethan began, "but we want to talk to you about a packet that was left in a collection plate at the church this morning. Did you happen to see who put it there?"

"Why do you ask?" Bowen replied.

"We're investigating a series of thefts that may be connected to a murder."

Bowen sighed and rubbed his hand across his chin.

"I've been expecting you," he said, "only not today, of course. I thought you might have the decency to at least let us have Christmas Day."

Seeing Bethan's look of confusion, he turned to Davies.

"You've really come about that Harry Saunders fellow, haven't you?"

"Why do you say that?" Davies replied.

"Because I killed him. I've been expecting you."

The atmosphere thickened as if all the air had been sucked

252

out of the room. Glynnis Bowen gave her husband a hard, hateful look and covered her face with her hands. The only sound was a faint hiss coming from the radiator under the window.

"Here you go, Jimmy," said Penny as she helped him on with his coat. "They've finished lunch at Mrs. Lloyd's so we'll run you over now." Penny exchanged a few brief words with Gwennie, and then she and Victoria guided Jimmy gently down the path and into Victoria's car. They drove slowly through the almost deserted streets, quiet and peaceful in the lull of a Christmas Day afternoon.

"Everyone'll be sleeping off all that turkey," Jimmy observed.

"Are you tired?" Penny asked him. "You could have had a little lie down, and then we could have taken you over for supper, perhaps."

"How do you know I won't be having a little lie down when I get there?" asked Jimmy with a cheeky grin.

"Aren't you a bit old for that kind of carrying on?" Victoria laughed.

"You're never too old," said Jimmy. "At least I hope not."

"Hello, Jimmy, and do come in," said Mrs. Lloyd graciously, with a sweeping gesture in the direction of her sitting room. "Now I know you've just had a wonderful lunch, but I wondered if we might offer you a warm mince pie and a glass of sherry. I have dry and sweet."

"Nothing for me, thanks," said Jimmy. "I couldn't eat another thing." Leaning heavily on two canes, he walked slowly but steadily into the sitting room, followed by a solicitous Mrs. Lloyd.

"Come in, you two," said Mrs. Lloyd to Penny and Victoria. "We've given Florence the afternoon off after all her hard work this morning. She's in here with the Evanses." Everyone laughed as a small, sharp bark emanated from beside Bronwyn's chair.

"Oh, sorry, Robbie. Yes, Robbie's here, too."

Penny and Victoria smiled at the room, and Penny reached down to give Robbie a pat.

"We can only stay a few minutes," Victoria said. "I've got to drive Penny back to hers and then get over to my cousin's and deliver the Christmas presents to the children. They've already texted me twice, asking when I'm coming. They're pretending they can't wait to see me, but we all know what they're really after."

A light silence fell over the group as they watched Mrs. Lloyd settle herself into a corner of the sofa.

"We had a lovely meal," said Bronwyn to no one in particular. "Florence did herself proud. Everything was just delicious."

"Indeed it was," echoed the rector.

Seated in a wing chair in front of the fireplace, Florence acknowledged their thanks.

Penny glanced at her, and then at the rather large book on the table beside her elbow.

She picked it up and turned it over.

"Are you reading this, Florence?"

"Yes, I am and quite enjoying it, too. He does a good job, that author does, of capturing the essence of Liverpool the way it used to be."

Jimmy leaned over to get a closer look.

"*John Lennon. The Life.*"

"Yes, there's a lot about Liverpool back in the old days, the way I remember it," Florence said. "I like reading about the old days. All those people and places. Beautiful old buildings, some of them. Long gone."

"Where did you get this book, may I ask?" said Penny. "It's not a library book or I might take it out of the library myself."

"Oh, it was given to me as a little gift," said Florence. "It's used; it came from the charity shop, but I don't mind that. I'm glad to have it. It must have cost quite a bit when it was new, by the weight of it."

Penny nodded. Careful, now, she thought. Take it easy.

"Who gave it to you, Florence?" she blurted out.

Florence tipped her head to one side.

"Why, Glynnis Bowen. She's very generous. She's given me quite a few nice things, hasn't she, Evelyn?"

Mrs. Lloyd nodded. "Well, nice if you like that sort of thing. Secondhand."

Penny caught Victoria's eye and stood up.

"Well, sorry to dash, but we have to be on our way. Victoria's very anxious to get over to her cousin's. Mustn't keep the kids waiting any longer. Come on, Victoria, let's be having you."

After hurried good-byes and leaving a somewhat startled Mrs. Lloyd standing in her doorway waving them off, Penny settled into the passenger seat and scrabbled about in her handbag for her mobile phone.

"What on earth was that all about?" demanded Victoria. "We didn't even say a proper good-bye to Thomas and Bronwyn."

"No, and I'm sorry about that," said Penny, "but we had to get out of there. Don't you see?"

"See what?"

"Glynnis Bowen. She gave the John Lennon book to Florence. That book was on the list that Bethan gave me of things that had been stolen from the charity shop. It was just so easy to remember a John Lennon book because everybody knows who he was."

She reached into her pockets. "Oh, where the hell is it?"

"What? Where's what?"

"My phone. I can't find my phone. Where's yours?"

"In my bag on the backseat."

Penny twisted around and tried to reach it. "Argh. I can't get it."

"Well, we're almost back at yours, you can ring when we get there. Who are you so keen to ring by the way, as if I didn't know."

"Gareth. I have to ring him and tell him about Glynnis."

"Tell him what?"

"That she killed Saunders and poor Brian Kenley."

"How do you work that out?"

"Well, I don't know why she killed Saunders, but she killed Brian because she was afraid that the photographs he took at Conwy Castle the day Harry Saunders was killed could incriminate her."

"And you know all this because . . ." said Victoria as she turned into the narrow lane that led to Penny's cottage.

"Because she stole the letter opener from Mrs. Lloyd. She must have taken it the day of Mrs. Lloyd's open house and then forgotten about it. And there it still was at the bottom of her bag on the day we went to Conwy Castle. And she stole the daffodil plate from the charity shop and gave it to Brian Kenley, just like she gave the book to Florence. And that's what I couldn't work out that day I went to see him, just before he was killed."

"All this is so hard to follow. You couldn't work out what?"

"I couldn't work out why he didn't seem bothered that the plate got broken. But now I see the reason he didn't care was he hadn't had it very long and it was just an old secondhand plate that Glynnis had given him. He couldn't have cared less about it getting broken, but I think he was upset because it happened when Glynnis was there. And then when I went over to see him, full of apologies about breaking his plate, he really had no idea what I was going on about."

"I'm not so sure I do, either," said Victoria, pulling up in front of the little path that led to Penny's front door. "Anyway, here we are. Do you mind if I don't come in? I do need to get over to see the children and I expect Gareth and Bethan will be back soon."

"No, that's fine," said Penny. "Gwennie and I'll do the tidying up, and you and I can catch up later or tomorrow. Right. Got to find my phone."

"It's only me, Gwennie," Penny called out as she pushed open the front door, to be greeted by a tail-wagging Trixxi. "Just got to make a phone call, and then I'll come through to help you."

She picked up her phone from the small desk near the window and pressed the key to ring Davies. Damn! It went to voice mail. "Hi," she said, "it's me. Call me the minute you get this. It's important." She paused a moment and then, just before pressing the key to end the call, added, "Really important."

She went through to the kitchen to find Gwennie seated at the small table eating a turkey sandwich. The dishwasher was chugging away, and the leftover food had been wrapped up and put in the refrigerator. A few large pots soaked in the sink.

"Hi, Gwennie."

"Hello, Miss Penny. You're back then. I wondered if I might have a word with you."

"Of course. May I join you?" Penny pulled out a chair and sat down.

"I've been thinking about what you were saying at lunch about the woman's body that was found in the ductwork in the spa and how she was related to the man who got himself murdered at Conwy Castle."

Penny nodded.

"Well, I remember back when I was a girl and my mother worked at the Hall and she mentioned once that the girl who worked in the kennels and stables had gone missing. And she had a boy, about six or seven, I think he was, a bit younger than me. I'm not sure if the dates are right, but it might be worth looking into. I called my sister and she remembers Ma talking about it. Caused a lot of anxiety at the Hall when she went missing. Mr. and Mrs. Gruffydd did what they could to try to find her. The girl's sister looked after the young lad, and eventually they moved away."

Gwennie took a sip of water. "Been a long time since I thought about that, but it might be worth mentioning to your police fellow and he can look into it."

"What was her name, Gwennie? Can you remember?"

"Juliette. I always thought that was such a pretty name. Juliette Sanderson, she was."

"I'll definitely tell Gareth, Gwennie. Thanks very much for this. It would be wonderful if we could give her name back to her after all these years."

She got up from the table. "I'd better just go and try to ring him again."

"And I'll make a start on those pots," said Gwennie, as the dishwasher changed gears, paused for a moment, then whirred into the final rinse cycle.

Penny turned back to Gwennie.

"I wanted to thank you for all you've done today, Gwennie.

And it was wonderful of you to arrive early to make a start on things."

"I didn't arrive particularly early," said Gwennie as she took a step toward the sink. "I said I'd be here at eight and I was here at eight."

Penny tipped her head.

"But I heard you moving about down here around seven thirty."

Gwennie shook her head.

"It wasn't me, Miss Penny. You must have been dreaming. Trixxi and I had our walk at seven thirty, just like we do every morning, and then we came here."

At the mention of a walk, Trixxi looked up at Penny with large, hopeful brown eyes and wagged her tail as Gwennie ran hot water into the sink and reached for the washing-up liquid. Penny hurried into the sitting room toward the desk where she had left her phone, but just as she picked it up, a small figurine caught her eye. As she took in the little shepherdess, holding her crook as a cuddly lamb peeked around her ruffled blue skirt, a rough voice barked out, "Switch that phone off and put it down."

She turned slowly to see Glynnis Bowen emerging from the kitchen, her left arm roughly around Gwennie's waist, and her right hand holding the tip of the carving knife to Gwennie's ribs.

Twenty-seven

You heard me. Switch it off and put it down," Glynnis ordered. Penny put the phone down beside the shepherdess figurine and then turned to face Glynnis.

"Glynnis. Please, let Gwennie go. She's done nothing to you."

"Of course I can't let her go," Glynnis said. "She'd go straight to the police, and I've had enough of them for one day, thank you very much." She laughed, a strained, high-pitched, desperate kind of noise.

"Oh, yes, they've taken Huw in for questioning." She practically spat out the name.

"Huw?" exclaimed Penny. "Why on earth? But he's not . . ."

Glynnis gave her a cold, dark stare. "Yes, Penny? He's not what?"

Penny said nothing.

"He's not the murderer, is that what you were about to say? Well, he's just confessed."

"Why are you here, Glynnis? What do you want from me?"

"Do you know, that's a good question. I'm not sure. But I do know you and I are going to have a long overdue chat."

"Let Gwennie go," Penny repeated. "She's done nothing."

Suddenly Glynnis released her grip.

"She can sit down in that chair over there," said Glynnis, gesturing with the carving knife, "but she's not going anywhere." Gwennie turned her pleading meerkat eyes to Penny, who nodded. "You, though, you stay right where you are. And don't move."

Penny watched as Gwennie sat gingerly in the chair nearest the desk and then turned to Glynnis.

"You've already killed two people, Glynnis, don't make it any worse for yourself. We both know Huw won't stand up under questioning, and it won't take the police long to figure out he didn't do it, so he's lying to protect someone, and the only person that could be is you."

Glynnis glared at her with mad, glittering eyes.

"No, Huw couldn't have done it. It'll all unravel, Glynnis. You'll see."

"What makes you so sure the police won't believe him?"

"Well, I worked out that whoever stole the items from the charity shop also stole my brooch and Mrs. Lloyd's letter opener. What are the chances there'd be two thieves at work in a town this size? But what really got me thinking was that business about putting a valuable diamond brooch on top of the Christmas tree in the charity shop. That was whimsical. Creative."

Glynnis smirked.

"Huw's a banker. He's logical. He likes everything orderly. He likes things to add up and balance out. From what I know of him, that just isn't something he'd do."

"So you've got it all worked out, then, have you?"

"Most of it," said Penny. "When I saw the John Lennon book that you gave Florence, I knew you'd given it to her. It was on the list of items gone missing from the charity shop along with the plate you gave Brian. Why did you give those things away, Glynnis? Was there part of you that wanted to get caught?"

"Caught? No? What would I want with them? I had no need of them. I just took them. I liked stealing things. It was exciting. But nothing was as good as taking your brooch! Now that was fun. And speaking of giving things away, I hope you noticed I left you a little something." She nodded at the table where the little shepherdess sat. "Left it there for you this morning. A little calling card, if you like." She smirked.

"How did you get in?" Penny asked, filled with revulsion at the idea of Glynnis walking around her home, picking up a book here, a picture there, touching her things.

"It was easy," gloated Glynnis. "Not much of a lock on that back door. I would have thought with a policeman for a boyfriend you'd have something a little better."

I will now, thought Penny grimly.

Glynnis sighed. "We might as well sit down."

She turned to look at the sofa behind her, and in that moment Gwennie snatched up the mobile phone from the desk and slipped it into her apron pocket. Penny gave her a slight nod and the hint of a smile.

"I think you were having an affair with Harry Saunders, and I know you killed him, but I don't know why."

263

"You're right. I was in love with Harry Saunders," said Glynnis, her eyes misting over. "He was exciting and rich. We couldn't wait to be together. Oh, I knew all about his dalliance with Mrs. Lloyd, but that meant nothing to him. He was just being kind to an elderly woman. Giving her a bit of a thrill. It was me he loved. He told me so, over and over, and I could see it in his eyes. I was going to leave Huw, and Harry and I were going to have a wonderful life together in San Francisco, where he's from."

"He told you he's from San Francisco, did he?"

"The Golden Gate Bridge, Chinatown, Fisherman's Wharf. It was going to be wonderful." She paused. "And then Huw had to go and ruin everything."

Despite herself, Gwennie leaned slightly forward.

"He insisted on showing up at Conwy Castle that day we were having our outing. That was the day Harry and I were going to make our final plans to leave all this behind. And then Huw, so jealous and controlling, had to come along to the art club outing. I think he was suspicious of Harry and wanted to confront him. Nobody wanted Huw there. Least of all me."

She sat back in her chair, the carving knife resting lightly across her knees.

"So when I saw him standing on the parapet, something just came over me and I still had Mrs. Lloyd's letter opener in my bag and I felt this great surge of anger and I pushed it into him and over he went." She choked back tears.

"Except it wasn't Huw—it was Harry," she sobbed. "The man I loved and I killed him by mistake."

She looked from one to the other.

"I know you'll think me the biggest fool, but in the heat of the moment, I panicked and I thought he was Huw."

"I can see that," said Penny. "They were both about the same height and wearing those green anoraks that just about every man in the area wears. So it was a case of mistaken identity."

Glynnis nodded.

"And Brian?" asked Penny. "You were worried there might have been images on his computer that could have incriminated you?"

"That's right. So at least I took care of those."

"No, you didn't, actually. The police have copies of the photographs Brian took that day, and if there's anything on them that points to you, they'll find it. And don't forget they have all that high-tech digital enhancement gadgetry."

Penny glanced at Gwennie, who was now sitting very straight in her chair.

"So you see, Glynnis, it's over now. I can see how desperate you are. Don't make things any worse than they already are. Let's have Gwennie make us a cup of tea. Would that be all right? If she went into the kitchen and made some tea for us?"

Glynnis, who seemed to have collapsed within herself, nodded, and Gwennie rose slowly and walked toward the kitchen, giving her apron pocket a little pat as she passed Penny.

"No matter what you think, Glynnis, Huw must love you very much to do what he did for you," Penny said, anxious to keep Glynnis talking now that Gwennie was safely out of the room.

"Oh, he loves me all right, in his boring, predictable way."

"But you must have known what he was like. Why did you marry him?"

"Well, I had to marry somebody, and eligible men aren't exactly thick on the ground around here. I'm not the independent kind of woman that you are. I needed a husband and he was the best on offer at the time. I knew I'd always have a roof over my head, so I settled for that. I knew I wasn't in for an exciting time."

She gave Penny a venomous look. "There was someone once, until you came along."

"Me?"

"Yes, you. Remember Tim?"

"Tim? But that was so long ago."

In her early years in Llanelen Penny had fallen in love with a local police constable, who had drowned in the River Conwy while rescuing a child. Thinking back on it, and knowing what she knew now, a terrible sensation crept over her.

"You didn't have anything to do with his drowning, did you?"

"Of course I didn't. I loved him. We were going to be married until you came along. And when he met you, it wasn't long until he dumped me."

"He did mention that he'd had a girlfriend, but I never dreamed that was you. And anyway, he said that relationship was over before he met me."

Glynnis gave a little snort. "That's what he told you, was it? Well, it wasn't over, and maybe we'd still be together if you hadn't ruined everything. I could have been happy. I might have had children."

She leaned forward. "So you see, Penny," she said, emphasizing her rival's name with bitterness, "you took all that away from me. If I'd been going to kill you, I would have done it years ago."

She slumped back in her chair, limp and drained, the carving knife still resting on her knees. A moment later she sat up and glared at Penny. "I'm not stupid, you know. Of course the police are on their way, and they'll be here any minute. But you know what? I don't care anymore. You're right. It's over."

As they sat in suffocating silence, Penny could feel the wild beating of her heart start to subside and return to normal. A few moments later they heard quiet voices in the kitchen, and then Gareth Davies quietly entered the room followed by Sergeant Bethan Morgan and Chris Jones, who had opened the Conwy Police Station door to Penny just a few nights ago. At a nod from Davies, Jones slowly reached down and grasping its blade, picked up the carving knife.

"All right, Glynnis, we're going to take you into custody for questioning," Davies said. "Do you have anything to say before we go?"

She looked wildly around the room and then asked, "What's going to happen to Huw?"

"We'll hold him for a bit longer while we continue the investigation, and then we'll see," said Davies. "He might be charged with wasting police time. Depends."

Davies gave a few instructions to his officers and they left, taking a docile Glynnis out the front door, which another officer had been guarding in case she tried to make a run for it.

Davies returned and wrapped his arms around Penny.

"All right, love?"

Gwennie appeared in the doorway and cleared her throat.

"I've left out some food for you, sir, in case you're hungry. There's salad and cold turkey and bread rolls. It was a pity you and your sergeant had to miss lunch, but what can you do? I guess when duty calls, you have to go."

Davies smiled. "I guess you do."

"Oh, there's just one more thing, Miss Penny. I'm going to spend the night at my sister's. She and her husband always invite a few of the neighbours round on Christmas night, and being true Welsh, they just can't help themselves and the singing starts, and wonderful to hear, it is. But you know my sister's view of animals. She's that house-proud, neither fur nor feather allowed past her front door. So if you wouldn't mind, I'm going to leave Trixxi here for the night with you. She's had her dinner, her water bowl's full, and I've made up a bed for her in the kitchen beside the Rayburn, just the way she likes it. I've left her lead by the back door. She'll want a walk about eight, but other than that, she won't be any bother."

"She'll be just fine with us, Gwennie, don't you worry."

Penny and Gareth exchanged a quick glance and he nodded.

"Gwennie, would you like Inspector Davies here to drive you home?"

"Thank you, but no. My sister wouldn't want the neighbours seeing a police car at the house. Begging your pardon and no offense meant, but she and her husband are much too respectable for that, thank you all the same." She looked from Penny to Gareth and back to Penny.

"Well, then, if there's nothing more you'll be needing this evening, I'll be off." As Gwennie pulled on her gloves, the telephone rang. Excusing herself, Penny answered it. She listened for a moment, exchanged a quick greeting with the caller, and then held out the receiver to Gwennie. "It's for you." As Gwennie approached to take the call, Penny tapped Gareth's arm.

"You must be starving. Let's see what Gwennie's left for you."

A few moments later Gwennie joined them in the kitchen, looking thoughtfully apprehensive.

"That was Mr. Emyr." Penny nodded. "Yes, he was calling to say he's been approached about the Hall and he's decided to sell it. He says he expects a quick sale, as the buyer is motivated, was the word he used. Yes, motivated. He says he's going to be traveling more and will live the rest of the time at the house in Cornwall." She looked from Penny to Gareth and finally to Trixxi, who was seated at Penny's feet. "I don't need to tell you that the Hall has been my whole life. I've never worked anywhere else, and my mother before me worked there her whole life, too. We took care of the family and we took care of the house." She shook her head. "How many times we dusted that banister, washed those floors . . ." Her voice trailed off, unable to keep up with her thoughts.

"So it looks as if I will be accepting that position you offered me at the spa, Miss Penny. I'll start in the new year, I expect."

"Well, we'll be lucky to have you, Gwennie. You'll start a new chapter in your working life with us."

Gwennie accepted the envelope Penny held out to her and then turned to go. And then she bent over, gave Trixxi a pat, and was gone, watched by a loving pair of Labrador eyes.

"Well, Florence, all in all, I'd say our Christmas was quite a success, wouldn't you agree?" remarked Mrs. Lloyd as she put her feet up. She had a glass of sherry on the table beside her, and she and Florence were settling in to watch the first episode of a new serial on television, involving the upstairs and downstairs lives of an aristocratic old family in a magnificent stately home.

"Yes, very successful," agreed Florence. "In fact, one of the nicest Christmases I've had in years. Certainly one of the most eventful. I enjoyed every minute of it."

"You did a wonderful job with the food and organizing everything," Mrs. Lloyd said.

"Evelyn, I wasn't born yesterday. When you start in with the compliments I know you're angling for something. So just come right out with it. What is it?"

"Ah, well, yes. It's just that I was wondering what you were planning to do about that job offer in Liverpool. You see, what with me losing all that money from Harry Saunders, things will be a little tight from now on, so I was hoping you'd be staying on here as I could do with the rent money. I am sorry to have to be so blunt, Florence, but that's the way it is, I'm afraid."

"That's all right, Evelyn, I quite understand. I'm very settled here now. I like the people, so I'm going to stay. There doesn't seem much point in going back to Liverpool." She turned to her companion. "But I think I'll do a bit more in the new year. You're right. I should get out and about more. I thought I might offer to teach old-fashioned cooking skills at the community centre. With all the ready meals and cooking not being taught to young girls anymore, it's getting to be a lost art."

"That's a lovely idea, Florence. I'm sure it'll be very popular. Especially with the young mums."

"Well, maybe not as popular as the dancing classes, but we'll see. By the way, I was reading the travel section in the newspaper and they had a story about America. I couldn't remember. Where did that Harry Saunders say he was from?"

"Palm Beach," said Mrs. Lloyd. "Or was it Palm Springs? Palm something or other, I can never remember. Someplace we'll never go, anyway."

She took a sip of sherry. "Which reminds me—"

"The program's about to start," Florence interrupted, "and I like to see it from the very beginning. We have to be quiet now."

Mrs. Lloyd did as she was told.

Penny unclipped the lead from Trixxi's collar as Gareth locked the kitchen door behind them.

"I think she enjoyed her walk," said Penny, taking off her coat. "That's the great thing about keeping a dog. It gets you out and about."

Gareth raised an eyebrow.

"You do know where this is going, don't you?" he asked. "With the Hall being sold and Emyr traveling, there's a good chance Trixxi's going to need a new home. And it won't be with Gwennie at her sister's place. You heard what she said."

"Neither fur nor feather."

"So, how do you feel about having her?"

"I don't know. I'll have to think about that. What do you reckon?"

"I really liked the sound of what you said."

"What did I say?

"You told Gwennie, 'She'll be all right with us.' I liked the 'us' part."

Penny smiled up at him. "What would you like to drink? Some wine? Beer?"

Davies hesitated.

"I know," said Penny. "How about cocoa?"

"I like the sound of that, too."

With warm mugs of cocoa on the table in front of them, Penny and Gareth sat together on the sofa.

"I love the painting of Conwy Police Station," Gareth said. "I've been wanting something you painted and this is perfect." After admiring the painting a moment more, he handed her a small package awkwardly wrapped in colourful red paper. "Here," he said, "I hope you like it."

Penny removed the red paper, revealing white tissue paper. She unfolded it slowly and pulled out a delicately carved wooden spoon. The handle featured a Welsh dragon and, above it, a hollowed-out heart. She read on the attached card that the heart meant steadfast love.

Davies pulled her closer. "You know what it is, don't you?" he said.

Penny nodded. "I do. It's a Welsh love spoon."

"I hope you know how much I . . ." He hesitated.

"Yes," said Penny. "I do know."

And with the curtains drawn against the long, silent night, shutting out the moonlight that shone so bright on the ancient snow-covered hills, and in the warm glow of the dying embers, they wrapped themselves around each other.

Penny knew that she had finally left her past behind and was ready to move forward into a future filled with love and promise. The sound of Trixxi's gentle breathing filled her heart with joy, and she reached out to stroke a black velvet ear.

Gareth stirred beside her and looked at his watch.

"Must you go?" she asked. "Do you have to? Why don't you stay?"

He groaned as his phone rang.

"Oh, why can't they give it a rest, tonight of all nights," he muttered, seeing who was ringing. "It's Bethan," he said. "Do you mind?"

"No," said Penny. "I want to know what's happened."

Davies pressed the green button.

"This had better be important, Sergeant."

He listened for a few minutes, never taking his eyes off Penny. A slow smile played around the corners of his lips, and then he replied. "We'll deal with it in the morning. Thanks for letting me know."

Penny sat up straighter. "What? Tell me. What's happened? It looks like good news. What is it?"

"A call from the daughter of a B and B operator in Llandudno. Visiting mum for Christmas. Seems the mother had a gentleman renting a room on a weekly basis who suddenly disappeared. She packed up his things in a hurry so the daughter could use the room over Christmas but wasn't sure what to do with the stuff. And then the daughter and her family arrive. The daughter had seen our television appeal, put two and two together, and called us. One of our officers collected the case, and lo and behold the key found in Harry Saunders's pocket opened it.

"There was a stash of passports. U.K., United States, and even a Canadian one. All in different names."

"Let me guess. Harry Saunders."

"That was one of the names, yes."

Davies leaned forward and handed Penny her mug of cocoa.

"But that wasn't all." He grinned at Penny, enjoying his moment. She raised her eyebrows and turned her head slightly as Davies nodded.

"There was an uncashed cheque drawn on a Chester bank in the amount of twenty thousand pounds."

Penny laughed and raised her mug.

"Merry Christmas, Mrs. Lloyd!"